CW00815769

BIG BROTHER

Simon Davies is one of the world's leading experts on privacy and technology. In 1990 he founded the international watchdog organization *Privacy International*, and since then has led campaigns across the world on a vast range of surveillance issues. He is a Visiting Law Fellow in the University of Essex and the University of Greenwich, and is Senior Research Associate in Chicago's John Marshall Law School. He now lives in London with his computer.

Also by Simon Davies

The Islands of Sydney Harbour
Shooting Up

SIMON DAVIES

BIG BROTHER

Britain's Web of Surveillance and the
New Technological Order

PAN BOOKS

First published in Great Britain 1996 by Pan Books Ltd
an imprint of Macmillan General books
25 Eccleston Place London SW1W 9NF
and Basingstoke

Associated companies throughout the world

ISBN 0 330 33556 1

9 8 7 6 5 4 3 2 1

A CIP catalogue record for this book is available
from the British Library

Typeset by Parker Typesetting Service, Leicester
Printed and bound in Great Britain by
Mackays of Chatham plc, Chatham, Kent

To the memory of Tony Kidson

CONTENTS

ACKNOWLEDGEMENTS

I would like to acknowledge the support, advice and encouragement of numerous people and organizations. First among these is the late Tony Kidson, who gave me inestimable support until the time of his tragic death in 1994.

Thanks to my good friends John Steel and Neil Quigley for companionship and encouragement when I needed it most, and to Dave Banisar for constant friendship, input and invaluable masses of data.

Nigel Burke spent many hours reviewing the drafts, a task which deserves special thanks and several wholesome dinners.

My appreciation goes also to Fleur Fisher, Steve Anderman, Kevin Boyle, Paul Vaughan, and to the staff of the Essex and Greenwich University Law Schools for having faith in me.

Marc Rotenberg, James Petts, Wayne Madsen, Colin Bennett, Jim Rule, Rafael Fernandez Calvo, Chris Pounder, Freddy Koster, Garry Armstrong, Phillip Edwards, Steve Saxby, Tim Dixon and Derek Johns, my agent, were terrific.

Elsie Lively, Alan and Marjorie Steel, John Hall, Steve Spicer, Paul Doyle, Paul Diamond, Patricia Wright, Ian Austin and Des Williams nurtured me into a new life in London, for which I am more grateful than I can say.

I would also like to thank a small number of organizations for their support. *Biometrics Technology Today, Data Protection News, Kable Briefing, Statewatch,* and *Security Industry* magazine supplied me with excellent information. David Hencke at the *Guardian* provided me with some very useful documents. The Electronic Privacy Information Center in Washington DC provided consistently superb material.

INTRODUCTION

Just on a generation ago, academics and human rights scholars throughout the world went through a period of intense speculation about the future. The pace of computer evolution had sent chills up the spines of old and young alike. For many people, the spectre of George Orwell's *1984* was a nightmare waiting to happen. Between 1970 and 1978, hundreds of books, papers and reports were written on the subject of the Orwellian vision.

Most writers concluded that these computers would vastly increase the power of governments and corporations. The individual would be diminished – made to be an insignificant cog with limited independence. Privacy would be decimated as the State intruded into more and more areas of private life. Ultimately, because information is power, democracy itself would be weakened.

It is more than a decade since 1984. Most of the gloomiest predictions appear – at first sight – not to have materialized. Computers have indeed become powerful beyond the wildest dreams of the early technologists, but the individual has survived. The Orwellian nightmare seems to have been contained. Most people go about their lives without giving Big Brother a second thought.

The technology that exists today has, nevertheless, two

faces. True, it has liberated many disabled people, given a voice to minority causes, and relieved isolation. It has made communications cheaper and more universal. It has created services like videophone, teleconferencing and electronic mail, all of which will give electronic communications greater relevance and depth. But technology has also been responsible for large-scale unemployment. It has created wholesale intrusion on our privacy. Computers have increased the power of large organizations. Electronic media have allowed the masses to view the wider world intimately, but the cost to individual life has only begun to be assessed.

This is a book about a new enemy in our midst. For although Big Brother is not the threat we imagined, something far more sinister has taken its place: complacency.

The Big Brother society imagined by the world in 1970 depended on coercion and fear. The society we are developing now is more Huxley-like than Orwellian. It is Brave New World. Instead of the repressive tyrants and their omnipresent intrusive technology, we are witnessing a process of mass pacification. Big Brother entailed conflict but ours is becoming a society based on Harmony Ideology. Technology is our friend – our partner. Compliance and agreement are the natural order. We have, after all, become components of a new order based on the surrender of information. The division between private and public organizations is fast disappearing as both spheres increasingly reach accord. Public interest, civil rights and privacy bodies become more ineffectual by the day as pragmatic solutions are struck by the key players. There is little disquiet over these trends and almost no discussion. That is the greatest danger of all.

The history of this state of affairs is fascinating. Ten years ago, a series of events began which silently changed the course of human history. One by one, governments and corporations across the world started to reach agreement on ways to link the information contained in their computers. Isolated, cumbersome machines progressively became part of a giant web of information touching every aspect of our lives. A Global Information Infrastructure – potentially the greatest force since the birth of the automobile – is being forged. And hardly a dog is barking.

Mass surveillance is developing in the UK not merely through video cameras, police systems and credit reporting agencies, but through a vast range of computer-based surveillance mechanisms. Most are designed to improve efficiency, to maximize revenue, or to serve law enforcement and national security. Increasingly the systems are linked so that information is shared throughout the government and the private sector. The justification is seductive and difficult to oppose. The danger in this rationale is that it knows no bounds. Within a decade the UK will have an ID card, a national CCTV surveillance grid, a DNA database containing most people's genetic code, and the most astonishing web of computer networks in Europe. Presently, the interests of the individual are hardly in sight.

Speaking at IBM's 'Citizen and the State' seminar in London in 1995, the former Deputy Commissioner of the Metropolitan Police, Sir John Smith, warned that Britain was becoming an 'Orwellian' society in which people were constantly under surveillance. Sir John argued that the growth of surveillance would inevitably provoke distrust of those who had allowed it to happen, and would distance the citizen from the State.

Bank accounts, once considered off limits to government

surveillance, will soon be open to full scrutiny. Since 1986, a variety of laws have been passed allowing accounts to be monitored by government on a case by case basis. The Criminal Justice Act now goes a step further by requiring all staff of financial institutions and banks to report to the government any customer who is suspected of being involved in any criminal conduct. The bottom line of this law, according to Derek Wheatley QC, is that bank staff will report 'every irregularity that might conceivably relate to crime of any kind', including tax evasion. The penalty for failing to report suspicions is up to fourteen years' imprisonment.[1]

Information is being shared more frequently between government agencies. The procedure of 'data matching', where computers of different agencies are linked, or tapes of information exchanged, is occurring throughout the world. It is likely to be a widespread practice in the UK, but no information has been provided to Parliament or elsewhere on the extent of the practice. The issue has hardly been raised.

Some countries have passed laws which limit such activity and provide meaningful protections. France maintains the right to ban hostile technologies. Germany, Hungary and Portugal outlaw national numbering systems, which they consider dangerous to human rights. The Scandinavian countries have enshrined very strong freedom of information laws. Quebec demands that private sector companies conform to strict privacy protections. Britain has few such legal limits upon surveillance. The Data Protection Act, enacted in 1984, requires computer users to register their databases of personal information with the Data Protection Registrar. Beyond this, the Act places few limitations on the use of computers by government or the private sector. It is, in every sense, a useless piece of legislation that provides the illusion of protection, and successive UK governments have done all in their power to derail efforts of reform.

Talk to the experts in this field and you will be bombarded by legalities. With furrowed brow they will passionately outline conventions, legislation and regulations. They will lecture you on definitions, connotations and exemptions. You will listen with growing bemusement about how such and such an information practice breaches such and such a data protection principle and you will learn all about how this may or may not be in contravention of so many other directives, codes or conventions. And in the end, you realize that these things hardly matter at all. The one element left out of this passionate legal debate is the public. Countless pounds are spent cutting deals in the backroom to erode our privacy and barely a penny is spent advocating the issue among the very people who are affected. The public is left with nothing but the consolation of hollow slogans about tax cheats, criminals, and the need for administrative reform.

It seems probable that the UK faces two options. It will become either an information society which has developed safeguards against abuses; or it will become a surveillance society controlled and dominated by powerful entities. At some point, the British public must convene a discussion on the subject. If not, the experience of a dozen countries indicates that the decision will be made *in absentia*.

CHAPTER ONE

FUSING FLESH AND MACHINE

The impressively named Neural Prosthesis Unit of the US National Institute of Health conducts its affairs from a featureless concrete office block in Bethesda, Maryland, just a stone's throw from Washington DC. Its function, in a nutshell, is to plant microchips into live human brains.

Even the most experienced medical professionals find it difficult to come to terms with the fusion of computer technology and brain tissue. Nevertheless, over the past decade more than 15,000 people worldwide have had electronic components implanted directly into their brains. In a procedure until recently confined to the fantasies of science fiction, microchips are now being routinely placed into brain stems and cortexes. Micro-engineered probes many times thinner than a human hair are buried deep inside the brain, fed by platinum wires lacing underneath the skull.

These leading edge medical procedures are part of a science called 'neural prosthetics', otherwise known as 'bionics'. The most common procedures are 'cochlear implants', in which hearing is restored to people who are profoundly deaf. More complex experiments have commenced with the intention of restoring partial sight for blind people, to control epileptic seizures, and to restore bladder control and hand grip for paralysed patients.

These are early days and the interaction between the chip and the brain is relatively simple but, as Neural Prosthesis Director Terry Hambrecht puts it, this is 'just the beginning'. In the future, microchips may have the ability to conduct an intimate two-way conversation with memory and even with the basic processes of thought and motivation. In medical and engineering institutes throughout the world these have become serious and well-funded programmes. Their intention is to use microscopic computer technology to explore, map, change and repair the most unreachable parts of the human brain.

Five thousand miles to the east, in the German university town of Tübingen, the Institute of Medical Psychology and Behavioural Neuroscience has created a bionic fusion of a different type. After completing a fifteen-year programme of experiments on electrical brain activity, the Institute recently announced that its patients have developed the ability to operate machinery remotely through the power of thought.

To achieve this, tiny electrodes are placed on the surface of the scalp. These measure electrical signals being emitted by the brain. By thinking in certain ways, subjects can change the pattern and intensity of their electrical brain activity. These signals, in turn, are transmitted to machinery which is programmed to respond accordingly. No buttons; no key pads; just the power of pure thought energy. The Institute reports that the process is 96 per cent accurate after only eight hours of training. Further 'automatization' through more intensive training, assured the Institute, will result in a 100 per cent success rate.[1]

The Tübingen Institute is one of several around the world experimenting with the procedure, which is commonly known as 'remote touch'.[2] The Defence Research Agency in the UK (formerly the Department of Defence Research Division) is working on a high speed 'brain to machine' link using infrared transmission of brain signals from scalp electrodes.[3]

In 1996, British neurosurgeons working with paralysed patients will take such brain-to-machine communications to a new level by implanting a device directly into the spinal cord at the base of a patient's skull. It is, says the team leader, 'instant and reliable'. In this case, the patient – although intelligent – is unable to communicate in any way. The procedure may allow him to correspond in a relatively complex 'Morse Code' with a computer.

The medical possibilities in harnessing thought power are immense. By merely thinking, patients will be able to control wheelchairs, electrically operated machinery and computers. Their thoughts will move artificial limbs. The limbs, in turn, will feed signals to the brain so the patient will 'feel' heat, cold and pressure. Within ten years, complex telepathy between humans and machines will be a reality.

THE SECOND GENERATION OF *HOMO CYBORG*

This fusion of flesh and machine has been a theme of science fiction for decades. The ultimate fusion is the classic 'cyborg' organism featured in such films as *Robocop* and *Terminator*. True revelations of present-day microchip implants bring the fusion a step closer.

To an extent the age of the cyborg is already common-place. Every three seconds, somewhere in the world, a human being becomes 'fused' with technology. The science of surgical implants is creating a new cybernetic species – part human, part machine.

Medical science has become blasé about placing objects into patients. Plastic hips, polythene penises, silicone breasts and bionic ears hardly raise an eyebrow. Heart valves, vascular grafts, chin implants and pacemakers have become part of everyday language. At least 6 million medical devices a year worldwide are surgically implanted in humans.[4] £8 billion a year is spent on implant technology and this figure is rising sharply as new techniques are approved. This first generation implant technology has now become a routine form of medical treatment.

Implant technology, however, is constantly evolving. Some second generation implants can now 'think'. They can interface with the brain, provide complex instructions to mechanical parts and read brain activity. The use of computer microchips also allows these implants to provide a mass of unique information about the host human. With the aid of a small radio scanner, microchip implants located underneath the skin can provide identification and medical data relating to the individual (see Chapter 3). A new generation of 'intelligent' materials and chemicals can fool the brain into believing they are part of the human body and thus become part of it. By far the most exciting development for research scientists is the creation of probes so fine that they can make contact with individual clusters of neurons deep inside the brain. With these devices the basic workings of the brain can at last be mapped.

Scientists have dreamed about this notion for generations. As far back as 1874 scientists unsuccessfully inserted an electrode into the brain of a woman whose skull had been eaten away by a tumour. Until recently, the technology has constantly frustrated researchers and has often been the subject of scepticism and derision. With the development of micro-electronics, however, the physical barrier has at last been overcome.

Neural prosthetics is making extraordinary advances, including inroads to the development of artificial vision. Dr Hambrecht's team recently restored very basic sight in a blind patient by implanting electrodes and microchips in the visual cortex area of the brain. A second, more complex operation is planned for 1995. A miniature camera records images which are converted into electrical impulses and fed directly into the brain. Within five years, artificial eyes will contain high resolution cameras controlled by thought power.[5]

THE UNIVERSE IN A GRAIN OF SAND

Many of these developments owe their success to advances in subminiature electronics. The field of micro-engineering has made surprising progress in the past decade, resulting in miniaturization on a scale that could scarcely be imagined until now.[6] Laboratories around the world are building an array of microscopic devices that promise to have a huge bearing on health care in the twenty-first century.

Already in use or well in progress are infrared microlights so small that a bundle of them would pass comfortably through the eye of a needle. The microlights could be used to monitor gases in the blood or breath and to detect tumours in very small volumes of tissue.[7] Silicon 'micromotors', one-third the width of a hair, are being developed to scrub out clogged arteries or perform delicate operations under computer control.

Ingestible sensor systems the size of a vitamin pill will record temperature, heart rate, blood pressure and stomach acid levels, and send the information back to external monitors sewn into the patient's clothing.

The extent of micro-engineering gets more astounding each year. Implantable timer-pump systems can detect conditions such as low blood sugar and automatically squirt a metered dose of insulin into the bloodstream. Microscopic pressure monitors that are about the size of two grains of table salt can be inserted into the heart and used to measure blood pressure on either side of a valve.

Beyond micro-engineering is a field which takes miniaturization to a more astonishing scale. Nanotechnology is the science of manipulation of atoms and molecules to form microscopic and sub-microscopic engineered structures. In this process, the limitations of size cease to be a critical factor. The extent of this science is virtually limitless. While micro-engineering is close to producing mechanisms invisible to the naked eye, nanotechnology may eventually use chemical combinations automatically to construct even smaller robots atom by atom. Fraser Stoddart, Professor of Organic Chemistry at Birmingham University, has successfully constructed complex molecules by manipulating individual atoms.[8] And, in what must have been the most bizarre promotional stunt of all time, American scientists recently created the letters 'IBM' by manipulating 35 atoms of xenon.[9]

Miniaturization will accelerate the development of *Homo Cyborg*. In the absence of any limitation on size the fusion of human and machine will be intimate. In our lifetime microscopic robots will pound an arterial beat, interacting with a variety of intelligent implants located around the body and communicating with external technology. The application at present is for people suffering chronic medical conditions. In the future, such technology may be as common as disease inoculation.

This growing intimacy with technology will in time become a dependency. Intricate devices tuned to the unique characteristics of each human may become a vital component of our bodies. Thus the fusion of flesh and machine will be complete. Scientists at ICL, IBM and Rank Xerox have independently developed organic based engineered computers, allowing them to construct machines out of living material, using protein strands as wires, and molecular movement as memory. The interdependency is limitless. Only the mystery of life itself stands in the way of a complete fusion of technology and people. This too is about to change.

MAPPING THE BUILDING BLOCKS OF LIFE

Mapping the human brain is rivalled in complexity only by the quest to map the very building blocks of life: our genetic coding. The Human Genome Project, funded by government and private interests across the world, is a fifteen-year programme to achieve this end. Costing around two and a half billion US dollars, this magnificent quest will crack the code of human life and lead to the creation of a genetic dictionary which will have profound implications for future generations. Scientists are inspired by the prospect of engineering genes to provide monkeys with the power of speech, breed plants which contain animal flesh, and create a stronger and disease-resistant breed of human.

The current state of DNA research now makes it possible easily to code a person's genetic identity. This technology has proved so useful that a growing number of companies in the US are using it to screen out job applicants with undesirable genetic characteristics.[10] The technology takes on a more sinister aspect when used in the pursuit of eugenics. In Western nations millions of parents will be capable of individually stopping the development of defective or unsatisfactory embryos. In other countries, the process will be somewhat more brutal. In 1995 China moved to prevent the birth of children who are unable to live 'independently'.[11] In the first instance, marriages between handicapped people will be illegal. In the future, mass genetic screening will broaden the prohibition, leading to a form of social engineering that borders on eugenics. Chinese officials have refused to rule out the possibility of 'encouraging' couples not to have children with even minor handicaps.

Closer to home, the national DNA computer database, launched by the government in 1995, will ultimately contain the genetic 'grid reference' of much of the population. Presently, the database stores the DNA code of anyone arrested for any offence punishable by imprisonment (and this means everything from shoplifting to murder). Following the lead of other such information systems such as the Police National Computer and the NHS Network, access to the DNA database will in all probability be extended to include security agencies, employers, health and social security agencies and insurance companies. As more uses are found for this genetic data, more people will voluntarily submit to testing.

Police, employers and the insurance industry would like to see everyone placed on the database. Even now, police are using DNA testing to screen large populations. When Cardiff police were hunting the murderer of a young girl in 1995, they asked the entire male population of a local housing estate to 'volunteer' for DNA testing. 'Just so we can eliminate you from our enquiries,' assured the police. The twist was that anyone who did not 'volunteer' was considered a suspect, and was therefore compulsorily tested.[12] In June, the tactic was used by London police after the rape of a girl in Great Portland Street. In that case, police had written to people with certain physical characteristics, again arguing that volunteering for the test would 'eliminate' them from further enquiries.

August 10 1995 was a red-letter day for the police. After precisely four months in operation, the DNA database scored its first 'hit'. The DNA 'fingerprint' from blood samples taken from the scene of an unsolved burglary in Derbyshire was automatically matched with a sample of saliva taken from a suspect two months previously.

Police were ecstatic. Not since 1902, when London burglar Harry Jackson was jailed on the evidence of his thumbprint found at the scene of a crime, has forensic science been so celebrated. The Derbyshire case, according to local Assistant Chief Constable Don Dovaston, marked the start of a revolution in policing. It will go down in history as the most important breakthrough in police work since the start of the fingerprint record system.

Is it an accurate measure of guilt? In short, no. There are many sources that claim probabilities of a false match of around one in 40 million. This may well be true, but the problem, according to the Office of Technology Assessment of the US Congress, is that the technology is hampered by substandard human input. The gathering of samples, their recording and labelling, and the treatment of the evidence are subject to exactly the same fallibilities, falsities and corruption as is any other police work.

Genetic science can offer solutions to the scourges of disease and old age. It can also provide one key to the successful detection and prevention of some crimes. The downside is that this science also provides the bedrock for mass surveillance and social engineering on a scale that can scarcely yet be imagined. The fusion of intimate genetic data with a mass of general information on our lifestyle, health and habits will provide limitless opportunities for monitoring and regulation of many aspects of our lives. Among these may be the determination of your 'suitable' categories of employment, establishing entitlement to health care, and determining the extent of your access to life insurance.

None of these uses could ever be put into practice unless there existed an information society in which people had become used to intimate details of their life being explored. Fortunately for the architects of genetic and bionic science, and their many corporate backers, those conditions are almost complete.

THE PRE-EMINENCE OF THE MICROCHIP

All societies throughout history owe their growth and prosperity to the existence of a Yellow Brick Road, upon which travels the most important political, cultural and economic activity of the age. In the past, the road was militarism, industrialization, religion or the trading routes. In the late twentieth century, it is computer technology. The modern Yellow Brick Road is paved with microchips.

Developed in the early 1970s, this remarkable invention, containing thousands of microscopic circuits and components, made it possible for information to be inexpensively stored and processed. Within a few years, the invention had facilitated a mass market in personal computers. By the late 1970s, the 'information society' was well and truly part of common language. The popular vision of the future changed almost overnight and the world economy went through a minor transformation.

The microchip was so cheap and adaptable that it found its way into simple domestic appliances. It could be used to control everything from vacuum cleaners to food processors. Within a decade this slim device came to symbolize power, progress, speed and knowledge. The world absorbed this new technology as voraciously as it absorbed the technology of the motor car.

Computers have now without question become one of the most pervasive forces in our day-to-day lives. Our contact with people and organizations is increasingly reliant on microchip technology. Without this basic component the telephone network, the banking system, the Stock Exchange, the airlines and virtually every form of transport, communication and corporate organization would suffer instant paralysis.

Despite its usefulness as a device to help make perfect pancakes, the primary function of the microchip is to facilitate the collection and processing of data. The microchip gives organizations the means to accumulate information about many aspects of our lives. In an economy whose prosperity is increasingly dependent on services rather than products, the efficient and creative processing of data is a crucial ingredient for growth. The evolution of government departments, large companies, and even the corner store inevitably involves management of information as a top priority. And these days, the management of information is the province of the computer.

Predictably, the efficient management of information depends on the ability of computer companies to create a working partnership between information technology and people. Without such a partnership, the delicate equation of economic growth would suffer.

ENGINEERING A NEW RELATIONSHIP

To grease this relationship between technology and people, the image of computers has had to become warm and benevolent. They look, sound, feel and act in gentle, 'user-friendly' ways. Their once sinister image has been softened by clever marketing, slick design, and persuasive reasoning. The new relationship is, of course, not entirely an illusion. Computers can speed up our transactions and lubricate our dealings with large, complex organizations. They can put us in touch with vast sources of information and help stream-line our personal affairs.

Without realizing it, we develop a symbiotic relationship with computers, usually without concerning ourselves with the world that lies behind them. As they become more familiar, we surrender increasing amounts of our personal data to them. Our connectivity with computers becomes stronger and closer by the day. The barrier of fear and uncertainty that once existed has all but vanished.

As we grow more comfortable with computers, we develop important bonds with them at several levels. First, we establish an understanding of trust followed by an exchange of knowledge. We must be 'personally' known to the computer. 'It' has to recognize us. There are already several 'voice recognition' programmes on the market, the function of which is to allow your computer to be controlled by voice command and for the word processing to be achieved without the need for you to use a keyboard. These programmes analyse your speech pattern and they can then interpret the spoken word as if it were typed on the key pad. This process is likely to become universal. Children will shake their heads in wonder when they are told of a time when computers could not recognize speech. The result is yet another step towards intimacy and bonding between human and machine.

In this way the human and the machine are becoming, in a sense, one 'information organism'. The concept of bringing human and machine into such unity is well known. It began with the motor car – once a cumbersome, lathe-like juggernaut and now designed and marketed as an extension of the mind, body and psyche. One difference between cars and computers is that intimacy with the latter involves the surrender of important values and rights.

In the short term at least the fusion of flesh and machine will be less dramatic than the wizardry of genetic and bionic fusion. While our brains and bodies may not yet be materially fused with technology, we are none the less quickly developing an irreversible bond with a complex web of computer technology.

We are becoming intimately known to computer systems, and as each day passes we unwittingly divulge to them more and more about ourselves. Once disclosed to a single machine, the data will be shared with other computer networks and databases. The barrier of geographical distance, language, or computer literacy will cease to matter.

FORMING THE SEAMLESS, GLOBAL WEB

Computer technology is now capable of tasks and functions that astound even the technologists. Simple tests conducted by the police or an employer can now determine which drugs you had last week. Computer programmes designed to improve workplace efficiency silently assess and profile your work performance. Meanwhile, data matching programmes minutely compare your files in a variety of government departments. As you read these words, information about you is being processed by the thousands of computer data bases held by governments, credit reference agencies, banks, insurance companies, the police, marketing companies and so on. The average Briton is on 200 computer databases.

The most important development in computers is not their size, speed or prevalence, but the phenomenon that most of them are coming together to form one mass – a sort of seamless technological web. This web is important for the organizations controlling the information systems. It will mean that computers will talk easily to one another, and it will ensure that all people are constantly visible.

The process of linking and matching computers is international. Immigration, telecommunications, social welfare and police systems are being linked. Travellers entering the United States can now place their hand on to a computer screen for 'biometric' verification. Their identity is instantly confirmed, and the immigration computer makes an international search to determine eligibility to enter the country. Traditional borders are made redundant by global information technology.

The world's telecommunications systems, too, are forming a seamless web. The Motorola corporation's 'Project Iridium' and other programmes are currently stationing dozens of communications satellites across the globe. As you move around the planet, the satellite will be able to track you through your mobile phone. By the time telephone companies introduce 'cradle to grave' universal personal numbers in a few years, every telephone customer will be permanently and limitlessly connected to the system. Vast amounts of 'transactional data' generated by the network will reveal precise details about your geographic movements, electronic transactions and telephone activity. These same satellites that make such a telecommunications system possible are also monitoring traffic on the highways. Soon they will have the ability to direct and track individual vehicles. Road tolling systems will keep a detailed record of a car's movements across entire continents. The culture of freedom on the open road is close to extinction.

The technologies themselves are converging. Thirty years ago, the television, the computer and the telephone were unique and individual technologies. Now they are merging into one single matrix. It is impossible now to be an expert in one aspect of technology without having a broad knowledge of the others. Beneath the cheerful colours and graceful contours of modern user-friendly devices is a vast gravitational force bringing all technologies together so that ultimately they too will form a seamless web. Your telephone will be your computer. Your computer will be your videophone and television. Your television will be your computer. We are no longer playing with gadgets or devices. We are dealing instead with a technological canopy. And the complex mass of information which you allow to be placed under this canopy will be passed on endlessly to be configured and reconfigured, distributed, sold and redirected in a thousand ingenious ways.

UTOPIA OR DYSTOPIA?

There are two ways of viewing this new relationship between humans and technology. We are certainly encouraged intellectually and culturally to see it as positive and necessary. The architects of modern computer systems have successfully argued that their technology can solve the ancient curses of social dysfunction and administrative expense. Bureaucracy, they claim, can be made more efficient through the automated management of information. Society can be made safer. Economies can run more smoothly and education can be conducted more effectively.

Some of these claims are valid but most are well orchestrated lies or illusions. The marketing of a modern supercomputer has a surprising amount in common with the tactics of a door-to-door vacuum cleaner salesman, and in many cases has about the same level of credibility. A study by the Congressional Office of Technology Assessment in the US found that computer systems, once implemented, often result in 'unforeseen costs, unfulfilled promises and disillusionment'.[13]

There are many reasons why we should not be relaxed about new technology. In spite of its carefully crafted image, information technology is neither friendly nor neutral and almost never benign. With notable exceptions, it is developed by unethical corporations, peddled by apathetic salesmen and implemented by large organizations as a means of maximizing control over the individual.

The widespread use of information technology is increasing the power and influence of government and corporations. One inevitable consequence is that the individual is subject to increased monitoring, regulation and control. Cash machines and electronic road tolls may be seen as useful or necessary, but they will establish a 'real time' geographic tracking system over the entire country. ID cards may be viewed as a weapon against criminals, but history shows that they will be used ultimately as a tool of authority against the ordinary citizen. Closed Circuit Television (CCTV) in town centres may reduce the incidence of bag-snatching, but it also creates a means of enforcing public morals and public order on an unprecedented scale. Our movements, transactions and personality are becoming known in a way that Orwell could scarcely have imagined. And yet our dependence on technological systems is greater than at any point in history.

The key rule to ensure personal autonomy and independence is never to get too familiar, reliant, or friendly with the power centres around you. In embracing the exciting new fusion with technology, we have broken this ancient law. One result is that we have now formally entered the first phase of the Post-Orwellian State. The future should offer an expanding gulf between the illusion of personal autonomy and the power of large organizations.

TURNING THE TIDE OF OPINION

The apocalyptic view of the future creates scant concern for most young people. After all, information technology has made possible so many of the beneficial features of modern life: great video games, cheap communication, powerful computers, and vibrant electronic media. To many people technology is merely an extension of their psyche.

But it was not always so. It is hard to imagine a time when the British public was ever passionately concerned about the existence of computers, much less terrified of them, but such was the situation in 1971. For fifteen years, the breathtaking growth of computer technology had fuelled public anxiety over the emergence of a Big Brother state. Huge repositories of personal information were being constructed and many people genuinely feared these would merge into a central databank.

Backbenchers in Parliament responded by introducing a variety of troublesome privacy bills, all of which were designed to clip the wings of computer technology. The government, in this case representing the interests of computer users, was keen to derail these hindrances. So, in 1971, as part of a deal to silence the backbenchers, it established a committee to investigate the subject of computers.

One of the first tasks of the committee was to conduct an opinion poll. The result was a surprise to everyone. Of all the concerns – nuclear war, economic depression or communist infiltration – none attracted greater fear and hostility than the threat that the government might construct a central computer databank.[14] A generation ago, George Orwell's vision of 1984 was a nightmare still waiting to happen.

Attitudes have changed dramatically in a mere quarter century. In the view of many people, computer technology hasn't turned out so bad after all.

The promise of a technological utopia has made sense to a population becoming weary of high taxes, inept organizations, big government and failing social institutions. Stage by stage, we made a contract with computer technology, the terms of which are that we would surrender our personal information to technology in return for a safer, cheaper, more efficient life.

Some of the promises came good. Many more were proved to be nonsense. Whatever the outcome, the upshot is that modern society has been de-sensitized to even the most extraordinary technologies. The fear we felt in 1971 – and the distance we kept from the technology – diminished as each generation of computers found its way into more common use.

It's no longer fashionable among intelligent folk to admit being 'scared' or even 'concerned' about computers. Smart people embrace technology. The most drab and unimaginative politicians are advised to climb aboard the Superhighway and get hip about new technology. Cabinet ministers without the guts or perspicacity to deal squarely with the policy challenges in their own domain publicly embrace computers and smart cards as a Great Solution. Young people, mesmerized by the magic of computers, fail to see the universe that lies behind the screen. But some people still feel the old nightmare as if it were forgotten wisdom from another age. Beyond the slick technology, there is an emerging Big Picture and it is not an entirely pleasant one.

The assumption that technology is entirely good for us is misguided and dangerous. Some technologies are just plain malevolent and their uses should have been outlawed years ago. Sadly, the people who know about the rancid underbelly of technology are so often reluctant to sound the alarm for fear of being branded Luddite or heretic. It is no exaggeration to say that there has been a conspiracy of silence about the threat of information technology. In the process, normally intelligent and thoughtful professionals have let us all down. The discourse and debate necessary in a free society has simply not taken place.

A generation ago the single greatest fear in British society was the development of an Orwellian state. In the public mind, the computer might well be the tool of totalitarianism. Now the technology that was so feared is in place. Each developed country has the technical capacity to numerically code and geographically track every member of its population. Every government has the ability to collect, store, cross-correlate and cross-match intimate details about all people. Our financial dealings, medical concerns, employment records and a hundred other aspects of our lives are already monitored. Banks, insurance companies, government bodies and credit agencies hold billions of items of personal information.

These 'regions' of data are being merged. As they join together a web of surveillance silently forms, fusing us with the technological infrastructure and monitoring each facet of our lives. As the web forms, fragile personal freedoms are compromised. The only thing capable of interceding in this process is the boundary that we call privacy.

THE LOST WORLD OF PRIVACY

Privacy is a little like freedom: the less you have of it, the easier it is to recognize. Like the concept of freedom, privacy has at least a hundred wildly different definitions. Even after decades of academic interest in the subject, the world's leading experts have been unable to agree on a single definition. One pioneer in the field described privacy as 'part philosophy, some semantics, and much pure passion'.[15] At least on that point, everyone agrees.

Some countries – France, for example – see the concept of privacy as a form of 'liberty'. Others, including Britain, view privacy as being preservation of a space around us. Some European countries interpret privacy as the protection of our personal information. A popular definition is expressed in the Oxford dictionary, which explains privacy as '*being withdrawn from society or public interest*'.

One school of thought argues that privacy protection is one way of drawing the line at how far society can intrude into your affairs. In that context, privacy is a question of power – yours, the government's and the power of the corporations. 'The bedrock of civil liberties,' social justice campaigner Patricia Hewitt once observed, 'is the setting of limits on the power of the state to interfere in the private life of its citizens.' Privacy can be viewed as a measure of how much surveillance and control can be established over our lives. It is a measure of how much we should become subjects of the expanding technological empire. Privacy can even be a benchmark to indicate how much autonomy a nation should have in the emerging international order.

Single parents, for example, might be concerned about

just how far the government should be allowed to ask intrusive personal questions about relationships and daily activities. A clerical assistant might wonder whether an employer should have the right to monitor telephone conversations or electronic mail, or to set up closed circuit video surveillance cameras in the office. People who deal in cash for legitimate reasons might feel that the government has no right to commence a routine investigation after they bank the proceeds of a garage sale. In each case, privacy can offer a useful formula.

A hundred years ago, a prominent US judge, Louis Brandeis, articulated a concept of privacy that urged that it was the individual's 'right to be left alone'. Brandeis argued that privacy was the most cherished of freedoms in a democracy, and he was deeply concerned that it was not specifically protected in the US Constitution. A century later the Constitution still gives only limited protection for privacy. In Britain privacy is given even less weight.

In 1975, the Californian Supreme Court ruled: 'The right of privacy is the right to be left alone. It is a fundamental and compelling interest. It protects our homes, our families, our thoughts, our emotions, our expressions, our personalities, our freedom of communion and our freedom to associate with whom we choose. It prevents government and business interests from collecting and stockpiling unnecessary information about us, and from misusing information gathered for one purpose in order to serve other purposes or embarrass us.'[16]

In Britain there exists no Bill of Rights to enshrine privacy and there is no specific privacy law. The Data Protection Act establishes some rudimentary rules about the handling of information, but sets up few barriers to the establishment of intrusive computer systems. Chapter 5 explains why this law has failed to achieve any real protection for Britain.

One of the pioneers of privacy, Alan Westin, defined privacy as the desire of people to choose freely under what circumstances and to what extent they will expose themselves, their attitude and their behaviour to others.[17] Arnold Simmel argues that 'the right to privacy asserts the sacredness of the person'. He believes a violation of a person's privacy is a violation of their dignity, individualism and freedom.[18]

Back in the 1970s, when academics were turning their attention to the importance of individual rights, privacy protection was seen as a key indicator of the strength of a democracy. These days, however, privacy is not a highly regarded concept. In the words of veteran privacy writer John Carroll, 'Privacy was not a virtue in the greedy 1980s, nor is it a cause for concern in the needy 1990s.'[19]

Part of the problem of developing a broadly accepted definition is that privacy is being portrayed more and more by governments and the corporate sector as being equivalent to selfishness or secrecy. Anyone standing in the way of government information strategies must have something to hide. The surrender of personal information has become a routine and automatic process. We scarcely give it a thought.

From my own perspective, as a privacy advocate, the definition has to be at least as potent as the forces which oppose privacy. So the definition of my own choosing (and my own making) is:

> The right to privacy is the right to protect ourselves against intrusion by the outside world. It is the measure we use to set limits on the demands made by organizations and

people. It is the right we invoke to defend our personal freedom, our autonomy and our identity. It is the basis upon which we assess the balance of power between ourselves, and the world around us.

DEFENDING THE UNDEFENDABLE

The construction of massive information systems is often justified on the basis of improving society. Every computer system lays claim to catching a crook or saving a pound. But at what point has the individual the right to call a halt to the uses of the technology? In its quest to track down every lost penny, does the government have an unlimited right to pry into our personal affairs? In its pursuit of crime, has the government absolute power to demand compliance? The answer to these questions will not easily be found. No one wants to stand in the way of genuine efforts to solve social and administrative problems. On the other hand, thoughtful people realize that the march of surveillance and intrusion, if unchecked, could go on endlessly. Thoughtful people also realize that the price we might pay for allowing total fusion with information technology, is a society so constrained by the machinery of surveillance that it stands the risk of falling prey to a hostile future government.

Privacy should be of vital concern to everyone because the technology to monitor and control our lives exists right this minute and there appears very little opposition to it. Public awareness is handicapped by the unfortunate reality that technological intrusion takes place with stealth. Slick public relations consultants and wordsmiths are employed to neutralize the language of privacy invasion.

Increasingly, as computers talk freely to other computers, we have to be on guard against the growing potential for abuse of our personal information. More important, we have to be on guard against becoming mere subjects of the new technological order. Information domination, like cultural domination, takes place invisibly and incrementally.

The case for privacy is a clear argument for restraining the use of information technology. Many of the privacy arguments that made sense twenty years ago seem in the modern day to be paranoiac and antisocial. From the perspective of the advocate for privacy, however, information is power – an equation that does not change from one millennium to the next. History demonstrates that information in the hands of authority will inevitably be used for unintended and often malevolent purposes. If any government is allowed, piece by piece, to assemble a complete linkage of computer technology, many of our traditional freedoms will be imperilled. The alarm will not be raised until the mechanism has become indispensable.

Privacy is one of the most important rights of a free nation. In Britain, we take it for granted. To understand why privacy is so important, you only have to imagine life without it. People who have no rights of privacy are vulnerable to limitless intrusion by governments, corporations, or anyone else who chooses to interfere in your personal affairs.

TIME FOR A RESURGENCE OF THE LUDDITES

The process of complaint, resistance and rebellion is a learned response. Children who have only ever known submission fail to grasp the concept of resistance. Populations trained to submit to the demands of an information society will have difficulty comprehending the importance of privacy. If the machinery of the information society is blessed by political consensus the options for the opposing voice are few.

It is now time for a neo-Luddite movement against technology. There exists too much sycophancy from the very people who stand to lose the most. All things considered, it is now appropriate to begin a programme of civil disobedience against information systems. Such a response is politically and intellectually valid. It is a genuine and reasonable response to an external threat.

This book will present the evidence to justify such a movement.

THE ULTIMATE SCENARIO

We are living in the second decade of the second phase of an unwritten strategy of planetary management. The first stage involved the establishment of a web of international agreements and conventions. The second stage involves the construction of a borderless, global information economy. The threat of nuclear, environmental and economic holocaust has hastened this process. Problems of terrorism, the arms trade and human rights abuses increase the urgency. Furthermore, the alleged costs of failing to implement a global information economy have been too great to ignore. 'The road to health for all lies through information,' proclaimed the World Health Organization. Few people in any field would disagree. Banks, telecommunications companies and governments follow the same line of reasoning.

Planetary management involves some radical changes. No event can happen and no decision can be made in isolation. Those days have gone. Our society is becoming tuned into consensus, compromise, agreement and conformity. Indeed, the BBC's James Burke has complained: 'Togetherness is the flavour of the millennium. It is beginning to be politically incorrect even to mention difference.'[20] Modern information technology assists this process by providing practical templates for social change and conformity.

The information revolution has three goals in mind. The first is to create maximum efficiency within each information system. The second is to achieve perfect compatibility and communication between computers. The third is to create perfect human identity. In its quest to achieve these aims, the computer industry must bring about a subtle but profound change to the human spirit and to our way of life.

Now that the bleak Orwellian image of computers has been softened and redesigned in gentle pastels, it is no longer fashionable to be pessimistic about these things. The harsh edges of technology have been smoothed; the whole concept has been made user-friendly. The result is that we routinely use the most fantastic machines without sensing the unusual. People of all ages feel no fear of technology. All around, there is an air of acceptance. Slowly, however, we are being fused with the technology. And, as we become fused with the technology, human identity becomes less distinct.

Whatever rationalization is adopted to defend the construction of the information web, one thing is clear: if present trends continue, your children will have very little to keep secret – and that is where the nightmare truly begins. For unlike the village system of other centuries, the new information web will not allow you to pull up roots and leave. You cannot start afresh in another town, go to the big city, or emigrate for a new life. The emerging web is unlimited and unforgiving. Unlike the character in *The Rise and Fall of Reginald Perrin*, there will be no second start for a population whose personal identity is irrevocably fused into the technological web.

There is no Big Brother enforcing compliance with this New Order. People will happily surrender their most intimate data. The nightmare vision that Britain sensed in 1971 is about to materialize.

CHAPTER TWO

MAKING A KILLING ON THE INFORMATION SUPERHIGHWAY

Until the 1970s computers were expensive, cumbersome and relatively stupid. They fulfilled a narrow role in businesses and research and they did so without style, speed or grace. Few individuals had the money or the inclination to own one. And, even if they did, its repertoire of functions was so limited that it was light years from either a learning tool or an entertainment centre. Compared with the staggering power and limitless features of modern day machines, the early computers really were quite anally retentive.

For the first few decades of its existence the state-of-the-art computer resembled a sort of metal-working lathe. Powered by banks of valves and supported by cumbersome steel frames, they did their business in bleak isolation, sinister and alone. Their sterile environment was probably fortuitous since these juggernauts terrified and baffled most of the population.

From the 1970s, two important developments occurred. First, microchip technology caused a breathtaking reduction in the size and the price of computers, so much so that by the early 1980s personal computers (PCs) were to be found throughout homes and offices. Their new-found power, coupled with a multitude of user-friendly software programmes, brought the computer into the private domain. The second development began about twenty-five years ago when computers started to speak with each other.

DIRT TRACKS TO THE SUPERHIGHWAY

In the early 1970s, having invested large sums in the development of computer research facilities, the US Defense Department was looking to ways it could configure a computer network so that it could function even when large chunks of it had been destroyed or paralysed. The Department developed the Advanced Research Projects Agency Network, ARPANET, which was, in effect, a web of computers across the country, each component of which had been programmed to act as a 'mail handler' for all the other computers.

The Defense Department's strategy was simple: when one computer wanted to send a message or file to another machine on the network, it prepared the data as an 'electronic envelope' which was addressed in a precise way. Each computer was instructed to 'pass the packet' until its destination had been reached. If the network was partially down, the packet would keep circulating in different ways until it found a clear passage through which to travel. The revolutionary part of this development was that this network had no 'central command' that could cause the complete paralysis of the system. Each computer and each packet of data acted as part of a collective intelligence.

In brief, ARPANET and its successor, the Internet, operate in the following way. The computer systems connected to the Net function independently of one another, although they communicate in a common protocol, or language. These separate computer systems are frequently referred to as nodes. Each node processes whatever commands or requests are currently before it, making requests to other computer systems when necessary. When one computer needs to send information to a node to which it has no direct connection, it sends the information to a computer system to which it is connected with a request that this second system pass the information along until it reaches the desired node. No specific route is designated. If a particular attempt fails, the various systems which receive the information will try alternate routes and will continue with such attempts until the information is successfully delivered. This lateral thinking transformed the handling of information in the most profound way since the introduction of the automated telephone exchange.[1]

Because there is so much flexibility in the way the Net organizes the transfer of its information, and because each node operates independently of the others, no particular computer system or group of systems is essential to the functioning of the Net. A direct although unintended result of this fact is that it is almost impossible to technologically regulate what goes on in the Net. In the words of one person, 'The Net interprets censorship as damage, and routes around it.'[2]

BUILDING BLOCKS OF THE SUPERHIGHWAY

The Internet has matured from its early ARPANET beginnings to a thing of vast proportions. The world's telecommunication systems connect nearly 10,000 smaller networks in 100 countries, and 30 million people through their PCs and workstations. The Internet grows at around 10 per cent every month as housewives, schoolchildren, small businesses, organized crime syndicates, government agencies and millions more clients swell its ranks.

The Internet is used for numerous purposes. It supports the use of electronic mail, allowing messages to be transmitted cheaply from one machine to any other machine in the world. It has news groups and bulletin boards where thousands of like-minded people can exchange views and ideas in a public forum. The Internet also allows information in the form of electronic files to be pulled from one machine (say, the NASA public database in the United States) to your home computer. Alternatively, you can use the Internet to browse through electronic libraries throughout the world. The cost of doing this is usually little more than that of a local phone call.

The advantages of the Internet, however, are also its disadvantages. It was always a free and open network, virtually a public resource. Anyone could use it provided they could gain access to a node computer, say at a university or research establishment. In time, a number of commercial access services such as Compuserve or America on Line sprang up, giving limited access to services on the Internet and policing the content of the data flowing through their systems. Once you had even this access, a vast network was yours and you could contact any other machine that had a similar connection. The funding for research and development as well as maintenance and expansion of the Internet was paid for by the large government and academic institutions that supported the high speed communications links between different parts of the network.

The high-profile players in the field, many of whom had become extremely rich off the profits of the computer business, likened the whole scene to the Wild West. They fondly described it as the 'Electronic Frontier' and painted folksy wordscapes of electronic pioneers wandering unfettered throughout the endless domain of cyberspace. There were, so the electronic squatocracy assured us, no rules out there, just plenty of space for hungry minds and fat wallets.

The only drawback to this cosy arrangement was that since no one owned the Internet as a resource, capital investment was limited. While the opportunity for profit was thin, so would be the investment potential. Large sections of the community would remain disconnected. More importantly, many facilities and services that required big investment would stay undeveloped because the infrastructure of the network simply could not cope with the technical demands. Video telephones, tele-medicine (using phone lines to conduct medical services), interactive television and high speed computer communication all need sophisticated digital and optical fibre technology to handle the vast amounts of data.

In the lead-up to the 1992 US election, vice-presidential candidate Al Gore capitalized on the potential for developing the Internet by calling for the construction of an Information Superhighway that would connect every US business, school and home, and which would revolutionize

American education and business. What Gore was proposing was that the Internet be developed using dollars from the
American corporate sector. His vision called for it to be
made bigger and faster, using Integrated Services Digital
Network (ISDN) or optical fibre technology piped into every
local area in place of the existing slow speed, low technology
telephone wires. In return for their investment, the
corporate backers would place 'toll gates' on the Highway
to reap revenue from the vast traffic of information that
would be generated through demand for the new services
and products created.

It was a radical shift from the egalitarian frontier so
fondly embraced up until the day before, but large numbers
of people in America and throughout the world went crazy
over the idea. A complex notion had been simply expressed.
Government and industry bodies in a dozen countries, eager
to cash in on the craze and wanting to link arms with the Al
Gore vision, set up Superhighway task forces. The concept
was known by different names – the National Information
Infrastructure, the National Research and Education Network, the National Public Network, and even the International Information Infrastructure. So thoroughly intrigued
are political leaders in the US by the rhetoric of the
Superhighway that conservative leader Newt Gingrich set
about making the legislative materials available on-line and
has called for a Magna Carta for the information age. The
rich, self-assured computer barons quickly abandoned their
frontier analogy and instead eulogized the Highway and its
potential to civilize the wilderness.

In Britain, the government scratched its collective head
over the fuss, but its mandarins lost no time in summoning
all those boffins who for the past ten years had produced

unintelligible reports about the information revolution. Delighted at this unexpected turn of events, they advised what they had aways advised: information technology should be taken more seriously. It should be government's primary tool for reform. Ministers were told that the rest of the world was leaping on to the information Superhighway. Britain should do so now lest it miss this priceless window of opportunity.

Now that the information revolution had been legit-imized, ministers were anxious to embrace it. Struggling technologists from many departments suddenly found their work was taken seriously at the highest levels. Information technology schemes recently ditched were revived, dusted off, and brought out for show. The Cabinet Office commissioned a major study of the potential for reform, while Downing Street set up a cross-government committee, GEN 34, to investigate the application of microchip (smart) card technology.

The information revolution in the form of the newly named Superhighway was, of course, already well under way. Cable companies such as Nynex were connecting cable to homes throughout Britain. The national telephone system was already being transformed thanks to digital technology. More than a dozen major schemes to introduce large-scale information systems had already commenced throughout government. The missing ingredient was a national infor-mation policy of the sort Al Gore had proposed. What private and government bodies needed was a set of national goals and standards that could form the basis for a total network of connections. Without political leadership on the matter such a policy could never evolve. Instead, the British government had become impaled on its free market rhetoric. Unable to set the pace, it signalled to companies that they could sort the Highway out for themselves. In the end, the government proposed that the private sector could build many Highways of its own choosing.[3]

The experts know that once the Internet has been transmogrified into the Superhighway, using high performance technology and countless new connections into the community, the activities taking place on it will increase. Interactions will become part of an information marketplace conforming to the rules of corporate strategy. This information marketplace, according to one group representing the telecommunications sector, is likely to include electronic invoicing, billing, listing, brokering, advertising, comparison-shopping, and matchmaking of various kinds. 'Video on demand' will not just mean ordering current movies, as if they were spooling down from the local videotape store, but opening floodgates to vast new amounts of independent work, of high quality thanks to plummeting prices of professional-quality desktop video editors. Customers will grow used to dialling up two-minute demos of homemade videos before ordering the full program and storing it on their own blank tape.[4]

There will be other important uses of the network as a simulation medium for experiences which are impossible to obtain in the ordinary world. One US group established to promote digital communication says: 'If scientists want to explore the surface of a molecule, they'll do it in simulated form, using wrap-around three-dimensional animated graphics that create a convincing illusion of being in a physical place. This visualization of objects from molecules to galaxies is already becoming an extraordinarily powerful scientific tool. Networks will amplify this power to the point that these simulation tools take their place as fundamental scientific apparatus alongside microscopes and telescopes. Less exotically, a consumer or student might walk around the inside of a working internal combustion engine – without getting burned.'[5]

According to its most enthusiastic supporters, the most significant change the Superhighway will create is a new mode of building communities – as did the telephone, radio, and television. People often think of electronic 'communities' as far-flung communities of interest between followers of a particular discipline. But, so say the promoters of the new network, digital media can serve as a local nexus, an evanescent meeting-ground, that adds levels of texture to relationships between people in a particular locale.

All this may or may not materialize. Australian telecommunications specialist Peter White has observed that such claims about the benefits of new technologies have been made and discredited many times before. When we look at the literature proclaiming the potential benefits of radio and television we can see that those media have been promoted as ways to provide universal access to education, improve the lot of the economically disadvantaged, elevate public taste and revitalize the democratic process through the creation of an informed citizenry.

Unfortunately these promises have not always been fulfilled. 'Parallel errors can be seen in the early discussion of the telephone system. At the turn of the century there was no understanding of the telephone as a potential tool for everyday social communication. Almost none of the pioneers predicted how the telephone would transform the way we live our lives. So new communication technologies don't always deliver their promised benefits. Even when benefits are realized, early forecasts of these have often been way out.'[6]

In the end, so say the sceptics, the Superhighway may become a euphemism for 500 channels of crap on cable TV. Consumers in Britain may be intrigued by that idea, but anyone confined to an American hotel room for a few days learns quickly that choice and value are not equivalent constants. Many of the channels on American cable are either forgettable B-grade movies, or reruns of sad shows from twenty years past. Promises of a new era of public access are unlikely to see the light of day. The Internet has already proved that too many cooks spoil the informational broth. Maybe everyone can have fifteen minutes of fame on the Internet by being his own publisher, but the noise to signal ratio is now so high that few people trust the content.

TOLL GATES ON THE SUPERHIGHWAY

There are many ways of interpreting the Superhighway. At one level, it is a scramble by big money corporations to cash in on the information revolution and establish a means of permanently taxing information. At another level it is a complex infrastructure which will be a vehicle for wholesale social change. A more cynical (but no less correct) view is that it is an over-hyped gadget of marginal importance. The reality falls somewhere between the three scenarios.

The Superhighway might be the means to create new products and services for a hungry economy. It might be the source of an entertainment and information reformation that enriches the lives of billions. It might strengthen democracy by creating a means of bringing government and the people into closer and more meaningful contact. It might do all of these things or none of them. The Superhighway, after all, is merely a metaphor for a basket of complex images and ideas. It is a means of expressing an astoundingly ambitious vision which has to do with bringing technology and information together. In the Superhighway vision, isolation is anathema. No machine should stand alone, no human should be disconnected.

The Superhighway will be constructed on the three piers of compatibility, convergence and connectivity. In other words, it will aim to make all technology conform to the same rules of input and output and will then seek to link *all* technology to *all* people for *all* purposes. At its most advanced point the Superhighway is a vast web that touches all machines, all forms of information and all humans. It brings them into harmony by creating common rules, common specifications and common goals.

Few strategies in the history of the planet have been this ambitious and few have offered such a rich diversity of rewards. The architects of the Superhighway are serious when they talk about 500 channels of TV, or the creation of electronic democracy, or universal video phones. They believe that the Superhighway can really bring the world into our living rooms in an interactive way. For this you will gladly pay by the minute or by the transaction.

The Superhighway is an important theme throughout this book, not because I believe all the hype associated with it, but because I am certain it is going to make possible a new era of surveillance and control. The Highway is, after all, a two-way thoroughfare. We hear much about the services that it will provide, but little about the masses of personal information that it will extract. We hear much about the spectrum of new opportunities it will offer, but little about the demands that it will make. The history of information technology is peppered with doublespeak, deceit and one-sided bargains that inevitably fall against the interests of the consumer. The Superhighway is hardly likely to perform any differently. Imagine, just for a moment, what a hostile power would do with the Superhighway.

If any example is needed to demonstrate the potential dangers of the Superhighway, the current epidemic of CCTV systems should provide it. As I outline in Chapter 8, by the end of the century Britain will have nearly half a million CCTV systems covering every conceivable activity in public and private spaces. The images will be digital, as will be the national photo archive that these cameras can connect with. CCTV images can be automatically scanned against the photo archive, thus placing a name, ID number and other related information alongside anonymous faces in a crowd. The visual images will be carried throughout the nation – and the world – along the very Superhighway that offers the promise of a stronger, safer democracy.

One of the most intriguing aspects of the Superhighway will be its international dimension. We naturally think of highways as national facilities, an assumption which high-lights the shortcomings of the analogy. In the next five years the Superhighway will be totally international and will facilitate the export of information on us and our activities to any country in the world, promoting questions of control, privacy and sovereignty. Often, personal information is exported because of international obligations. Britain is locked into a vast array of international agreements and conventions on the sharing of information. The *Mutual*

Administrative Assistance in Tax treaty, for example, obliges Britain to surrender personal tax information to all other signatory countries. Other countries have not been so ready to part with their citizens' data. A wildcat campaign by the Australian Privacy Foundation forced the federal government to distance itself from the tax treaty.

Until the 1980s, information exchange between countries was impossible on any large scale because computers could not be made to talk easily with one another. This is changing. There is now international agreement on the harmonization of computer hardware and software, and this process (known as 'open systems planning') will ensure that in the future, vast quantities of computer information from virtually any source can be transferred, processed and analysed by any other computer in any other country. This *open systems* plan will create the effect of a vast international computer network, reducing the isolation of nations and of information.[7]

This harmonization of computers is assisting the accumulation from all parts of the world of information that previously remained separate. The genealogical records of much of the world are being collected by the Mormon Church for storage in a vast computer in Utah. Its extraordinary memory contains information on the ancestral records of each one of us. Through hundreds of terminals this information is processed and assessed. Mormon agents have collected this personal information from the public records of governments throughout the world. How the information is used is a closely guarded secret. The claim, however, by former American intelligence agents that the Mormon Church is being used as a recruiting base for new CIA operatives is fuel for concern about how this sort of information is used, and the importance of openness of such systems.[8]

THE HIGHWAY TO HEALTH

The Superhighway is a metaphor for the convergence of machines and databases scattered throughout Britain and the world. Each sector – police, banks, airlines and defence – is building its own laneway on the Superhighway. Among the most impressive of these projects is the one which will computerize the National Health Service. If it is successful, Britain may well end up with the most efficient and cost-effective health system in the world. If it fails, the quality of NHS health care and the confidentiality of medical information within it will be imperilled.

The Management Executive of the NHS recently embarked on an ambitious plan called the Information Management and Technology Strategy (IMTS). The plan aims to standardize all information and technology throughout the health system. In five years, if the plan succeeds, all computers throughout the NHS will be able to speak with each other. Information on all aspects of health care and health records will be available in computerized form and will be distributed throughout the health service.

This means that, eventually, diagnostic and clinical information on any patient will be available instantly wherever it is needed – X-rays, pathology results, clinical notes or hospital information. By 1996, more than 90 per cent of GPs will have access to this system, as will all major NHS organizations.

The simplest way of picturing this project is to imagine a

vast information 'spine' running through the entire NHS. Computers in all areas of health care will feed information into this spine through telecommunication 'nerves'. This data can then be tapped anywhere else along the spine. It means that as well as personal medical information being made available reliably, quickly and cheaply throughout the system, health planners and administrators will potentially have a huge quantity of quality information at their fingertips.

To achieve this goal, the Management Executive plans to reissue all NHS numbers in a new format (currently there are twenty-nine formats being used). This means that by 1996, every member of the population will have a unique number. This number, together with personal details such as name, age and address, will be recorded in one of a series of linked administrative registers. This is the heart of the system. All medical information on patients will then be 'attached' to their unique number, which will then become the central reference throughout the NHS. The number, in effect, becomes an information 'skip' into which is placed the medical data.

If an NHS worker or a doctor needs information on any aspect of a patient's health record or history, this can be instantly obtained by inputting the new NHS number through the computer system. The information will be 'pulled' through the network from wherever it is stored. In the jargon of health informatics, this is known as 'seamless' health care.

This particular wind of change is not unique to Britain. It is blowing through most of the world's advanced health systems. In Australia it is known as the Health Communications Network (HCN), which the federal government envisages as being like a telephone system. In the United States it is called the 'Computer Based Patient Record' using the Superhighway. Same system, different imagery.

The potential benefits of the system are enormous. Administrative and clinical savings could amount to billions of pounds a year. In the US it has been estimated that the savings from computerization of the health system could be between 10 and 30 billion dollars annually. Clinical savings arising from such factors as reduction of duplication of tests might amount to as much as 40 per cent of this figure. Administrative savings would account for a similar amount.

The scenario, however, is not entirely rosy. Some studies have found that nearly half of all clinical computer systems fail because of poor design, user resistance, or incompatibility with existing work practices. One 1990 survey of 620 US hospitals indicated that hospitals use less than one-fourth of the capabilities built into their computer systems. Planners are often out of touch with the people who will be required to use the system on a day-to-day basis. Managerial and fiscal motivations driving such plans seldom take into account the many minor factors that can render a computer impractical in the work environment. The costs of building a network are vast, and the end result is invariably less positive than the architects promised. There appears to be a general rule that the more complex a system becomes, the more permutations of failure are created.

In Australia, where a similar project has commenced under the auspices of the Federal Government, the medical profession is sceptical. Some state branches of the Australian Medical Association, suspicious of government control, have formally opposed the initiative. The view of some doctors is that a centrally controlled health information system will inevitably be used against the best interests of medical independence and medical confidentiality. Ultimately, a computerized health network would work against the interests of patients.

The confidentiality and privacy issues are thorny. Countering any potential benefit of computerization is the risk that the network could all but destroy medical confidentiality. A system which allows sensitive personal information to be made available quickly and simply to a large number of people and organizations brings with it grave risks to privacy.

The UK Department of Health flew in the face of conventional security opinion in 1992 with a decision that encryption was not necessary, because (it claimed) the risk of hacking was 'minimal'. The upshot is that everyone's records will be openly published in a way that will make them widely available. The million or so users of the new system will have to be 'authenticated' before accessing data, but the system's information will not be technically secure. The British government's concept of information protection is centred around the idea of security: making sure that personal medical information is seen only by those who are authorized to see it. The medical profession is concerned that as time passes, more and more people will be 'authorized' for reasons which have little to do with primary health care.

This minimum privacy policy is setting the government on a collision course with the medical establishment. The Council of the British Medical Association (BMA) fired a shot across the government's bows in October 1995 with a warning that doctors might have to boycott the system unless the government radically strengthened its privacy and security safeguards. A doctor's duty to confidentiality, warned the BMA, is more important than considerations of speed and efficiency of health information. And with all information channelled on to the new health Superhighway, medical practice can be better controlled and monitored, patients can be more easily surveilled, and the data more readily sold off to private interests. The BMA withdrew cooperation from the network.

The BMA is not alone. In Massachusetts, where the government and the private sector are establishing a similar data network, the local branch of the American Civil Liberties Union (ACLU) issued a press release condemning the scheme and warning, 'It is more and more the case that the "outsider" is being brought inside. Insurers are combining with providers, pharmaceutical companies with HMO pharmaceutical prescription management corporations, etc. It is now common for a corporation that seeks information held by another entity to buy out or form a strong contractual link with that entity.'

TURNING THE SUPERHIGHWAY INTO A
   ## SNOOPER HIGHWAY

Anyone with concerns about the surveillance activities of law enforcement and national security agencies has ample justification to fear the Superhighway. The technology is a one-stop-shop for snooping. Intelligence agencies are delighted with the potential of the Superhighway. It will contain vast amounts of sensitive information. And because of the ordered convergence of this information, it will be easy for the agencies to extract masses of data about our day-to-day activities. Much of this 'transactional' data can be accessed without the requirement of a warrant.

There are many agencies here and overseas that have an interest in snooping on the Superhighway. The United Kingdom supports seven intelligence agencies which have the responsibility of protecting national security and gathering intelligence information. The best known of these are MI6, which has parallel general intelligence responsibilities to the CIA, and the signals intelligence agency Government Communications Headquarters (GCHQ) located in Cheltenham.

The agencies are large, well resourced, and influential. GCHQ has over 5,000 staff, and its access to government is absolute. Virtually all domestic law includes exemptions for national security, and departments are generally careful to ensure that national security interests are observed, so as not to force an open challenge against an administrative decision. All national security agencies make their views known through the Joint Intelligence Committee, chaired by the Cabinet Secretary.

These affairs are conducted, in the words of one former MI6 operative, 'on a wink and a nod'. Bureaucrats and ministers rarely, if ever, challenge a 'request' by the Joint Intelligence Committee.

The national security interests of the UK are intimately entwined in a complex web of international arrangements and agreements, binding us to the national security interests of other nations. In 1943, the British and US governments signed a pact, appropriately called the British–United States (BRUSA) agreement, which established procedures for the sharing of information and facilities in the intelligence efforts of the two countries.

Immediately following the Second World War, in 1947, the governments of the United States, the United Kingdom, Canada, Australia and New Zealand signed a National Security pact known as the Quadrapartite, or United Kingdom–United States (UKUSA) Agreement. Its intention was to seal an intelligence bond in which a common national security objective was created. The five nations carved up the earth into five spheres of influence, and each country was assigned particular targets (Britain, for example, was responsible for intercepting the Chinese, through its Hong Kong listening post, while the US was given other responsibilities to cover from its listening posts in Taiwan, Japan and Korea).[9]

The UKUSA Agreement standardized terminology, code words, intercept handling procedures, arrangements for cooperation, sharing of information, and access to facilities. It is generally understood to be the most secretive agreement in the English-speaking world, and creates an intelligence dependence which British journalist Chapman Pincher described as 'so great and [its] cooperation so close that I am convinced security chiefs would go to any lengths to protect the link-up'.[10]

One important component of the agreement was the exchange of data and personnel. The link means that operatives from, say, the New Zealand signals intelligence agency GCSD could work from the Canberra facilities of Australia's Defence Signals Directorate, to intercept local communications, and pass on the contents to the Australian intelligence agencies, without either nation having to formally approve or disclose the interception.

The strongest alliance within the UKUSA relationship is the one between the US National Security Agency (NSA) and GCHQ. It is widely understood that the NSA contributes several hundred million pounds each year to GCHQ to fund its main 'listening station' at Menwith Hill. In return, GCHQ provides full access to the NSA and its operatives in the UK.

According to James Bamford's study of the NSA, *The Puzzle Palace*, the relationship between the two agencies is so intimate, that they could be considered to be one organization:

> Sharing seats alongside the NSA operators, at least in some areas, are SIGINT (signals intelligence) specialists from Britain's Government Communications Headquarters (GCHQ). According to the former Menwith Hill official, the two groups work very closely together. 'In fact,' he said, 'the cooperation was so smooth that when the Brits would put down their earphones for their ten am tea break, the Americans would simply cover their positions.[11]

Cooperation between the two agencies is not confined to the interception of non-English-speaking countries. It is one of the worst kept secrets in Whitehall that the NSA conducts large numbers of unauthorized wiretaps on British citizens, and passes on the information to GCHQ. Such exchanges are not covered by law (GCHQ operatives also work out of the NSA's headquarters at Fort Meade in Maryland, and reciprocate the activity). In 1994 the Home Secretary authorized 871 new wiretaps, yet Menwith Hill is reported to have 40,000 active telephone lines connected to it. This tactic has been used for decades, but the Superhighway gives the potential for total surveillance of countless individuals.

One hot potato in national security is that the UK–US

link-up has the effect of ensuring that US national security interests are instantly reflected in UK domestic policy.

THE ENCRYPTION CONUNDRUM

GCHQ, the Home Office, MI5 and MI6 often exhibit differences of opinion about priorities and strategies, but all agree that the widespread use of encryption (scrambling of information) on the Superhighway has the potential to inhibit, and possibly imperil, law enforcement and national security. All agencies agree that encryption should be the sole province of trusted parties such as the Foreign Office and the Department of Defence, but encryption in the general community should be resisted. Some elements of the intelligence community believe that encryption should be made illegal in circumstances where it makes the communication immune to wiretapping. Technically, most forms of encryption can be cracked using linked Supercomputers, though this is a costly and time consuming process.

The intelligence agencies argue that the growing use of cheap, commercially available encryption systems will seriously diminish the ease of interception of communications. Accordingly, an 'understanding' has been reached in Whitehall that the government will not institute any national encryption system to make information secure from interception and hacking.

The effectiveness of the pan-governmental understanding was successfully tested in 1993 when GCHQ convinced the Department of Trade and Industry to oppose the strong A5 encryption system intended for the GSM mobile communications network. Then, in 1992, GCHQ again worked on the Department of Health to ensure that the emerging national health data network (the IM&T strategy) was not encrypted. This was despite reports that former health minister Brian Mawhinney had wanted encryption.

The UK situation is not unique. In the United States, the National Security Agency has achieved an identical – though less binding – policy. One common national security objective is to ensure that the flow of data within and between the UK and US is kept 'wiretap friendly'. Because the gathering of intelligence information depends on access to open flows of data, national security agencies have traditionally resisted the development of encryption systems that would scramble data, and make its interception difficult or impossible.

The NSA has fought the encryption battle on two fronts. First, it has pioneered the introduction of a technology known as the 'Clipper Chip', which provides secure scrambling but which also gives spy agencies a 'back door' through which to read the scrambled data. Second, the government has introduced a Digital Telephony law which requires all manufacturers of communications equipment to conform to standards that would ensure all communications lines are wiretap friendly.

The Clipper Chip is the government's solution to the encryption dilemma. It involves the development of an 'official' form of encryption built into a fingernail size device that can be attached to telephones or computers. The unique algorithm, or code, generated by each device is registered with a government agency, along with the name and details of its user.

The 'key' to decode the encryption is split into two parts, each of which is held by a different agency (the National

Institute for Standards and Technology, and the US Treasury). Only when the appropriate intercept authorization is presented, will the agencies release the components of the key. When the two halves are joined, the agency is able to decipher the code.

This is known as a 'twin escrow' system. It is not a perfect solution from the perspective of security agencies, principally because it inhibits the ease of access that they formerly had. Nor is it a perfect solution from the perspective of users, who believe it is a weaker and less secure means of encrypting data. It is, nevertheless, being promoted as the compromise solution. With its Clipper Chip plan, the government has taken the first step to a compulsory official encryption registration scheme, ensuring that the Superhighway can be monitored with relative ease. In 1995, the Electronic Privacy Information Center, a public interest group in Washington DC, acquired FBI documents under the Freedom of Information Act, which outlined a two-stage plan for mandatory state-controlled encryption.

WHO CONTROLS THE SUPERHIGHWAY?

It is easy to be carried away by the earnest rhetoric of politicians and corporate moguls as they sell the Superhighway as a tool of benign social engineering. It is easy to believe that the harnessing of information, at any price, must be good, and that the proliferation of technology is necessary and socially desirable.

Not everyone goes along with this popular wisdom. American consumer guru Ralph Nader believes much of the information revolution is dangerous and retrograde. Sitting on a Spartan armchair in a corner of the vast, empty, ornate conference room of the Carnegie Center in Washington DC, he tells a different story.

Nader is one of a tiny élite of thinkers who can consistently pick trends. Since his ground-breaking 1965 investigation into the car industry, *Unsafe at any speed*, Nader has been at the forefront of consumer rights. The problem, he argues, is that while corporations and their marketing strategies continue to gain influence and momentum, opposition to their plans is increasingly paralysed. The traditional political divide between left and right has been neutralized by the tendency of liberal groups and corporations alike to seek comfortable consensus – easy middle ground that cuts out extremes and limits reform to the interests of the most powerful players in the equation.

He calls this the emergence of 'harmony ideology', a process which, according to America's civil rights and consumer community, has crippled the Clinton Administration's reform agenda and is doing the same across the world. Britain's Labour Party, according to Nader, is falling prey to the same influences.[12]

Nader's views are in stark contrast to the claims made by proponents of the Superhighway, who argue that modern information technology will strengthen democracy, enlighten the individual, and usher in an era of personal freedom and choice.

'Not so,' replies Nader. 'This is the multinational corporate epic, and the corporation has no ethical compass.' Part of the price, he believes, will be personal privacy, which will be sacrificed because of back-room deals between the corporate sector and weak-kneed government. In the Nader analysis, the Superhighway is the product of converging vested interests seeking to exploit a gullible public.

SHADES OF A CORPORATE CONSPIRACY

On the other side of Washington DC is the headquarters of the Center for Strategic and International Studies (CSIS), a vast and supremely influential hub of what used to be called the military–industrial complex. The man behind the desk in front of me had just been hired by the CSIS to help run a new effort to control the world's information economy.

Ever since the information Superhighway was created, the world's telecommunications and computer companies have been moving to force governments to back away from establishing any rules or regulations. Until now they have not been able to speak with one voice. Now, under the banner of the CSIS, a consortium of the world's leading companies have formed the Global Information Infrastructure Commission (GIIC). Headed by the president of Mitsubishi, the chairman of EDS (a multinational computer giant that is moving to buy many of the British government's computer records), and the vice-chairman of Siemens Corporation, the GIIC intends to create a conglomerate of interests powerful enough to subsume government interest in regulating the Superhighway. In Britain, the effort is not necessary because government has already opted for a hands-off, corporate-driven approach.

The whole effort is being bankrolled by the World Bank, which in early 1994 bought the line from CSIS that unregulated economic investment was more important to developing economies than social and political reform. The corporates, argued CSIS, can deliver this economic reform along the Superhighway, and they can do it best if they, and not the governments, take the lead. Indeed, the slogan of the GIIC is 'Forging a new contract for public and private sector cooperation'. Shades of Nader's harmony ideology.

Listening to the rhetoric of the CSIS and its moneyed interests makes very clear the claim that Nader made – the individual is being cut out of the whole deal. Corporations and governments have formed an alliance which will shape the emerging information economy to their ends. The individual and the consumer are hardly on the horizon.

TAKING THE CONSPIRACY TO THE ULTIMATE LEVEL

The new deal between government and private sector interests has become transparent at the highest levels. The 1995 summit of the G7 (the seven richest industrial powers) linked arms with the richest corporations on earth to form a consensus about how the Superhighway should be built. Predictably, this supremely influential gathering agreed to a set of principles that would maximize growth, development and profit. Relatively little attention was paid to the negative impact of the Superhighway on developing countries and on the rights and privacy of citizens of developed countries. Martin Bangermann, Europe's Commissioner in charge of information technology, remarked, 'We will not achieve the information Society unless we give the free market a free rein.'[13]

Back home in the UK, while it is a simple matter to uncover passion about the private sector culture that dominates the political landscape, it is mighty difficult to find concern about the sort of technology which is the focus of these companies' efforts. The use of such technology here does not inflame general sentiment.

The Superhighway, by whatever name it is known, offers a tantalizing view of the future. The technology can be turned to public good, or to the interests of powerful élites. Just as important, the information generated on the Highway can be used to promote free choice, a democratic vision, and a vibrant information market. Alternatively, it can be harnessed as a means of creating a surveillance society which pursues control, maximizes corporate profit and limits personal privacy and freedom. Just how the mechanism will achieve those ends will depend on the awareness and consciousness of the British people.

CHAPTER THREE

IN SEARCH OF PERFECT IDENTITY

Phoenix psychologist Charles Jenkins is embarked on a bizarre mission. He is part of a US consortium which will shortly launch an identification microchip designed to be implanted into humans. The chip will be inserted behind the shoulder, underneath the first layer of skin, and will be 'ideal', so claim its promoters, for the senile, the insane – and even for small children.[1] The chip will contain basic identifying information on the 'host' human. The consortium will also offer a toll-free number to provide further information on the patient, including more detailed identifying information. No more lost babies or grannies. No more wandering, unidentified nutters.

Mr Jenkins and his colleagues also have their sights on the rest of us. Their chip will contain a medical profile to aid paramedics at accident scenes. Diabetes, allergies, heart conditions, or even deafness can be deduced with a hand-held scanner. An attractive proposition indeed. Perhaps the ID chip could be taken a step further, becoming a substitute for all those cards and PIN numbers. Given the fallibility of conventional ID cards, the implant option is a novel idea waiting to gain respectability.

Civil liberties bodies in the United States have turned their attention to the risk that this form of technology might one day be used as a general human identifier. 'It's coming,' Louis Rhodes of the Arizona Civil Liberties Union told the *Phoenix Gazette*. 'Kids will be first. Then perhaps criminals on intensive probation. Then others.'[2]

This fear may not be entirely without foundation. Authorities in Britain and elsewhere are desperate to find cheap alternatives to imprisonment. Extensive responsibilities are to be handed to a private company to develop and enforce a 'community detention' scheme for prisoners.[3] In this programme, offenders would be electronically 'tagged' with an ankle bracelet. The bracelet is designed to sound an alarm if the offender leaves a designated area – usually a house or place of employment.

The tagging concept was the brainchild of an Albuquerque judge, who was inspired by a Spiderman comic in which the hero was tagged and tracked by his arch enemy. It seems, however, that attaching a physical object to a human is an inferior means of achieving this goal. Trials of the technology were undertaken in Nottingham, Newcastle and London in 1989, with the embarrassing result that 40 per cent of offenders tore their bracelets off and absconded. With the bracelet removed, the offender has total freedom of movement. So far as the authorities are concerned, the bracelet is in its proper location, so all is well.

It is feasible that an implant procedure could improve this outcome. An implant inserted via a twelve-gauge needle deep inside the abdomen or neck would be impossible to remove without a surgical operation. A proportion of offenders – particularly first-timers – would volunteer for deep implantation if it saved them from the rigours of imprisonment. Given the prevailing attitude to law and order, public opinion is likely to be on the side of the technology.

THE FIRST GENERATION OF HUMAN ID IMPLANTS

In non-criminal society, hundreds of people have already been implanted with ID implant technology. One of the most vexing problems in the field of conventional medical implants (breast implants, plastic penises and so on) has been the tracing of data about medical procedure and product data relating to the implant. Years later, if a patient visits a doctor because of problems with a hip joint or a chin implant, medical information such as the manufacturer of the implant and the name of the surgeon who performed it may not be available.

The problem has been solved by installing an ID chip implant on to the primary implant. This is, quite simply, a microchip on which all relevant information has been encoded. Called SmartDevice, the chip is manufactured by Hughes Identification Devices, a subsidiary of Hughes Aircraft Co. In the event of complications with an implant, a doctor could retrieve the information from the chip using a 'gun' that emits a radio beam. The gun operates in much the same way that decoders in supermarkets decipher bar coding. The information on the chip will link with a global registry.

LipoMatrix Inc. has been issued a patent for the use of

SmartDevice in medical implants and has begun putting them into its soya bean oil breast implants. SmartDevices are already in several hundred breast implants tested since October on women in Britain, Italy and Germany.

The use of ID chip implants in humans may become far more general. The difficulties relating to medical problems with implants apply also to general surgery. If people are happy to accept an ID implant as part of an appendectomy or cancer surgery, these devices will soon become general across the entire population.

FIRST, THE ANIMALS

This form of information implant was first used for the identification of animals and is now common throughout the world. Microchip implants roughly the size of a grain of rice have been used since the mid-1980s to provide identifying data on animals. The technology was used initially in the US to track salmon (and has subsequently been used in the UK to catch salmon poachers). A veterinarian can implant the chip in an animal in seconds for about £20 with no more complexity than a common injection. It emits a unique wave which can be read by a small scanner. The technology is now used in more than twenty countries and is useful in a range of circumstances – tagging rare animals, identifying livestock and for wildlife research.

The most popular use for the technology in recent years has been for the identification of domestic pets. Around 200,000 dogs and cats have been implanted in the UK and the number grows by more than 1,000 a week. Most animal care organizations support the procedure. Battersea Dogs home, for example, microchips every animal leaving the Home. The chip reveals the dog's vaccination history, as well as showing details of its owner.

If the Commons Select Committee on Agriculture has its way, all dogs and cats in Britain will eventually be microchipped. In late 1994 the Committee recommended replacing quarantine controls with universal vaccination for rabies, suggesting that the vaccination system should be enforced through microchipping and 'pet passports'. Some governments, including those of Singapore and Hong Kong, are considering making the use of microchips mandatory.

FROM BIONICS TO BIOMETRICS

It is tempting to dismiss the idea of human ID implants as a doomed notion. While some people will instinctively recoil from the idea, it is wise to recall just how far we have already travelled down the road to a fusion of flesh and machine – and how easily the fusion can be justified. Entire populations that in the time of one generation have revolted against various forms of technology and information gathering cheerfully accept them in the next.

As I mentioned in Chapter 1, 12,000 people in the United States have had their brains 'wired' as part of cochlear implants designed to restore hearing. As chip grafting becomes capable of relieving an increasing number of conditions, people will accept it as a legitimate and 'friendly' procedure. It is, after all, not the technology *per se* that offends people in the modern age, but the purposes to which it is put.

The effective running of the Superhighway requires a number of conditions, and accurate identification of humans is at the top of the list. Indeed, the evolution of information technology for decades has sought to develop perfect identity of human subjects. With perfect identity lies the hope of perfect efficiency. Or, to put it another way, perfect identity is the single most important condition for the establishment of a controlled society.

Even if the spectres of child abduction, incapacity or disappearance are not convincing enough bogeys to motivate the population at large to adopt 'perfect' microchip identification, there are other less invasive technologies that achieve the same result. If you can't put the machine into the human, why not put the human into the machine?

Governments and corporations across the world are doing just this. The process is known as biometry – the process of collecting, processing and storing details of a person's physical characteristics. The most popular forms of biometric ID are retina scans, hand geometry, thumb scans, fingerprints, voice recognition, and digitized (electronically stored) photographs. Spain is planning a national fingerprint system for unemployment benefit entitlement. Russia has announced plans for a national electronic fingerprint system for banks. Jamaicans will shortly need to scan their thumbs into a database before qualifying to vote at elections. Blue Cross and Blue Shield in the US have plans to introduce nationwide fingerprinting for hospital patients. This may be extended into more general medical applications. In Europe, tests are under way with equipment that puts a person's fingerprint information on to his or her credit card, so a device at the point of purchase can compare the card's data to a fingerprint to assure that the use of the card is legitimate. In Australia, the technology is being used in automated-teller machines.[4] As it becomes more viable, biometric technology is likely to be adopted as the identification of choice for large, complex organizations.

GIVING WELFARE A HAND

In January 1994, senior officials of the UK Department of Social Security met with their chief, Peter Lilley, to discuss ways of reducing welfare fraud, estimated to cost more than £2 billion annually. The DSS recommended a number of options. Surprisingly, the Department ended up supporting an initiative potentially far more controversial than an ID card. Its favoured option was to create a computerized database of the hand prints of every person receiving a government benefit. These would be stored in digitized form in a central computer. Whenever a person applied to a government agency for a benefit or subsidy, a hand print would be taken to determine whether that person already existed in 'the system'. The Department estimated that as many as 30 million people would have to be 'palm printed'.

The Department's reasons for recommending this strategy are largely to do with its ramshackle administration, a woe which it shares with many other agencies. Identification procedures are haphazard. Many clients simply do not have the necessary ID documents. While the problem of false or multiple identities is generally overstated, it nevertheless remains a political and administrative nuisance.

The accurate identification of individuals has always been a key concern for governments and private sector organizations. The development of identification systems is important to organizations because it offers one contributing solution to fraud and administrative inefficiency. Such initiatives can offer benefits to the client as well as to the administration. For these reasons, all organizations strive to achieve 'perfect identity' of their clients.

Conventional forms of identification have always been subject to fraud and manipulation. Card systems are the most vulnerable. Fake 'blanks' of even the highest integrity cards are generally available in Singapore or Thailand within weeks of issue.[5] The general availability of sophisticated computer machinery has placed the ability to forge such documents into the hands of a much wider group of criminals than would have been the case in earlier years.

The greatest problem facing benefits organizations, however, is the existence of multiple identities. Since most card systems rely on a pre-existing numbering or registration system, a lax identification procedure in the pre-existing system will give rise to a corresponding slackness in the card issue.

Many current number systems are inadequate. The Social Security Number (SSN) in the United States has become a *de facto* national identifier, despite admissions by the Social Security Administration that between 4 and 10 million false or illegal numbers are in circulation. The government of Sweden, which instituted the first national number system fifty years ago, is now claiming that the system facilitates fraud. Limitations are now being set on the uses of the number, and the Swedish Data Inspectorate is moving to break the number's 'monopoly'.

The development of high integrity identity systems is, however, fraught with problems. An overly rigorous identification procedure could prove unpopular, forcing some people to drop out of the system and inviting a degree of civil disobedience in others. On the other hand, lax and ineffective procedures leave organizations vulnerable to fraud. A key focus of information systems security in recent years has been to create ways of establishing accurate identity without the trappings of Big Brotherism.

There are three conventional forms of identification in use today. The first is something you *have*, such as a card. The second form is something you *know*, such as a password or PIN number. The third is something you *are* or something you *do*, such as a fingerprint, handwriting, or voice print. This latter form of identification is known as biometrics.

Biometric technology offers the prospect of highly accurate identification, but involves some difficult technical and public relations problems. In Western nations, the use of fingerprinting invites the stigma of criminality. Technical difficulties also dominate the use of sophisticated identification technology. Many systems do not live up to expectations because they fail to take into account the needs of people, or because the manufacturers provide inadequate testing under sterile conditions.

Flawed identity checking is very costly for organizations. It results in unnecessary duplication, fraud, and client disruption. A high integrity universal biometric system would, from the perspective of information users, be an ideal solution. Yet, from the perspective of privacy and autonomy, the move to such a universal form of identity carries enormous risk. There is a possibility of 'statelessness' arising where the system requires an increasing level of compliance which some people simply cannot or will not accept and thus end up being denied a range of services. Errors or failure in one part of the system may lead to a

domino effect involving suspension of benefits or entitle-
ments in other areas. Most importantly, the autonomy and
freedom of individuals may be compromised because of the
scale and nature of information collection.

Although biometry is increasingly seen as a solution to
fraud and inefficiency, not everyone is happy about the
technology. Daniel Polsby, a law professor at the US
Northwestern University, warns that a loss of personal
privacy will be the price. 'If the technology becomes as
efficient and cheap as expected, it almost certainly will be
widely used. The possibilities of abuse are mind-boggling,'
Polsby says. 'With this technology, the government can
compile a dossier on a person that tracks his every purchase
and movement. That sort of thing is possible now, but it is
too labour-intensive and expensive.'[6]

Government officials in the Netherlands say that biometrics has a 'real chance' of being accepted as a form of ID.
According to the Chip Card Platform, which is coordinating
the ID card, there has been a political change in recent years
and an understanding among the public of the role of
information technology. Officials do, however, acknowledge
that this change of attitude has taken them by surprise.[7]

In recent years, biometric technology has attained a
remarkable level of sophistication and reported accuracy has
been achieved at a level which far surpasses all other forms
of identification. The Iriscan system, for example, conducts
a scan of the eye and, according to claims made by the
manufacturer, is generally accurate to 10 to the 15th power
on the first scan, and 10 to the 22nd power on the second
scan. In other words, the chances of the match being
incorrect are one in 15 thousand trillion.[8] The figure may be
out by a vast amount, but the accuracy of the procedure is

still without parallel in the field of identification. Iris recognition does, however, suffer from the shortcoming that many people feel very sensitive and protective of their eyes and find such technology disquieting. Research is currently under way to scan the eye at a range of up to three metres.

Currently, the most popular form of biometry is fingerprinting. The Biometric Technologies Company of the US is in the final stages of developing a biometric fingerprinting system using neural networks. Laboratory tests commissioned by the manufacturer are showing an accuracy of 99.99 per cent, and a false rejection rate (rejecting genuine clients) of 0.1 per cent. Known as Printscan 3, the device is expected to be released in the early part of 1995 at a cost of US$600 per unit.[9]

The Japanese telecommunications giant NTT recently announced the development of a fingerprint recognition method that appears to be exceptionally fast and accurate. The technique can be used in conjunction with ordinary information processing and communications systems. Recognition of a fingerprint takes place in an average of 2 seconds on a personal computer or 1 second on a workstation, with accuracy above 99.9 per cent. Along with many other diverse applications, it can be used to confirm that the bearer of a credit card or ID card is the rightful owner. National computerized fingerprint systems are now being developed in several countries. The first national system was developed in Australia in 1987 using Fujitsu technology.[10]

The development of hand geometry, involving a scan of the shape and characteristics of the entire hand, has been a useful approach in situations where there is public sensitivity to fingerprinting. Hand geometry is already employed in over 4,000 locations including airports, daycare centres, nuclear research establishments, computer facilities, sperm banks, hospitals and in high security government buildings in Europe and the US.[11]

FINGERPRINTING THE POPULACE

The provincial government of Ontario in Canada is considering a biometric scheme which it hopes will eliminate fraud and duplication and streamline the functioning of all government agencies.

The Client Positive Identification strategy has been pioneered by the Community Services Department of Metro Toronto, an agency which hands out around 2 billion dollars Canadian (£1 billion) per annum on welfare services. The Department is steering a government-wide exploration of a biometric system which may eventually be used for all government benefits and services.

A committee representing virtually all Ontario departments has been established. It is currently discussing the mutual identification and administration concerns and the potential for creating a universal strategy for dealing with these problems.[12]

Although planning is still in the preliminary stage, officials are hopeful that a biometric register of thumb scans can be established by 1996. The register would be accessed by all Ontario agencies, and scanners (readers) would be located at many 'convenient' locations. The idea is to create a 'once and for all' identity which would then be valid for all government services and benefits. Discussions are under way with Federal agencies to see whether this programme can be integrated with immigration systems. The motivation behind this interface is that there is currently great concern over the issue of US citizens illegally using Canadian health care facilities. Nearly 12 million Ontario Health Benefits Cards have been issued to a population of 10 million, resulting in grave concern over the possible misuse of the numbers. Ironically, US authorities have criticized Canadians for crossing the border to use the 'superior' American health system.

The specifications set out in government documents describe a system that will digitize and store photographs and hand geometry, interface with existing information systems, and produce a plastic identity card with magnetic stripe.

The project manager for the strategy believes that the plan is technologically and organizationally possible, but 'politically tricky'. The Privacy Commissioner for Ontario has expressed grave reservations, but his involvement to this point has been minimal. It appears that the departments are compiling as much data as possible on the topic before formally presenting the plan to Cabinet.

A HAND ACROSS THE BORDER

In 1993, the US immigration authorities opened an intriguing new immigration lane in New York's John F. Kennedy Airport. What distinguished it from the traditional immigration procedure was that this new lane was entirely controlled by computer technology. Remarkably, it could automatically identify and process a passenger in as little as twenty seconds.

Known as FAST (Future Automated Screening for Travellers), the lane identifies passengers from the characteristics of their hand rather than from their passport and photograph. It then connects with the standard immigration computer systems to determine the passengers' status.

These automated immigration lanes are appearing throughout the world – in Toronto, Frankfurt, Amsterdam, and on the US–Mexico border – as part of an international experiment intended to revolutionize the world's immigration systems.

The project, called INSPASS (Immigration and Naturalization Service Passenger Accelerated Service System), has for the past fourteen months been operating as a voluntary system for frequent travellers. More than 65,000 people have so far enrolled in the system, a figure which increases by almost 1,000 a week. Governments in twenty-six countries – including the UK – are coordinating with the project.

If the INSPASS trial is successful, the technology may ultimately make conventional ID cards and passports redundant. And, as a trade-off for faster immigration processing, passengers will have to accept a system which has the potential to generate a vast amount of international traffic in their personal data. Ultimately, a universal immigration control system may be linked to a limitless spectrum of information, such as police and tax systems. An increasing number of countries are already subscribing to a 'Blue Lane' information exchange system in which passenger information is transmitted in advance of the journey.

An in-house evaluation of the system has given INSPASS the green light. INS officials are now confident that a universal project can be established, using common international standards and a smart card system that can cope with either a hand geometry or a fingerprint scan. According to staff working with the INSPASS project, all European governments are committed to the goal of automated immigration processing.

The thorny question is whether such a system might ultimately be manipulated by governments and airline companies anxious to receive more information about passengers.

HOW INSPASS WORKS

INSPASS is available to frequent travellers to and from the US, who are US or Canadian nationals, or nationals of the thirty-two countries involved in the US visa waiver scheme. The countries participating in the trial are Andorra, Austria, Belgium, Bermuda, Canada, Denmark, Finland, France, Germany, Iceland, Italy, Japan, Liechtenstein, Luxembourg, Monaco, the Netherlands, New Zealand, Norway, San Marino, Spain, Sweden, Switzerland and the United Kingdom. Travellers who visit the United States at least three times a year are 'invited' to apply in writing for INSPASS registration. Applicants then attend one of the INSPASS enrolment centres at JFK or Newark airports, where they are interviewed, and their identity confirmed.

This completed, the traveller places the palm of a hand on to the surface of a scanner, which then records intricate measurements and details of the hand's shape and contours. These are converted into a 'template' and stored on a card (currently a paper card, but soon to be a smart card). Fingerprints are also taken and recorded at this point.

Whenever INSPASS members enter the two test airports,

they bypass the main immigration queues and go straight to the INSPASS 'Kiosk'. Once inside, the card is presented to the terminal, which confirms its status. The hand is then placed on to a scanner. This matches the biometry of the palm with the 'template' encoded into the card. The Immigration Information systems are consulted. Once the last of five green lights appear at the tips of the fingers, the glass exit door opens and the passenger continues to the baggage claim and customs zone.

FUTURE IMPERFECT?

To date only limited testing of biometrics has been carried out by independent agencies. Best known is the work of the US Department of Energy's Sandia National Labs, which released the results of its second round of tests on biometric devices in mid-1990. Encouraging as they are, these tests have to be questioned since they assessed equipment from only six US vendors out of several dozen in the marketplace. Hardly a truly representative sample of internationally available biometric products.[13]

None the less, these tests are currently the only comprehensive evaluations available. They showed that dynamic signature verification (DSV) is by far the cheapest of the evaluated product types, although these latest tests also reveal that DSV rejects a disturbingly high proportion of properly enrolled individuals. Hand geometry had a very low rate of false rejections, especially if more than one attempt was made, and was very much better than signature dynamics in this respect – but it costs more than twice as much. The poorest performer was voice verification, exhibiting very high false rejection rates and a relatively high false acceptance rate. Voice verification systems have been implemented by a number of financial institutions in association with the introduction of telephone banking services. Voice-based services are clearly seen by the banks to offer the most immediately rewarding area of biometric systems,[14] but the astounding accuracy of other biometric systems will ultimately make them the identification of choice for government and private sector alike.

A DISASTER WAITING TO HAPPEN

The benefits of large-scale computerization are erratic, unpredictable, and usually less satisfying than expected. No vendor or systems designer can predict with certainty the extent to which a system will succeed or fail. Computer failures compound disproportionately to the size and complexity of the system. While there are numerous examples where information systems within particular areas of government can deliver savings and additional benefits to clients and users, the case for multi-faceted computer integration of complex systems (i.e. the creation of a nationwide integrated biometric and administrative system) is less convincing.

The system for the Europe-wide Schengen police information sharing system has been constantly paralysed because of unforeseen human and technical problems. The FBI's and the UK national police electronic fingerprinting systems have also suffered. Where computer systems fail to deliver expected performance or returns, it is invariably clients and customers who suffer.

It is true, of course, that government service delivery is often inefficient. It is equally true that the relevant information is fragmented and inconsistent. However, it does not follow that a centralized plan of action can resolve the many factors that contributed to these circumstances. In a perfect world, shortcomings can be identified and solutions implemented with equal effectiveness. Sadly, the experience internationally is that attempts to resolve inefficiencies in the health, police or Social Security sectors often result in unforeseen problems and costs.

A 1993 report commissioned by the United States Department of Health and Human Services noted that there existed a vast gulf between the promise and the reality of savings from computer systems.[15] A study by the Congressional Office of Technology Assessment found that computer-based information systems, once implemented, often result in 'unforeseen costs, unfulfilled promises, and disillusionment'.[16]

The pursuit of perfect identification involves a number of important technological, organizational, social, legal and political issues. Modern identification systems rely on technology that is far from proven. Biometric systems have not been tested on a nationwide basis. They are, to a different and perhaps lesser extent, subject to the same problems that exist at present in more conventional ID schemes.

The administrative and IT systems that form the basis of such ID schemes have been shown in several countries to be much less accurate and cost-effective than was originally estimated. Years after the governments of the United States and Australia developed schemes to match public sector computers to save money, there is still no clear evidence that the strategy has succeeded in achieving its original goal. The audit agencies of both federal governments have cast doubt that computer matching schemes deliver savings.

There are a great many complexities involved in the introduction of modern identity systems. The integration of computer systems and the merging of information brings with it the need for major organizational restructure. The use of identity procedures also changes the nature of relationships and transactions between clients and departments. Flawed technology has caused grief for organizations that rely on a consistent relationship with their client base. History shows that many organizations are not prepared to take these factors into account.

Any discussion of the risks involved in an integrated ID scheme will intersect considerably with concerns over computerization in general. The vulnerabilities of a computerized biometric system – at a human and organizational level – are very similar to the vulnerabilities of any integrated information system. All modern nationwide ID schemes are part of a larger information strategy. ID cards or biometric templates are used for several purposes and are the basis of the sharing of data among organizations.

Problems of privacy and confidentiality are perhaps the most important non-budgetary problems created by these proposals. On the one hand, computers offer the promise of creating secure communications through encryption of information. On the other hand, they tend to be a conduit for the distribution of information to a great many locations, and they thus increase the risk of unauthorized access and unforeseen use. Systems designers are often fixated by the theme of security without glancing at the larger picture of how data are collected and distributed.

There exist a number of obvious privacy problems with any system that entails the establishment of a central registry, or even a distributed, but interconnected, repository of personal identities. It is uncertain whether the establishment of a repository of identification data would be covered by many data protection laws. A biometric print may be considered in the public domain, or it may find its way into general use by way of implied consent of the individual. In this way, people may find that they are required to provide a biometric print in many unforeseen or unintended future circumstances.

Identification systems throughout the world have a history of being ultimately used for unintended purposes. The Social Security Number in the US and the Tax File Number in Australia, the Dutch SOFI number and the Austrian Social Security number have been extended progressively to include such facets as unemployment benefits, pensioner benefits, housing entitlement, bank account verification, and higher education. There is a very real possibility that anything as widespread as a general-purpose biometric system could mutate. The mere existence of a multi-purpose system of this magnitude will create irresistible opportunities to collect vast amounts of personal information.

At a society-wide level, the creation of a biometric system involves a number of risks. Privacy advocates have, traditionally, resisted the establishment of monolithic information systems. Informational chaos and functional separation among agencies have ensured that the individual does not become too closely dependent on the correct functioning of a single system. Variety, choice, and chaos also have the effect of ensuring that the free movement, rights, and free choice of individuals are not compromised by errors in the system.

General purpose biometric systems carry with them two essential dangers. The first is that a problem in identifying a person's hand may affect one's dealings with a range of agencies which use the biometric identifier. This is the same problem that accompanies general-purpose ID cards which are lost, stolen or damaged, or which have in some way been 'flagged' by the system. The inherent danger is that while a card carries the presumption of fragility and temporariness, a hand does not. Alternative means of identification may not be built into the system.

The second problem involves the less tangible impact on the individual and society. The result may be a real or perceived increase in the power and influence of government administration. Biometrics, more than other ID schemes, may imperil the sense of individuality.

Biometry is, in many senses, a natural extension of this technological evolution. Like the modern automobile, it signals an intimacy with the client. Whether the public senses a danger in the establishment of such a fusion will depend on its sensitivity to privacy. Given the evidence from recent times, it is likely that this awareness is thin on the ground.

CHAPTER FOUR

NUMBERED LIKE CATTLE

Despite some very occasional creeping misgivings, most of us are comfortable with the idea of being numbered: National Insurance numbers, Social Security numbers, NHS numbers, passport numbers, driver's licence numbers, bank account numbers, right the way through to credit card numbers and insurance claim numbers. They meld into the affairs of our day unnoticed.

Managing all these numbers is a chore, but it's a state of affairs most of us have learned to accept. Indeed one of the safeguards of our privacy and of our day to day freedoms is the sheer variety of numbers in use. Each number, after all, is only the visible part of a complex personal identification system. Each system is controlled by a vast computer network. While these many different systems work independently on their individual tasks, the risk of a Big Brother society is minimized. A large number of separate information systems engenders a more diffuse concentration of authority and control and a less centralized stockpile of our personal information.

While we have a dozen different credit, identification and

authorization numbers in our wallet, it is improbable that they will all malfunction at once. If, for example, we encounter a problem with one organization and have our card or our benefits cancelled or our affairs placed under suspicion, the existence of separate systems means we are unlikely to suffer a domino effect involving other organizations. Privacy lawyers call this ideal situation 'functional separation'. We feel this concept in action when, after having one credit card refused at a restaurant, we can – with an exclamation of relief – reach into our wallets to produce another. The linking together of all credit card systems would – if we allowed such a scheme to go ahead – probably result in simultaneous cancellation of all cards. This threat also applies to our dealings with government departments. An alleged failure to pay a tax debt should not result in a cancellation of a pension or passport.

Some countries, such as Germany, Portugal, Austria and Hungary, have recognized potential dangers to the extent that they have constitutional limitations on the establishment of a single national number. In any modern society, they argue, a spectrum of different systems is a necessary safeguard.

But what happens if you start to link the government's information systems? What if you decide that the computers that run Social Security should be linked to the ones running the NHS? What if you then link these to the Inland Revenue and then to the police? What if you decide that in the quest for administrative efficiency and effective law enforcement, the information from all computers throughout the nation should be linked? One network, one number, one identity. In effect, you end up with the equivalent of a single Super Department covering all key elements of your day-to-day life.

This process has already begun. It is known quite simply as 'data matching', and it is one of the prerequisites of the emerging Superhighway. At its most common and brutal level, data matching touches the lives of nearly everyone through the mechanism of the TV licence.

THE TV NAZIS

The scene is familiar to millions of people: an officious-looking man stands at your front door, clipboard in hand, and demands to see your TV licence. You feign innocence, have a mild panic attack, and finally blurt out one of the dozen or so standard excuses.

It doesn't really matter what you say. The licence inspector already knows, of course, that you don't have a licence. The most sophisticated population database in Britain has told him so. He is just going through the motions, hoping for a quick confession and an easy case.

Every year, 400,000 TV licence dodgers are caught and prosecuted. That's almost 1 per cent of the adult population of Britain. And every year, the people who catch them become more powerful and more intrusive. In the quest to catch the licence-dodging villains, as many as 3,000 search warrants are issued each year and hundreds of millions of pounds are levied in fines.

This arcane system, intended to fund the operation of the BBC, is enforced not only by a massive computer network and an army of inspectors, but by the familiar fleet of TV detector vans and hand-held scanners, both of which can detect signals emitting from the horizontal sweep oscillator in your television. This technology is now capable not only of pin-pointing the exact location of a television within your home, but also detecting precisely what you are watching.

The organization which enforces television licences is an imaginatively named company called TV Licensing, the trading name of a division of a Post Office direct marketing subsidiary, Subscription Services Ltd. TV Licensing's job is to enforce compliance with the licensing system. Like so many private sector companies of its type, it does so with Terminator efficiency.

These licence enforcers are under increasing pressure to catch dodgers, and in the process they are building an unparalleled surveillance system over the entire country. At the core of the operation is a sophisticated computer called the Licence Administrative Support System, or LASSY for short. It holds details of every household in Britain. LASSY cross-references information with numerous other information systems, including Post Office and census databases.

Every time you notify the post office of a change of address, LASSY gets to hear about it. Make an innocent enquiry to the TV licence people and LASSY is all ears. Buy or rent a television from any dealer and LASSY faithfully stores and processes that information (all dealers are required by law to report the names and addresses of purchasers). The lists and databases from all these organizations are matched against the TV Licensing company's own database.

The 1,400 staff of TV Licensing divide their time between feeding LASSY with data and pursuing those who the system identifies as suspects – and that's anybody who doesn't have a licence. The licence inspectors have extraordinary powers and are required to take statements and evidence for prosecutions.

Recent legislation strengthened the hand of the licensing authorities, increased the penalties for evasion and demanded that all televisions would be subject to the licence fee – even if they are tuned only to cable or satellite and are unable to receive the BBC. The licence is now regarded as a common tax on technology.

Despite their apparent success at enforcing this regime, the licensing authorities are about to suffer an embarrassing turn of events. Television, computers and other technologies are slowly merging. The functions of a television will be assumed by other multimedia computer appliances. Steadily, they will merge to form one technology. Indeed, Apple computers has already marketed Apple TV in the US. Other companies have introduced drop-in cards which give a computer TV receiving capability. Within a few years, TV reception will be standard in many machines, as it is currently with video recorders. A television will cease, as such, to be a television. When the screen disappears in a few years, the TV Licensing people will be in a real fix.

When this sort of product becomes popular in Britain, the technologies of television, video recorder, telephone, high definition monitor, cable and optical CD will merge into an indistinguishable matrix. The TV Licensing people and the government are going to have to make an uncomfortable choice – either license all the technology or lose revenue. Tighter surveillance, more extensive information, stiffer penalties and greater powers. Such is the inevitable result of trying to license technology.

There are two possible scenarios for the future of Britain's TV licensing system. It will either crumble and decay as a result of the evolution of technology, or its enforcement will become an instrument of unparalleled surveillance, using increasingly powerful information systems to track and monitor people's use of technology. The science of data matching will be stretched to its limit as more and more sources are invoked to track defaulters.

MIXING AND MATCHING

Data matching (also known as parallel matching, bulk matching, record linkage, cross matching, joint running or computer matching) is the process of automatically comparing and analysing records of a person from two or more sources. Thus, the records of the Department of Social Security can be matched against the records of the Child Support Agency, or the records of Scotland Yard can be matched against the computer files of the Education Department. The government is then able to search for discrepancies between the files. It can reveal whether you are giving conflicting information to different agencies, or whether you have failed to reveal information, or even whether you have the sort of profile that indicates you are likely to commit a future offence.

In the wake of a 1993 local government programme involving the automatic matching of student grant files, the UK government recently commenced matching its DSS records with those of local government bodies. Its aim is to detect the incidence of benefit fraud. All major government departments are interested in following suit but have so far been held back by the continuing spectre of rationalization and the lack of a coherent national strategy to deal with computerized information. The private sector is also jumping aboard, with insurance companies and building societies looking to match their data to reduce fraud, over payments, and multiple mortgage applications.[1] It is now certain that in the next five years the government will move to harmonize its records throughout departments (and areas of the private sector). This will make matching a technical possibility.

If it does so, one inevitability will soon become apparent. Any data-matching exercises created within government are certain to fail and to cause great damage and distress. To get some idea of the pitfalls of computer matching, it is a useful exercise to look back a few years.

The genesis of computer matching goes back to 1977, a time when the United States bureaucracy was just glimpsing the possibilities of computerization. The Department of Health, Education and Welfare (now the Department of Health and Human Services), decided to automatically match all its computer welfare records against the Federal Payroll Files. It was a massive undertaking, with the aim of exposing welfare fraud, and was heralded as a milestone in law enforcement. The ambitious plan was to allow these new-fangled computers to conduct the searches themselves, rapidly and accurately matching the data on one set of files with the data on another. If a person had conflicting information in different agencies, the computer would detect this. Simple and logical.

'Project Match', as it was known, came up with 33,000 'raw hits' – instances where the information on a person's welfare file did not square with the employment file (indicating that the person was working and receiving benefits at the same time).

The office celebrations were toned down a touch when it was discovered that the majority of these hits were not valid.

Still, 7,100 valid cases were uncovered. Sadly for the participating departments, much of the information was either false or irrelevant and only 638 cases ended up being referred for internal investigation.

Of the 638 investigations, only fifty-five resulted in a prosecution, and of these, a mere thirty-five minor convictions were secured. No conviction resulted in a jail term, and less than $10,000 in fines were levied.[2]

No one may ever know the extent of the distress and humiliation this caused to tens of thousands of honest people but ironically, while the result of this multi-million-dollar exercise was so obviously a failure, the relevant departments hailed it as a great success. This deception has always been a feature of efforts to match computer records, not just in the United States but in all countries.

Privacy advocates have every justification for scepticism about these ambitious computer projects. Their dangers are vividly illustrated in the experience of fraud detection programmes in the United States and Australia, in which recent controversial data-matching strategies were carried through Parliament on the basis of figures which were later demonstrated in audit to be unsupportable.[3] As a result, a major Australian Commonwealth scheme (the Law Enforcement Access Network) has been abandoned.[4]

In the United States, a 1993 report on data matching from the US General Accounting Office has caused some embarrassment among agencies. The report advised that government departments involved in data matching had failed to assess adequately the cost/benefit or impact of these schemes. In response, Congressman Gary Condit of the House Government Operations Committee issued a press release which said, in part:

Most federal agencies have done a lousy job of complying with the Computer Matching Act. Agencies ignore the law or interpret it to suit their own bureaucratic convenience, without regard for the privacy interests that the law was designed to protect. As a result, we don't have any idea when computer matching is a cost-effective technique for preventing fraud, waste, and abuse. I support reasonable computer matching that saves money. But if we are losing money, wasting resources, and invading privacy, then it makes no sense.

In theory, the Computer Matching Act provides the safety rails for data matching and also requires that matching programmes include an analysis of the costs and benefits of the matching. One of the purposes of the Act was to limit the use of matching to instances where the technique was cost effective and therefore in the public interest. The GAO found many problems with implementation of this requirement, including poor quality or non-existent analyses. In 41 per cent of cases, no attempt was made to estimate costs or benefits or both. In 59 per cent of cases when costs and benefits were estimated, the GAO found that not all reasonable costs and benefits were considered, that inadequate analyses were provided to support savings claims, and that no effort was made after the match to validate estimates.

In Australia, where the government has announced a policy of information harmony (breaking down the barriers between departments), most departments are now moving to some form of data-matching programme. In 1993, more than thirty major projects were in progress. The number of matches in some of the key programmes is quite staggering. The new DSS programme envisions as much as 375–750 trillion (375–750,000,000,000,000) attempted file matches per annum.[5]

Impressive as this may sound, the Australians, like their American counterparts, quickly discovered that data matching didn't live up to the promises made by the companies supplying the hardware and software. A $17 million matching exercise conducted in 1994 by the Australian Tax Office, involving comparisons of 20 million files, did not identify any cases of tax evasion.[6]

In the process of matching, hundreds of thousands of innocent people are placed under suspicion. The Australian DSS matched 137 million files, and discovered 2.2 million discrepancies, of which 189,442 were then selected for further internal investigation. About 40,000 of these people were subsequently contacted by letter and, following their responses, 26,000 cases were dropped. The remaining 14,154 are currently subject to further investigation and although it is unclear at this point how many will result in court action, it is likely to be a tiny fraction. In 1992, the department had given evidence to the Parliament's Inquiry into Fraud on the Commonwealth that in one data-matching exercise, action was taken against only sixty-one of 2,334 people under investigation for fraud. Presumably the other 2,273 people were investigated without just cause. The failure rate of these matching programmes has remained unchanged since 1977.

THE GREAT DECEPTION

The justification for data matching often hangs on the problems of benefit fraud, yet estimates of the extent of fraud on benefits agencies vary widely. In Canada, the

Toronto Social Services Department, for example, officially estimates fraud by way of false identity at less than one-tenth of 1 per cent of benefits paid,[7] whereas the Australian Department of Social Security estimates the figure at ten times that amount.[8] Estimates of fraud vary widely between one-tenth of 1 per cent of total benefits, to as high as 4 per cent.[9] Britain's 'popular' estimate of £1–2 billion is, in international terms, at the high end of the spectrum. Little wonder that there is such variance. Virtually no coal-face ethnographic research exists, and the data that do exist are drawn principally from internal and external audits, management reviews, and highly selective, retrospective studies.[10] Many methodologies have the effect of assessing risk, rather than quantifying actual fraud. No standard guidelines have yet been developed to assess the sort of information technology used in fraud control and identification. Additional problems are found with the definition of fraud and the terms of audit, which often do not match the parameters of internal departmental cost/benefit analyses.[11] In summary, estimates of fraud involve a breathtaking amount of creative accounting or, to express it another way, guesswork.

Some government departments argue that the process of matching computers in different departments has a deterrent effect in combating fraud (if people think they are likely to be caught, they won't attempt to commit fraud in the first place). Although the deterrent effect has not been quantified by research, most privacy and civil liberties bodies agree that it is a natural consequence of any surveillance system. They also argue that the deterrent effect is an unacceptable imposition because it casts an Orwellian chill across the entire society. A more tangible argument to justify computer matching is that not to do so will result in loss of revenue to the government. It is an argument that can easily be countered if the evidence is laid out.

Times are tough, it's true. Every penny lost to fraud is a penny that could have helped a single parent or a struggling school. Computer matching is difficult to oppose because people have come to believe that information held by government agencies is the property of the government. What is more, it is silent and invisible, and so does not raise the ire of the community.

COMPUTER MATCHING: THE DISTURBING REALITY

At first glimpse, the idea of automatically matching one set of computer records with another seems to be fairly innocuous. Surely no one could object to the government checking its files to weed out the cheats? The reality is far more complex.

Data matching is the technological equivalent of a general warrant on the entire population. It is no different to the notion of police being empowered to enter your home in your absence, search through your papers and take what copies they wish. The comparison might sound extreme, but it will become more poignant in future years as a greater amount of information about us is stored on computer. In 1986, the United States Office of Technology Assessment concluded that 'Computer matches are inherently mass or class investigations'.

Despite the (slight) possibility of computer matching yielding revenue for the government, there are several fundamental problems with the process. The first and perhaps most important is whether a government has a right to place a population under this form of surveillance (known as 'dataveillance'). Civil libertarians argue that even if savings are possible, we should not lose sight of the principle that no government has an absolute right to do as it pleases with our personal details. Data matching is directly equivalent to arbitrary investigation without cause or suspicion.

Within this broad concern, there are three distinct human rights and privacy dilemmas. First, data matching is based on an assumption of guilt. Each member of the population, according to the rationale of the data-matching programmes, is a suspect and therefore a potential criminal. The presumption of innocence no longer exists. A computer-matching programme therefore reverses the entire basis of the judical system.

Another fundamental problem with computer matching is that it breaches the privacy principles held in law throughout the world. One of the most important of these principles demands that information supplied for one purpose should not be used for another purpose unless the individual concerned has given consent. The reality is that governments in nearly all countries create exemptions for revenue or law enforcement – a sad indication of how useless the law can be on this issue.

One of the most dangerous long-term outcomes of a mass data-matching programme is that it tends to encourage governments to create a universal population numbering system. Since the greatest practical problem for computer matching is the way people identify themselves, such a numbering scheme would be most attractive. It would save the trouble and expense of maintaining many numbering systems.

Even in the absence of a single national number, the data-matching programmes, if fully linked, can create the effect of a single number. Data matching can contain processes to merge various numbering systems, applying criteria for determining whether a number from one sector adequately matches a number from another. There is, in effect, a 'working number' or 'working identity' applied or created by the data-matching system.

The second key area of concern relates to the accuracy of the information being matched. The key assumption under-lying any data-matching programme is that information from each of the sources is parallel and compatible. Such is never the case. Even apparently identical items of informa-tion or categories often have different meanings in different systems. Such items as *de facto, marriage, child, dependent, spouse, income, living costs, permanent* or *temporary* can be used in various ways by different departments, and people often quite legitimately use them differently according to a changed circumstance. A person's information may also quite legitimately vary between departments because of the date the information was originally provided. Data matching often does not take these discrepancies into account when determining if a person's file is a 'hit'. The decisions are made on a clinical basis, with the computer-matching staff being unaware of the broader context of each case.

Once a person has been flagged (marked for scrutiny) by the system, it is invariably the case that the onus is on proof of innocence by the person rather than proof of guilt by the government. Once an investigation proceeds, information that may be wrong or out of date is then liable to be communicated to people with no direct involvement in the case, resulting in possible harm or embarrassment to the subject. Continuing reports of false matches by the Child Support Agency are likely to be a harbinger of similar blunders in more automated matching systems.

One of the most alarming aspects of widespread data matching is that it provides the opportunity to develop a comprehensive profile on each member of the population, allowing organizations to make judgements on the basis of accumulated data. Indeed, data profiling is already being conducted in several countries, though virtually no assessment exists of the practice.[12]

Profiling involves the amassing and automatic analysis of personal information from diverse sources in order to predict people's behaviour or actions. The practice can be used for numerous purposes, for example, identifying students with high propensities for particular artistic or sporting skills; patients with high likelihood of suffering particular diseases or disorders; individuals likely to commit a crime of violence against persons; adolescents with a significant likelihood of attempting suicide; taxpayers who are likely to be materially mis-stating income or expenses; and travellers likely to be carrying or trafficking in drugs.[13]

The Office of Technology Assessment of the US Congress noted that most US federal agencies had applied the technique to develop a wide variety of profiles including drug dealers, taxpayers who under-report their income, likely violent offenders, arsonists, rapists, child molesters, and sexually exploited children.[14]

In his definitive work on the subject of profiling, Australian academic Roger Clarke details the chilling step-by-step process by which an automatic profile is created.

- Describe the class of person, instances of which the organization wishes to locate;
- Use existing experience to define a profile of that class of person. This is likely to be based at least in part on informal knowledge, references to the literature of underlying disciplines and professions, and discussions within the organization and with staff of other organizations with similar interests. (It is also likely that profile construction will be supported by analyses of existing data-holdings within and beyond the organization, whereby individuals who are known to belong to that class are identified, their recorded characteristics examined, and common features isolated);
- Express the profile formally, perhaps including the use of weightings to reflect the degree of correlation between the characteristic and the target, thresholds below which the correlation is low and above which it is high, and complex conditional relationships among the factors (e.g. factor x is indicative, but only if factors y and z are both above particular threshhold levels);
- Acquire a set of data concerning a relevant population; for example, in the case of customers: the organization's customer database and/or the databases of mailing list suppliers; in the case of employees: the personnel database, and/or that of staff placement companies; in the case of students' propensities in the arts and sport: school, club and perhaps medical records; in the case of patients: medical records from doctors, clinics, hospitals and registries, and/or family history information, e.g. from Utah; in the cases of potential criminals and of adolescents: school records, welfare agency databases, and/or the medical and psychiatric records of doctors,

clinics and hospitals; in the case of taxpayers: the historical record of tax returns, cash flow information from employers, financial institutions and other organizations, and statistical analyses of those and other databases; and in the case of travellers: inbound and outbound flight and voyage movement records;

- Search the set of data for individuals whose characteristics comply with the profile. This is highly likely to involve computer support, especially where the data-set is large (e.g. taxpayers), the processing complex (e.g. psychosocial analyses), or the time available short (e.g. lists of aircraft passengers);

- Take action in relation to those individuals; for example: mail selected advertising to selected customers or prospects; call students, employees or prospective appointees for interview; counsel patients or students and/or their parents and teachers; counsel adolescents and potential violent criminals, and their families, associates and workmates; subject tax-payers to audit; and interview passengers and/or conduct luggage- and body-searches.

The essential issue here is that data matching coupled with data profiling creates the effect of a single society-wide computer even if no single master computer exists. To understand this fundamental point, you only have to think of a computer as a mass of separate parts, each of which can communicate in a set way with the other parts. A large computer, in fact, is many smaller computers all communicating in harmony. Data matching is an extension of this process. The matching process allows one computer to talk easily with others, thus creating the effect of one giant computer.

This, perhaps more than any single point, is the one that should be foremost in the minds of our more aware and sensitive politicians. Data matching is not just a more efficient way for computers to speak; it is the systematic development of a vast, multi-faceted database that reaches into every aspect of our lives. Privacy advocates have always been deeply concerned that the linkage of computers will set into concrete a set of conditions which are inimical to a free society.

This dataveillance is likely to produce a chilling effect on the population when people begin to feel they are under constant surveillance. It has many features in common with the 'environment of deterrence' philosophy favoured by many police forces and employed with vigour through the use of CCTV systems in public places. Once this chill has set in, it will be difficult to reverse. A brief stay in Russia or the former Eastern Bloc should be enough to convince any visitor that the spectre of surveillance continues long after the machinery is dismantled.

A United Nations study entitled 'Human Rights and Scientific and Technological Development' warns:

> . . . the increased expansion of computerization of personal data may result in a 'dossier society' which would have 'dehumanizing' effects on the individual. The relative inflexibility of computer based record keeping resulting from the computers having been designed to use certain preconceived categories, coupled with the constraints that some computerized systems put on the freedom of persons concerned to provide explanatory details in responding to questions, have been considered as contributing to the dehumanizing effect of computerization.

While complex data-matching programmes in the public sector are inherently likely to fail, causing massive hurt and embarrassment, single-purpose matching programmes within organizations have a much greater chance of success (though they are occasionally no less dangerous to privacy). Matching exercises are undertaken by direct marketing organizations, police, political parties, banks and major employers. They often involve public information such as electoral records, phone number data, council records and company records. These are matched and merged with mailing lists, target lists and census data. People who blithely participate in surveys, opinion polls and customer loyalty schemes should be aware that their personal information is invariably sold on to companies which broker the data to other lists. These in turn are matched and cross referenced.

Often, industry groups such as banks and insurers will match their databases to detect irregularities. The insurance industry now has a system called the Computer Underwriting Exchange (Cue) which lists all insurance claims. Direct insurers commonly refuse cover for people who have claimed in the past three to five years, and so a central system of policies and claims is useful. Across the entire industry, more than a fifth of applicants are refused household insurance for allegedly failing to own up to past claims.[15]

The danger in such a centralized system is that customers can easily be blacklisted across the entire industry. One mistake – innocent or not – can result in years out in the cold. And factual errors in such a system can be disastrous. The most well-known and extensive data-matching programme, the credit reference system, has caused damage to millions of people because of identification and notification errors.

Once the privacy genie has been let out of the bottle, it will never return. Within the next ten years, all the world's major computers will be able to communicate with each other. A telecommunications computer in Ohio will be able to talk with a bank computer in Brussels. Russian defence computers will be replaced with conventional systems that are designed to link with computers in Europe and America.

The taxation systems of all developed countries will use compatible hardware and software, as will the computers of all communications and immigration agencies. Police agencies worldwide are already making their choices of systems on the basis of their ability to communicate easily with police computers of other national and international law enforcement organizations. The Police National Computer (PNC 2) was designed for compatibility with the Schengen police system in Europe. The new police computer strategy (ISIT) is also compatible with European and international police systems.

A trend is emerging internationally for nations to reach agreement on the transfer and exchange of information stored on these systems. It may be only a matter of time before the computer-matching epidemic touches every facet of human activity in every part of the globe.

As governments implement these programmes, it would be wise to remember Edmund Burke's advice: 'The true danger is when liberty is nibbled away, for expedience, and by parts.'

CHAPTER FIVE

THE FAILURE OF LAW

Commander Rodolfo Shahani has spent most of his life passionately committed to the revolutionary goals of the Philippines New People's Army. As an 'Insurgent' he was held responsible by successive governments for undermining the political stability of the nation.

Now Commander Shahani has a new obsession. He is in charge of a gleaming new enterprise in the former US base at Subic Bay. His mission is to use the cheap Philippine labour market to convert American medical records into computer files.

Throughout Manila and other major cities of the developing world hundreds of new companies have sprung up specializing in the processing of foreign data. Huge factories of data entry staff, computer programmers and typists are slowly converting the Western world's trillions of paper documents into computer files. Container loads of sensitive personal information – health records, police files, insurance data, credit card accounts and government records – are dispatched from all over the world for processing in remote regions which have little or no legal protection.

Welcome to the Global Village, a meeting point of Superhighways, where conventional borders disappear before our eyes and where our most intimate personal information is shunted around the globe behind our back. Our information, which we give willingly for one purpose, can now be downloaded to a computer on the other side of the world and merged with other unrelated information to create all sorts of profiles, marketing lists, blacklists and 'geodemographic' data. Modern marketing depends on more precise targeting of individuals. Not only is this offshore processing much cheaper for companies and governments, but it usually circumvents the troublesome data protection laws that are springing up in many countries.

According to the data processing industry, the clients for this new industry come from all Western nations – including Britain. The financial and legal advantages in the Third World have made the development of data havens increasingly attractive. The Caribbean, for example, enjoys a £70 million a year revenue from this activity. China, India, and the South Pacific are not far behind.

Until late in 1994, the Philippines had been expecting a very special new customer – the United Kingdom Home Office. For two years, the Home Office had been planning to send over all criminal records on paper files for conversion on to computer disk. At the last minute the government decided to abandon the plan.

The sudden loss of such a major contract doubtless came as a blow to the Philippines, but it will ultimately make scarcely a dent in the burgeoning industry. Data processing is big business in the Philippines. Revenue in 1993 was 800 million pesos (£20 million), and is growing rapidly. The government is planning to help the industry by opening up the communication facilities of the former US base at Subic Bay. High speed teleport and satellite links connect the data-processing operations with clients in developed countries. Gigabytes of sensitive information are flashed across the world without legal constraint. Huge contracts are negotiated hourly.

MEANWHILE, BACK ON THE FARM

Wilmslow, Cheshire, is a world and a half away from this action. Here in its idyllic rural setting nestles the office of the Data Protection Registrar, the official responsible in law for monitoring these sort of activities. The Registrar enforces a law which calls for fair play in the use of information. Data, according to the law, should be collected, processed, and distributed in such a way that it does not do any harm to the individual 'data subject'.

Sadly, the Registrar's office is not familiar with the cutting edge of the offshore data industry. This should come as no surprise, since the Registrar's office is scarcely familiar with so basic a technology as electronic mail. (The Registrar describes data matching as a new technology, even though it has been used for a quarter of a century).[1] As such, no one knows the extent to which British companies and government agencies are sending our data overseas. The Registrar's office has never investigated the issue. It should have done so long ago. Offshore data processing is worth at least a billion pounds annually to the developing nations, and the clients come from all over the world. Although most of the trade originates in North America, contracts from European organizations are steadily growing in number.

Britons should be worried about this trend. The Data Protection Act was enacted ten years ago with the intention of protecting our privacy. If data operations are moved overseas, an informational Pandora's box is opened. First, information can be configured in ways that would be illegal in this country. Second, our personal information will be vulnerable to more blatant forms of abuse – hacking, theft, blackmail and sabotage.

Anyone looking for protection from this trade will get no comfort from British law. The Data Protection Act, expressed bluntly, is a joke. It is doubtful whether at any time in its ten-year history it has stopped one intrusive information practice. Data users can do more or less as they please, provided they register the correct details and pay their money. Even so, a recent investigation by the National Audit Office (NAO) estimated that up to 100,000 data users had not registered their computer systems. Other estimates put the figure at 2–300,000.

Those who are registered need have no fears about heavy-handed treatment from the Registrar. In the year to May 1994 two search warrants were issued in the course of investigations. There were thirty-six prosecutions for offences under the Act, nearly all of which involved companies. Nine cases resulted in acquittal, discharge or admonishment. The average fine for the remainder was £460. Compare this with the enforcement system for television licences, which obtains up to 3,000 search warrants and prosecutes 400,000 people annually. The Data Protection Registrar has the ability to embarrass transgressors, but virtually no illegal activity is ever discovered. The situation highlights the extent to which individuals are caned while corporations get tickled by the feathery end.

When the Act was promulgated in the mid-1980s, the British Medical Association eloquently described it as 'a load of holes joined together'. The changing nature of technology has made the law even more hopeless as a mechanism. Registration of databases is an archaic idea that belonged to another era. Data is now international. If a law ever started to bite, companies could quickly and easily move their operations offshore. Jamaica Promotions, the industrial development agency for Jamaica, uses the slogan 'If you can't move it from the ground floor to the fifth floor, then move it from the ground floor to Jamaica – it's cheaper.' The promotion has paid off. Jamaica now has a £5 million teleport facility to service its burgeoning data-processing industry. Needless to say, Jamaica has no data protection law.

Britain has a history of intolerance of privacy and data protection, leading to a state of privacy protection which Geoffrey Robertson QC describes as the 'worst in the Western world'.

These issues of privacy are paid at least lip service in other European countries. In June 1995 the European Parliament passed a Europe-wide directive which will give member states the discretion to block the transmission of our personal data to countries which do not have an adequate level of privacy protection. In the process, European authorities are trying to convince all trading partners to pass strong data-protection law. The iron fist in the velvet glove is that if they fail to do so, Europe will simply not allow its masses of data to flow across the border.

These threats, however, are hollow. Many European countries have had these powers for years and have seldom used them. The UK Registrar, for example, has always had the power to block data but has done so only once in the past decade. The fact is that the political, financial and legal repercussions are too complex. Personal data is more or less free to travel wherever it wants.

Having said that, Home Secretary Michael Howard spent much of 1994 lobbying his opposite numbers in Europe to have the new European law derailed. He almost succeeded. The directive passed through the Council of Ministers in February with Britain in opposition. Howard and other ministers managed to gut the directive, forcing a range of exemptions, including political canvassing. Howard has been lobbied extensively by the corporate sector which he freely admits representing. It is no wonder companies want to maintain the existing conditions. *International Management* says the UK is Europe's main 'data haven', hosting 70 per cent of western Europe's multinational data sets.[2]

Such information is highly sensitive. Government data, collected when individuals pay taxes, receive benefits, or buy licences for such things as cars and televisions, is especially attractive to marketing companies. In the UK, a financial squeeze has raised state agencies' incentive to sell their data. Tax information is already being processed by the US based company EDS, while it and other companies have vied for ownership and control of data on the Police National Computer. Other potentially lucrative information exists in the by-products of electronic payment systems, such as itemized credit card bills.[3] According to 'The Holloway Report', an investigation of company outsourcing in Britain, the business is going through boom times. EDS alone has an annual revenue from Britain of around £500 million. The American based Computer Sciences Corporation quadrupled its revenue in just one year to reach £160 million by 1995.

It is of fundamental importance to decide whether we are happy to have our personal details known to the Global Village or whether we should rigorously enforce our sovereignty. The next step – as the US has already shown – will be offshore service delivery. Your telephone call to an airline will be dealt with not by someone in Britain, but by a low-waged worker in a remote data haven. What happens beyond that is anyone's guess but it's certainly clear that the existing law will never properly address the situation. Even where privacy Acts are governed by a dedicated and forceful regulator, the opposing forces are so overwhelming that it is often impossible to stand in the way of the most sophisticated data practices. David Flaherty, now Privacy Commissioner of British Columbia in Canada, says, 'There is a real risk that data protection of today will be looked back on as a rather quaint, failed effort to cope with an overpowering technological tide.'[4]

Without considerable positive discrimination, a privacy commissioner can do little. Flaherty has observed: 'The public is being lulled into a false sense of security about the protection of their privacy by their official protectors, who often lack the will and energy to resist successfully the diverse initiatives of what Jan Freese (one of Europe's first data protection Commissioners) has aptly termed the 'information athletes' in our respective societies.'[5]

THE DATA PROTECTION ACT

In theory at least, the law which is supposed to protect our privacy is the Data Protection Act. In reality, this piece of legislation, and the Registrar who enforces it, are paper tigers.

For ten years, since the creation of the Data Protection Act, the Home Office has consistently fought to erode the Act and the Registrar, who is the single person responsible for watching over privacy in the UK. At every turn, the Home Office has argued inside and outside Parliament that the provisions of the Act need to be watered down. At every opportunity, the Home Office has pushed for limits to be placed on the power of the Registrar.

In February 1994, on the eve of the retirement of the then Data Protection Registrar, Eric Howe, the Home Office succeeded in having its own Director of Information appointed as the new Registrar. Elizabeth France has worked for the Home Office for twenty-three years, virtually her entire professional career.

Ms France, of course, must be judged in time on the record of her actions, but the fact that the media failed universally to comment on this unusual appointment speaks volumes for the insignificance of the position of Registrar. Instead of being seen as an effective and respected protector of privacy rights, the Registrar is more generally seen as a low-level functionary – a view which has some basis in fact. Government agencies rarely seek the advice or support of the Registrar, and the Registrar rarely troubles them.

There are, nevertheless, some advantages to having a Registrar. There is no question that some of the more offensive activities of government departments are reined in as a result of its existence. Individual citizens are given some protection over the way personal files are used. In theory at least, we can gain access to many of our files – even if it is with a financial cost.

However, even within its narrow scope, the Data

Protection Act has serious limitations. One of the broadest deficiencies is that it is not really a privacy law; it is an information law. That means that instead of it being concerned with the full range of privacy and surveillance issues, it deals only with the way personal data are collected, stored, used and accessed. It is not concerned, for instance, with visual surveillance, drug testing, use of satellites or denouncement campaigns, of all of which the UK has more than its share.

Another problem relates to publicly available information (that is, information and records such as land titles and electoral rolls that are available for general public inspection). The Data Protection Act has no interest in this sort of information and it can thus be used in whatever way a government or private organization chooses. The situation shows once again that law on its own is an inadequate mechanism to deal with modern surveillance techniques.

A particularly serious problem with the Act is that it allows a great many privacy violations to occur in the name of law enforcement or taxation. The Registrar can do nothing to prevent such uses. If a scheme has been established to assist law enforcement or to pursue public revenue collection, the Act has only a limited application.

Perhaps the gravest limitation of the Data Protection Act is that it does next to nothing to prevent or limit the collection of information. The Act merely stipulates that information has to be collected by lawful means and for a purpose 'directly related to a function or activity of the collector'. Thus a virtually unlimited number of information systems can be established without any breach of the Act.

The deficiencies go on and on. The law does not prevent third parties from getting access to our information without our permission. It does not provide the Registrar with even the most rudimentary powers of a regulator. Finally, it gives the Registrar no scope to deal with international issues, thus making the UK data protection, by definition, parochial and archaic.

It would be a mistake, in any event, to assume that law is going to solve all our privacy problems. The Dutch privacy expert Jan Holvast recently explained that privacy legislation 'corrects the mistakes and misuses but it does not attack the way in which technology is used. On the contrary, experiences with data protection law in several countries show that these laws are legalizing existing practices instead of protecting privacy.'[6]

The world wide watchdog group Privacy International warned in its 1991 report: 'Protections in law, where they exist, are sometimes ineffective and even counter-productive. Extensive information holdings by government are invariably allowed under exemptions and protections in law. The existence of statutory privacy bodies, rather than impeding such trends, sometimes legitimates intrusive information practices.'

Despite the existence of data protection legislation (or, perhaps, because of it), Britain in the 1990s is shaping up to be one of the world's most advanced surveillance societies. There is an ingrained hostility to privacy within the bureaucracy, an ideological opposition to private sector privacy protection from within the Conservative Party and suspicion of it from all parties. People have come to the belief that opposition to the government's plans would be hostile to its best intentions. 'If you have nothing to hide, then you have nothing to fear' is a justification that we might have expected from the government of a totalitarian regime rather than from a liberal democracy. Government has hit upon the perfect solution for justifying the establishment of massive computer surveillance systems. First, establish a watchdog with rotting teeth. Second, proclaim that anyone opposing the reforms is working against the interests of the nation. By limiting the requirements of privacy law and glorifying the goals of fraud recovery, the government has successfully nobbled both the Registrar and the public advocacy bodies.

The risk inherent in all legislation is that instead of it conferring rights for people and restricting the actions of government, the law ends up being used to allow governments to do as they please under the cloak of legal protection. Such was the risk with data protection law. There was, from the outset, a danger that some ministers and government departments would use the Act and the Registrar as a smoke-screen for intrusive government activity. The ploy is an old one, and used throughout the world. A government department 'consults with' the Registrar and, regardless of the outcome, uses that 'consultation' to imply some sort of endorsement or protection.

In Australia, for example, the manipulation was very clear. Senator Amanda Vanstone, addressing the Privacy Commissioner during a Senate Committee hearing, warned: '. . . there are occasions when we hear members of the Executive basically using your position, if you like, as a soother [for the development of numbering schemes, etc.], and saying "Look, this is all right. The Privacy Commissioner has looked at it and he said it is OK." '[7]

Senator Vanstone later added: 'The reason I am concerned about it is that sometimes people who do not necessarily have a big interest in this area [privacy] – do not know much about it – have your position waved as a magic wand of approval.'[8]

In the United Kingdom, departments are very fond of justifying the planning procedure of each intrusive scheme by alerting all players that the Registrar has been consulted. Consulting the Registrar is invariably an exercise in diplomacy, since the law gives her little scope to do anything other than quietly advise the architect that she might be concerned over a legal technicality.

It would, of course, be useful to the cause of privacy if the Registrar used language consistent with the threat posed by information practices, yet for the past decade the Registrar's advice, reports and public utterances have been cloaked in qualified legal jargon; boring, insipid and uninspiring.

LEGALIZED PRIVACY INVASION

How information is used becomes a very cloudy matter under the Act. Information should be used only for the purpose for which it was given but, so far as the Act is concerned, 'purpose' is the purpose nominated in the Data Registration form lodged with the Registrar. The *Sunday Times* recently disclosed that a number of major High Street organizations had legitimately registered database information that would have been illegal under the law of most other European countries (sexual preference, religious belief, etc.). A doctor may feel that information should legitimately be shared with an insurer. The insurer, however, could legitimately share that information for as many 'purposes' as it had registered.

OTHER MECHANISMS FOR PRIVACY
  PROTECTION

In 1994, the world's oldest privacy protection organization
was dissolved. Holland's Stichting Waakzaamheid Persoons-
registratiie (Privacy Alert) had, for twenty years, provided a
powerful and effective focus for privacy issues in the
Netherlands. Although the decision of its Board of Directors
to wind up the organization involved financial issues, it is
also a reflection of changing social attitudes to privacy. It
seems there was simply not a strong enough commitment to
support the group through hard times, despite clear
evidence that Holland is facing severe and widespread
privacy problems. Indeed, the winding up of Privacy Alert
comes at a time when Holland is establishing a single
national numbering system, an identity card, and a vast
array of new police and administrative powers.

The Dutch situation is replicated around the world. Non-
government privacy organizations charged with the responsibility of raising awareness of privacy concerns have
increasingly failed to achieve broad public support for their
message. The loss of Privacy Alert is an important symbol of
changing times.

Considering that privacy is said by many civil rights and
libertarian groups to be one of the great emerging social
issues of this century, it is mystifying that so few advocacy
organizations have flourished. The Dutch group was easily
the world's most successful non-government privacy organization, yet it failed to survive the most crucial period of its
history. Other organizations elsewhere have suffered the
same fate.

The problem may well be that privacy is a complex and

highly technical issue entrusted to the care of a few experts – mainly lawyers. Under their patronage, the solutions to privacy invasion are formulated in a technical and legalistic manner. It is rare for energy to be devoted to the political dimension. This is a shortcoming of the privacy field.

During 1990, in an effort to galvanize the privacy issue worldwide, more than 100 leading privacy experts and human rights organizations from forty countries linked arms to form a world organization for the protection of privacy. Members of the new body, which took the name Privacy International, had a common interest in promoting an international understanding of the importance of privacy and data protection. Meetings were held throughout that year in North America, Europe, Asia and the South Pacific, and members agreed to work towards the establishment of effective privacy protection throughout the world. A Working Group of 120 leading privacy experts and human rights organizations was established to develop organizational guidelines.

Even though the effort ran on a shoestring budget (and still does), the formation of Privacy International is the first successful attempt to establish a properly structured world focus on this crucial area of human rights. As an international network, the organization is able to raise the alarm about dangerous technology and unwarranted surveillance.

Privacy International has been most prominent in North America and Asia, where it has liaised with local human rights organizations to raise awareness about the development of national surveillance systems. The network has also been used by law reform and human rights organizations in more than twenty countries to assist national or local privacy issues. In Thailand and the Philippines, for example,

Privacy International worked with local human rights bodies to develop national campaigns against the establishment of government identity card systems. In 1995 Privacy International announced that it would organize an annual 'Big Brother award' to go to the government or organization most offensive to privacy. PI is also utilizing the Internet, publishing details of companies which peddle surveillance technology to Third World dictatorships. In late 1995 it published a report on the global trade in surveillance technology and its links with the arms industry.

The problem Privacy International and other groups face is the increasing difficulty of convincing the public that privacy solutions must be forged outside of the big institutions such as government and corporations. People are seduced by law and by high-sounding commitments about public interest. Few people are interested in supporting the bottom line of privacy because it involves making a sacrifice of either convenience or access to services. The protection of privacy requires the same level of personal sacrifice involved in environmental protection. Without that level of sacrifice, privacy advocacy is doomed to remain an academic pursuit and privacy protection will remain the province of highly paid lawyers and toothless regulators.

CHAPTER SIX

THE IDENTITY CARD: BLUEPRINT FOR AN INTERNAL PASSPORT

Chiang Mai in Northern Thailand is a place of ancient customs and fixed values. Along the endless stretches of forests and rice farms, peasants work with much the same crude technology that their ancestors used for centuries. The intricacies of the automobile are known only to a few. For most, the telephone is still magical. Here in Chiang Mai, people neither know nor care about such things.

The farmers of Chiang Mai, however, are unwitting travellers on the information Superhighway. Over the past three years – to their unending bemusement – they have all been issued with high-tech, plastic identity cards. The card is part of a national strategy to computerize the Thai government and to keep track of the population. Every Thai adult has a machine-readable ID card containing a digitized thumbprint and photograph, details of family and ancestry, education and occupation, nationality, religion and information relating to taxation and police records.[1]

The card can be scanned by any police or government official to activate a sophisticated nationwide network of computers throughout the Thai government. By using a person's population number, which is registered in all agencies and banks, it will soon be possible instantly to secure information from police, social welfare, taxation, immigration, housing, employment, driving licence, census, electoral, passport, vehicle, insurance, education and health record databases. This remarkable system is called the Central Population Database.[2] It is the world's second largest relational database, surpassed only by the system in Salt Lake City owned by the Mormon Church.

For a government obsessed by the urgency of economic growth, this system is a cornerstone of national development. From the perspective of the military dominated parliament, it offers an opportunity to monitor and track the entire population. The ID card is the visible part of the technology and the only part that most Thais understand. Behind the card lies a strategy to construct a web of information which binds every aspect of a Thai citizen's life.

Few people in Thailand are fretting about these developments. Bangkok yuppies are anxious to ape the most sophisticated features of Western life. Politicians are anxious to show the world that Thailand is a truly advanced society. The military wants more information. Ordinary working people are too preoccupied with mere survival even to care.

The media is not convinced that such a massive information system will pose any threat whatever to the rights of citizens. One dissenter, the English language paper the *Bangkok Post*, published a two-page investigative article on the project. It warned: 'The population database will considerably strengthen the power of the Interior Ministry, already the most powerful and largest government agency in the country, and of the police, who are also governed by the Interior Ministry.'[3]

The *Bangkok Post* had every reason to sound the alarm. The new database system has the potential to retard Thailand's already fragile democracy. A 'Village Information System' monitors information at a local level. It is linked to electoral information, public opinion data and candidate information. Such a mass of related information in the hands of any government would put the opposition at a fatal disadvantage.

ID CARDS – A GLOBAL TREND

Political and economic factors such as these have been the key motivation behind the establishment of official identity cards throughout the world. The type of card, its function, and its integrity vary enormously. Around ninety countries including France, Germany, Italy, Spain, Portugal, Greece, Belgium, the Netherlands and Luxembourg have official, national IDs that are used for a variety of purposes. Among those which do not have a national ID card are Britain, Sweden, Finland, Austria, Ireland and Denmark. There are many and varied reasons why a country chooses not to have an official ID card. Some are cultural, some are constitutional. One Irish official explained to the *Daily Telegraph*: 'There has never been any attempt to introduce one because no one would ever carry it.'[4]

In most cases, the cards have become an accepted part of life. In Asian countries, for example, people are proud to show their ID card. In Singapore, the card is like an internal passport, necessary for every transaction. In Pakistan, the card is widely viewed as a protection against police harassment. In Germany, many people say they like the card because it helps streamline day-to-day activities. Interestingly, the more the card is requested by a burgeoning number of authorities, the more convenient it becomes.

Despite their prevalence, support for ID cards is by no means universal. Attempts to introduce national cards in such countries as the United States, New Zealand, Canada, Bangladesh and Australia have encountered widespread opposition and governments have been forced to seek back door approaches to creating an identifier for the population.

Despite these notables instances, a growing number of national governments have in recent years explored the adoption of the Thai ID model. Among these are such developing countries as India, Taiwan, and Malaysia. Canada, the United States and the United Kingdom are currently considering the adoption of a national ID card, while the Netherlands and France have recently announced national card schemes.

The use of specific purpose cards for health or social security is widespread. Most countries that do not have a national universal card have a health or social security card (in Australia the Medicare Card, in the United States the Social Security card). The reverse is also true. In Sweden, while there exists a ubiquitous national number, there is no official identity card.

Generally speaking, however, the key element of any modern ID card is the number. The number is the common element within all databases and is the key to access all this personal information. With this number governments can establish computer-linking programmes that merge information on many aspects of a person's life.

THE JUNK SHOP ID CARD

The 1994 Tory Party conference received more than forty motions calling for ID cards. For some conservative MPs, an ID card would be a simple and effective solution to so many of the problems that had dogged their government for fifteen years.

It came as no surprise, then, when Home Secretary Michael Howard told the conference that the government would proceed with a card. The announcement was well received at the conference, though some hard-liners heckled when Howard suggested that the card might be voluntary. Michael Howard was building on strong political foundations. His announcement came almost a year to the day since John Major declared his support for a national ID card.

Opinion polls on the subject brought a mixed result. Most indicated a clear support for the introduction of a card. Others reveal a different picture. MORI conducted a poll in mid-1994 which asked whether people would support an identity card containing bank account details, fingerprint, photograph, driver's licence and national insurance details. The poll revealed that while 37 per cent of people approved of such a card, 48 per cent disliked the idea. And while 16 per cent of the survey said they 'liked strongly' the idea of a card, more than double – 33 per cent – said they strongly disliked it. Curiously, most of the Conservative supporters polled disapproved of the card, while Liberal Democrats were overwhelmingly in favour. Perhaps the most surprising element of the survey was the revelation that young people – aged fifteen to twenty-four – were most strongly in favour of an ID card.

The MORI poll was commissioned by computer giant ICL. Like most other technology companies, ICL was very much in the market to produce and market a national ID card. Indeed, since the Prime Minister's 1993 declaration of support for a card, it seems that half the world's computer companies have launched an all-out sales offensive on the British government.

Within weeks of the Prime Minister's comments, the Department of Social Security and the Home Office were awash with glossy brochures, fancy technical reports and slick promotional videos. ID cards are big business world-wide. Half a billion cards and countless computer systems to run them have made this a lucrative industry with an aggressive marketing philosophy.

Most of the bumph received by the government promised a technical solution to many of Britain's social and administrative ills. New smart card technology and advanced computer design would make ours a more efficient, safe and prosperous society. ID cards and the numbering system thereon could be the key to a streamlined and harmonized government administration.

Civil servants responsible for dealing with these promotional pitches were sceptical. None of the competing companies were able to produce evidence that their systems actually worked. Technical specifications had not been externally assessed. Studies of the social impact of identity cards were nowhere to be seen. As for the political dimension, none of the competing companies even gave this a mention. For bureaucrats working in an ancient environment, these were important issues.

The warnings were ever present. In 1995 the police-automated national fingerprint system was shut down because the technical specifications did not match the organizational requirements of the police. A nasty legal battle ensued between the police and the supplier, IBM.

The problem facing the DSS and other agencies was that their political masters were far more easily persuaded. The computer industry's glossy promotional strategy has been accompanied by an equally slick lobbying effort of MPs. Ministers wanted these companies to be taken seriously by the departments. After all, they were promising all sorts of rewards for the constituency.

Using these tactics, the computer industry has enjoyed astonishing success worldwide. After the Control Data corporation had successfully targeted the Thai government to accept a national ID system, it worked on the prestigious Smithsonian Institution in the US to have the Thai government awarded a prize for 'brave use of technology'. The Thai mandarins were then able to hold the award aloft like some modern-day Holy Grail in answer to critics of their system.

The computer giants have had less success in the Philippines, where their wild promises and widespread palm-greasing were countered by a small but well-engineered campaign by local human rights activists. Instead of focusing on the risks of misuse by officials and police, the local groups concentrated on the fiscal component. Assisted by Privacy International, which had campaigned across the world against ID cards, local activists warned the Philippines Senate that the cost estimates provided by computer companies were less than a half of the comparable figure for overseas countries. The plan to introduce a card fell on these grounds.

The sales pitch of computer companies makes complex technology look like child's play, and that's where the conflict arises with departmental administrators in White-hall. A card system needs two additional components: a national number and a vast computer system, both of which are administrative nightmares. A national ID number in use throughout government would, in theory, create greater efficiency but would cause terminal chaos throughout the civil service. The attitude of most civil servants seems to be that these fancy card and computer systems could spell real trouble. A litany of computer failures has already cost departments countless millions.

Some officials have come to view the ID card idea as a solution looking for a problem. Others imagine it to be a tool to improve the efficiency of law enforcement. Inland Revenue and other government agencies don't seem to mind one way or the other. Police, generally, are ambivalent. The view of the Home Office has always been sharply divided. ID cards mean different things to different people. The simple icon imagined by many among the Tory right is nothing like the complex Thai-style system we are likely to end up with.

From the day John Major announced his support for a card, one fact became increasingly clear: support for an ID card could be on no other basis than gut instinct. No government agency has ever undertaken a serious study of the likely feasibility of ID cards or the computer systems that would drive them. The Home Office admits it has never commissioned a study. A technical feasibility study currently being conducted by the Cabinet Office has no interest in the wider dimensions of the issue.

Indeed no one had a clue how an ID card would work or even whether it would work. At a briefing session with officials at the Home Office, I was told the department did not have a clue about the law enforcement potential of a card. The following week, the police division responsible for writing the police response to the ID card proposal admitted to me that it did not have 'one shred of evidence' from overseas.

The complete absence of any credible data on identity card systems is one of the reasons for uncertainty in the mind of government about their adoption. In 1992, the view of the Home Office ministers was that the financial cost of an ID card would be unacceptably high and that such an instrument would have only a marginal impact on the fight against crime. The following year, Downing Street justified the Prime Minister's support on the basis that a card was needed to combat Social Security fraud. Then in 1994, the DSS concluded that it had 'no use' for an ID card, and that it would pursue other forms of benefit verification.

The division of opinion within government became public when, in January 1995, confidential ID card planning documents were discovered in a £35 government surplus filing cabinet in a junk shop in the London borough of Camden. The contents included Cabinet papers together with a confidential memo to John Major which outlined the proposed design of the smart card, a seventeen-page report on Whitehall's plans for smart cards and details of a key Cabinet option for smart cards.

The papers, which the Cabinet Office confirmed were genuine, refer to a meeting of GEN 34, a Cabinet committee set up by the Prime Minister 'to consider the developing technology of card systems, and the potential demand for such systems from government departments'.[5]

A letter to Mr Major from Lord Wakeham, then Lord Privy Seal, written on 25 May last year, discloses that ministers – including Mr Howard – were opposed to the introduction of national identity cards. At a subsequent Cabinet committee meeting, however, Mr Howard changed his mind.

Lord Wakeham writes that Mr Howard 'explained this morning that there had been growing interest in the case for a national identity card, and signs that the general public now find such a card more acceptable than in the past. He suggested that the time may now be ripe for a government document to test opinion on the subject.'

At the time Lord Wakeham – since replaced as committee chairman by David Hunt – warned Mr Major: 'I ought to record that some concern was expressed that an identity card would be contrary to our deregulatory stance and could prove unpopular. Also, chief police officers remain opposed, which could cause presentational problems.'[6]

The Cabinet papers reveal that the dominant view among planners was that police and civil rights concerns could be resolved if the ID card was made voluntary. Because of these difficulties, ID card proponents have to this point done little more than test the water of public response. But Britain's entry into Europe, together with the growing public anxiety over crime, has quickly forced the ID card idea on to a higher rung on the political agenda.

Pressure is also being applied from overseas. Such countries as France and the Netherlands have passed legislation requiring foreigners to produce identity, and Britain may pass similar legislation before 1997. One aim of Europol (the newly established Europe-wide police agency) is to have all European citizens issued with identity cards which are recognized and accepted in all other countries. The International Monetary Fund (IMF) also routinely builds ID cards into the economic performance criteria for

Third World nations. Implicit in these schemes is a strategy to equip all ID cards with magnetic stripes or chips which will access a range of computers.

The emergence of such problems as football hooliganism, terrorism, tax fraud, benefit fraud and illegal immigration ensures that most arms of government are likely to support the ID card option. However, attractive and logical as the ID card may appear to its supporters and proponents, the international experience is clearly that they are costly, cumbersome and dangerous.

In May 1995, the Home Office released its Green Paper on the ID card. Given the fact that the Home Office has conducted no research into the subject of ID cards, it was hardly a surprise to anyone that the consultation document lacked substance. Indeed, it was a clever device to confuse the public. The document offered numerous models for a card scheme, including voluntary cards, multi-purpose cards and compulsory cards, in several formats. No particular format was recommended, though the document appeared to give special weight to a compulsory, multi-purpose system, observing that such a card would maximize the benefits to the individual, and improve law enforcement. The same 'moving target' tactic was adopted four months later by the government of Ontario, with the identical result that opposition was neutralized.

THE ID CARD'S ROCKY ROAD IN EUROPE

Although the modern identity card has reached its evolutionary peak in Thailand, Western nations are not far behind. A plan being adopted in the Netherlands demonstrates how developed countries are getting in on the act.

Dutch authorities began researching and planning a national ID and numbering system about eight years ago. At the time there were two numbering systems, one for municipal registration and one for taxation purposes. The intention of the Dutch government has been to merge these numbers and then place the number on to an official national card.

Two factors have played an important role in the development of Dutch policy and practice in this area. The first is that throughout the 1970s and early 1980s there was a very great sensitivity about matters of privacy and personal autonomy. A campaign of mass civil disobedience in the early 1970s resulted in the scrapping of the national census and this forced a change in the direction of all information gathering in Holland.

Meanwhile, however, the Netherlands became a signatory to the Schengen police information sharing agreement and this established the foundation for pioneering work in cross-border information sharing. The two opposing influences have worked to a pragmatic centre.

In the mid-1970s, the Dutch government established a Tax number, which for many years was used exclusively for this purpose, but in 1989 it was extended to Social Security and, later, to house rent allowances, pensions and the registration of students' financial support. Although in 1989 the circumstances in which the number could be used were precisely laid out, the extensions were accepted without much debate. They were, after all, justified on the basis of fighting crime and fraud. One curious element of ID card promotion is that while it thrives on the spectre of crime, the card proponents have never been able to figure exactly how an ID card can prevent common crimes. The crimes of greatest interest to them are crimes not against the individual, but against the exchequer.

The new numbering system being established by the Dutch government is SOFI (Social Security and Fiscal number). It uses as its base the existing municipal registers – 650 separate regional databases which are networked (full networking will be finalized at the end of 1994). Recent studies have discovered a 99 per cent accuracy in these records. To arrive at this figure, a full audit of a city of 80,000 was carried out. The registers will be used as the basis for issuing the full spectrum of documents, including passports, licences and ID cards. Unlike the UK, where several numbers are in use for different purposes, a single Dutch number will be used for all intra-government information transactions.

Information relating to the population will be forwarded from the registers to the Tax Office, which will then create a number and return it to the municipal system. New numbers, wherever possible, will be issued at birth as part of a programme of cooperation with health facilities and hospitals.

From July 1994, all citizens were required to obtain an ID card from their municipal registry.

The newly developed ID is quite a simple card, although there are already plans for a more sophisticated smart card complete with digitized photographs. The present cards contain the name, address, photo, signature, number of issue and the SOFI number. The government plans to introduce digitized photography in the future and is discussing the concept of hand geometry (but not fingerprints). Biometrics is currently a controversial public issue.

The introduction of the card is, once again, justified with the argument that an open society such as the Dutch will need a new form of control after the opening of the borders. In the meanwhile, Parliament has accepted the law introducing the obligation to identify oneself in numerous situations including, for instance, at work, at football stadiums, on public transport and in banks. While the card is voluntary in name, it is in effect a compulsory instrument that will be carried at all times by Dutch citizens. Moreover, foreigners can always be asked to identify themselves to authorities at any moment and in any circumstance.

Ironically, Japan recently came under fire from the United Nations Human Rights Committee for the same practice. The Committee had expressed concern that Japan had passed a law requiring foreign residents to carry identification cards at all times. The eighteen-member panel examined human rights issues in Japan in accordance with the 1966 International Covenant on Civil and Political Rights. Japan ratified the covenant in 1979. 'The Alien Registration Law,' the Committee complained in its report, 'is not consistent with the covenant.'

The French have always had a turbulent relationship with ID cards. The French Ministry of the Interior recently announced the creation of a national smart ID card. The reason given for this initiative is that in recent trials no fraudulent smart card was detected, while the old-style paper card was easily forged.

Until the late 1970s, French residents were required to possess a national identity document. This was made of paper and was subject to the risk of forgery. In 1979, however, the Ministry of the Interior announced plans for a higher integrity 'automated' card encased in plastic. The card was to be used for anti-terrorism and law enforcement purposes. The card, to be issued to all 50 million residents of France, was to be phased in over a ten-year period. New laser technology was to be used to produce the cards.[7]

At first there appeared to be little resistance to the proposal, but in a fashion similar to the Australian experience (see Chapter 7), political and public resistance grew as details of the plan emerged. Although no identity numbers were to be used (only card numbers), there was some concern over the possible impact of such cards. France's information watchdog, CNIL, managed to suppress the machine-readable function of the proposed cards, though optical scanning made magnetic stripes somewhat redundant. Publications such as Le Figaro expressed concern that the cards and related information could be linked with other police and administrative systems.

Public debate intensified in 1980, with the Union of Magistrates expressing concern that an ID card had the potential of limiting the right of free movement. In response to these and other criticisms, the ruling of CNIL was that no number relating to an individual could be used, but that each card would carry a number. If the card had to be replaced, a new number would apply to that particular document.

In 1981 the Socialists were elected and the fate of the ID card was reversed. In an election statement on informatics, François Mitterrand expressed the view that 'the creation of computerized identity cards contains a real danger for the liberty of individuals'. His concern was echoed by the minister for the Justice, Robert Badinter, who explained that

ID cards presented a real danger to the individual liberties and private life of citizens, and the new Minister of the Interior then announced the demise of ID cards in France.[8]

Five years later, in 1986, a new conservative government reintroduced plans for the national ID card. The Ministry of the Interior, claiming urgency because of terrorism, drew up plans for a machine-readable card which would involve a fingerprint on the application form. The CNIL approved this proposal, but certain rulings meant that the card would not be compulsory because individuals would retain the right to identify themselves by any means. Additionally, the digital storage of fingerprints was disallowed. More important, perhaps, was the ruling that the ID card machinery cannot be linked to registers, nor can data stored on the card be given to third parties.

When the card was introduced on an experimental basis in 1988, there was a very strong adverse reaction by media and civil liberties groups. The ID scheme, however, was ultimately approved.

STRIKING THE BALANCE

Few people would oppose serious and effective strategies to reduce fraud and criminality. The experience overseas, however – as the following chapter vividly illustrates – is that there exists a vast gulf between hope and reality in the realm of ID card schemes. The cost/benefit calculations of agencies involved in such proposals are shown, invariably, to be wildly optimistic. The legal and civil rights implications are far more complex than governments want to admit. A recent survey of identity cards in fifty countries conducted by Privacy International found claims of police abuse of the cards in virtually all countries. Most involved people being arbitrarily detained after failure to produce their card. Others involved beatings of juveniles or members of minorities. There were even instances of wholesale discrimination on the basis of data set out on the cards.

Despite a degree of instinctive support for the ID card, many countries have witnessed bitter and prolonged public opposition to these schemes. An Australian government proposal in 1987 to introduce a national ID card resulted in mass protests and political upheaval. The card was abandoned that year by the government. A similar proposal by the New Zealand government in 1991 ended much the same way. It is virtually impossible to predict the point at which a population will turn against a card scheme – a factor which has come to plague the proponents of identity card schemes throughout the world.

CHAPTER SEVEN

THE DARK SIDE OF IDENTITY

In 1986, the Australian government announced its intention to introduce a national identity card. There, like most other places, the public initially accepted the idea without question.

It was, after all, a simple matter of weeding out tax evaders and welfare fraudsters. 'Only cheats and criminals would oppose it,' chanted the Parliament. 'Law-abiding citizens will want to support this.' In time, 'Nothing to hide, nothing to fear' became a sort of national mantra. Few people wanted to stand in the way of efforts to catch the guilty. Early opinion polls showed an 80 per cent support for the card.

Indeed, so popular was the idea that the government agencies wanting to use the card as a basis for their administration leaped from three to thirty. The proposed purpose of the card was extended to catch assorted criminals and illegal immigrants, and was to be used for financial transactions, property dealings, and employment. The list grew and grew: health benefits, passport control, housing. This growth in unintended purposes was given a catchy name: function creep.

This was to be a new era of government efficiency and fiscal responsibilty. A time for justice and equity for all. A billion dollars or more a year would be reaped by the ID card system.

Then something unexpected happened. The public started to debate the downside of these cards. Questions about the civil liberties implications remained unanswered. Doubts were cast. More and more prominent Australians from the left and the right warned that this card was not a path of least resistance to solve societal problems, but a slippery slope to a totally regulated society and even to a police state.

As the Australia Card Bill was subjected to increasing scrutiny, the surveillance nature of the scheme received more attention. One academic described the components of the Australia Card as 'the building blocks of surveillance'.[1]

The most obvious of those building blocks were the card, the unique number, the Australia Card Register (containing all the information and acting as an information exchange) and the telecommunications links between different agencies and arms of the Card scheme.

The Australia Card was to be carried by all Australian citizens and permanent residents (separately marked cards would be issued to temporary residents and visitors). They would contain a photograph, name, unique number, signature and period of validity.

Not so obvious, however, were the extensive reporting obligations throughout the government and the community, the automatic exchange of information throughout the government, the ease of expansion of the system, and the encouragement of the private sector and state governments to make use of the card and its number. Like the British Poll tax plan some years later, where 'prefects' would be appointed in each house to report to the State, the Australia Card would require mass reporting by individuals and organizations. All finance sector employees would have been forced under threat of jail to report suspicions to the government.

A Parliamentary Joint Select Committee, convened to consider the implications of the issue, raised a wide spectrum of concerns that eventually came to haunt the government. The majority of the Committee, including one government member, came down against the proposal, warning that the scheme would change the nature of the relationship between citizen and State and create major privacy and civil liberties problems. The committee pointed out that the cost/benefit basis for such a scheme was speculative and rubbery, and that all common law countries had rejected such proposals.[2]

Several well-known Australians joined the condemnation of the scheme. Sir Noel Foley, formerly chairman of Australia's largest private bank, Westpac, stunned his colleagues with the blunt assessment that the card would pose 'a serious threat to the privacy, liberty and safety of every citizen'. Australian Medical Association president Dr Bruce Shepherd went as far as to predict: 'It's going to turn Australian against Australian. But given the horrific impact the card will have on Australia, its defeat would almost be worth fighting a civil war for.'

Americas Cup winner Ben Lexcen – a national hero – threatened to leave Australia for ever if the scheme proceeded. Rock singer and conservation leader Peter Garrett called it 'the greatest threat Australia has ever faced'.[3] Communist author Frank Hardy was seen on the same platform as the right-wing Ben Lexcen. The Council for Civil Liberties linked arms with the Libertarians. Fuelled by the unique alliance, newspapers and talk-back shows recorded a logarithmic increase in public concern. Within weeks, a massive movement was under way.

The letters pages of most newspapers reflected the strong feelings of Australians. 'We won't be numbers!' was a typical letters page headline, with others such as 'I have no intention of applying', 'An alternative is the ball and chain', 'Biggest con job in our history', 'Overtones of Nazi Germany', 'I will leave the country' and 'Passive resistance gets my vote'.[4] The cartoonists contributed to the strong feelings, with some constantly portraying the then Prime Minister Robert Hawke in Nazi uniform.

A major national opinion poll conducted in the closing days of the campaign by the Channel Nine television network resulted in a staggering 90 per cent opposition to the card. The normally staid *Australian Financial Review* produced a scathing editorial which concluded, 'It is simply obscene to use revenue arguments ('We can make more money out of the Australia Card') as support for authoritarian impositions rather than take the road of broadening national freedoms.'[5]

As news of the specifics of the ID card legislation spread, the campaign strengthened. If you were in employment without an ID card, it would be an offence for your employer to pay you (penalty $20,000). If you were then forced to resign, you could not get a new job, as the law would make it an offence for an employer to hire a cardless person (penalty $20,000). Farmers without ID cards could not receive payments from marketing boards for their produce (penalty $20,000). A person without an ID card would be denied access to a pre-existing bank account and could not cash in investments, give money to or receive money from a solicitor, or receive money in unit, property or a cash management trust.

Cardless people could not buy or rent their own home or land (penalty $5,000), nor would benefits be paid to the unemployed, widows, supporting parents, the aged, the invalid or the sick.

If your card was destroyed for any reason that could not be proven as accidental, the penalty would be $5,000 or two years' imprisonment or both. A $500 penalty would be imposed if you lost your card and failed to report the loss within twenty-one days. Failure to attend a compulsory conference if ordered to by the ID card agency would result in a penalty of $1,000 or six months' jail. Failure to produce your ID card on demand to the Tax Office would invoke a penalty of $20,000.

By this time, the card's architect, the Health Insurance Commission, was well and truly on the nose. Talk-back radio hosts had become fond of quoting a paragraph of an HIC planning document on the Australia Card:

> It will be important to minimize any adverse public reaction to implementation of the system. One possibility would be to use a staged approach for implementation, whereby only less sensitive data are held in the system initially with the facility to input additional data at a later stage when public acceptance may be forthcoming more readily.[6]

The campaign organizers stressed the pseudo-voluntary nature of the card. While it was not technically compulsory for a person actually to obtain a card, it would have been extremely difficult to live in society without it. By mid-September, the government was facing an internal crisis. The left of the party had broken ranks to oppose the card[7] while right-wing members (particularly those in marginal seats) were expressing concern within caucus.[8] Deputy Prime Minister Lionel Bowen urged the Party to tread with caution, and suggested that a re-think might be necessary.[9]

There were some very persuasive and pragmatic arguments against the card, many of which related to the vast administrative problems that would be generated. It was estimated that up to 5 per cent of cards would be lost, stolen or damaged each year. Hundreds of thousands of people would suffer serious and prolonged disruption of their affairs.

In the initial months, people saw the ID card as being no more than yet another form of identification. The idea, however, that your life could literally be paralysed without it made people very nervous. As with ID cards in many other countries, identification was only one component.

Within weeks, in the face of major protests, a party revolt and civil disobedience, the government scrapped the ID card proposal.

The campaign raised several very substantial privacy and data protection fears. These included matters of data security, function creep, incursions related to data matching, improper use and disclosure of data, erroneous data, the establishment of central control and tracking, and the development of an 'internal passport'. Coupled with the government's inability to establish that the system would actually tackle major problems such as the underground economy, even the most conservative government supporters became sceptical. The final sin committed by the government was plain arrogance. Australians felt that if they were to be subjected to a national identification system, they should have a say in its development. To be characterized as a 'noisy minority' did not sit well with those who had genuine concerns about the proposal. The government's policy of trivializing the criticism was perhaps its major error.

THE KIWI CARD

On the evening of 11 September 1991 viewers of New Zealand's popular TV3 television network watched in amazement as a senior bureaucrat, disguised in shadow, revealed that their government was in the final stage of secretly planning a high-tech universal ID card. The card would link major government departments and would have the capacity to track the financial dealings and even the geographical movements of New Zealanders. The plan was to be known as 'social bank', and the card would be a 'Kiwi Card'.

What followed was a memorable national crisis of confidence. Cynicism and disillusion with the government was already at perhaps its worst point ever in New Zealand history, but the smell of a conspiracy made the relationship between the beleaguered citizens and their conservative government even more uneasy. The media ran hot with the issue. Hundreds of people turned out for public meetings in Auckland and the government began to feel the heat of mass protest.

Branding the reaction as 'absolute hysteria', Prime Minister Bolger angrily denied claims that work was proceeding on such a scheme.[10] He was immediately contradicted by the deputy head of the Social Welfare Department, and also by former Prime Minister David Lange, who revealed that work on a 'smart card' (a card containing a computer chip) had been going on for four years.[11]

The senior bureaurat who started the whole affair (whose name was withheld but who was said to be the head of a major government enterprise) warned that although the government intended to introduce the card merely as a health benefits entitlement for low income people, the card would later be extended to all people and for all government benefits. The card would be required to open and operate a bank account and would ultimately be demanded by employers (those people who did not produce their card would almost certainly be required to pay the highest tax rate). Perhaps the most disquieting aspect of all was that there appeared to be absolutely no limits, safeguards or restrictions on the use of the Kiwi Card. It could be demanded by anybody – police, government officials or banks – for any purpose.

The shadowy figure on TV3 dominated the media for weeks. Public concern reached an extraordinary intensity as more and more questions were asked about the capacity of this new scheme to change the country for ever. The Prime Minister's assurances seemed to have the effect of throwing fuel on to the fire. Within a week, a large and turbulent public meeting in Auckland had formed the New Zealand Privacy Foundation to fight the proposals.[12]

The foundation's first act was to distribute a provocative leaflet. In a country where the concept of privacy was still in its adolescence, the foundation tried to convince the New

Zealand public that privacy was not the suspect or selfish concern that the New Zealand government had recently insinuated. The right to privacy, warned the foundation, is the right to draw the line at how far a government – or anyone else – can intrude into your personal life. 'The defence of privacy is the defence against surveillance and control. If we sacrifice or surrender that right, freedom has lost one of its most precious safeguards.'

The foundation went on to warn that a country with no constitution and no parliamentary house of review could ill afford to accept the promises of politicians – conservative parties or otherwise. 'When governments in New Zealand propose any measure to monitor or control the population, New Zealanders should demand an exhaustive justification. This simply has not happened.'

A great many issues were debated in the days and weeks following the revelations of the anonymous public servant, but none were more passionate than the debate over the right of government to hold so much power over the citizen. Surely the people had a right to draw the line at how far their government could go?

The Privacy Foundation worked long and hard at persuading the New Zealand public to remember that in any democratic nation it is the government that is accountable to the people, not the other way round. Governments that argue on the basis of 'nothing to hide, nothing to fear' are resorting to a flimsy and dangerous argument. No civilized population, the foundation argued, should be blackmailed into accepting a revenue measure.

Cracks began appearing in the government. National MP Grant Thomas crossed the floor of Parliament on the issue to vote against the card and later told Agence France Presse, a press agency, that the scheme could well 'creep into every aspect of our privacy'.[13] One senior government minister met with me privately and expressed his concern.

The campaign forced the government to introduce privacy legislation and to modify the Kiwi Card proposal. Ultimately, however, most features of the original scheme were retained. The hot buttons which stimulated public debate were cooled as soon as a compromise plan was announced. This pattern of public response emerges time and time again where ID cards and computer networks are introduced. In a consensus-based society, people do not feel comfortable taking a hard and uncompromising line on schemes designed to combat crime and fraud. Any compromise move by government has the effect of neutralizing a campaign of opposition.

MYTH AND REALITY

In 1994, in an attempt to discover the problems caused by ID cards, Privacy International compiled a survey containing reports from correspondents in forty countries. The summary below addresses the problems raised in virtually all systems.

TWELVE REASONS WHY ID CARDS ARE A BAD IDEA

I. They won't stop crime
Law and order is the main motivation behind current efforts to introduce an ID card in the UK. Home Secretary Michael

Howard told the 1994 Tory Party conference that he believed an ID card could provide an invaluable tool in the fight against crime.

Howard's claim has received little support from academic or law enforcement bodies. The Association of Chief Police Officers (ACPO) said that while it is in favour of a voluntary system, its members would be reluctant to administer a compulsory card that might erode relations with the public. Dutch police authorities were not generally in favour of similar proposals in that country, for much the same reason.

According to police in both countries, the major problem in combating crime is not lack of identification procedures, but difficulties in the gathering of evidence and the pursuit of a prosecution. Indeed, police and criminologists have not been able to advance any evidence whatever that the existence of a card would actually reduce the incidence of crime. In a 1993 report, ACPO suggested that street crime, burglaries and crimes by bogus officials could be diminished through the use of an ID card, though this conflicted with its position that the card should be voluntary.

In reality, it appears that only a national DNA database (such as has just been opened in Britain) or a biometric database (such as is being proposed in Canada) might assist the police in linking crimes to perpetrators.

There is a powerful 'retributive' thread running along the law and order argument. Some people are frustrated by what they see as the failure of the justice system to deal with offenders, and the ID card is seen, at the very least, as having an irritant value.

2. They won't stop welfare fraud

Benefits agencies around the world have identified problems relating to fraud. Three levels of fraud are often expressed, in order of significance, as (1) false declaration, or non-declaration, of income, (2) criminal acquisition of multiple benefits using false identification, and (3) more conventional fraud and theft of benefit payments.

There also exist numerous other factors which contribute to benefit overpayment, including clerical error and genuine misunderstanding about the terms of payment.

No one knows the true extent of fraud. Virtually no ethnographic research exists, and the data that do exist are drawn principally from internal and external audits, management reviews, and retrospective studies.[14] Many studies assess risk, rather than quantifying fraud. Estimates of the extent of fraud on benefits agencies vary to a far greater extent than do the conditions in each recipient population.

The Parliamentary Select Committee on the Australia Card warned that the revenue promises were little better than 'qualitative assessment' – in other words, guesswork. The Department of Finance refused to support the Health Insurance Commission's cost/benefit estimates. Revenue was constantly revised downward, while the costs continued to rise. The Department of Social Security insisted that the ID card would have done little or nothing to diminish welfare fraud. In evidence to the parliamentary committee investigating the proposal, the Department said that much less than 1 per cent of benefit overpayments resulted from false identity. The Department decided that it would pursue other means of tackling fraud. The DSS in the UK argued against ID cards on the same grounds.

The Australian DSS estimates that benefit overpayment by way of false identity accounts for 0.6 per cent of overpayments, whereas non-reporting of income variation accounts for 61 per cent. The key area of interest, from the perspective of benefit agencies, lies in creating a single numbering system which would be used as a basis for employment eligibility, and which would reduce the size of the black market economy.

3. They will not stop illegal immigration

The immigration issue appears to be the principal motivation behind ID card proposals in continental Europe, the United States and some smaller developing nations.

The abolition of internal borders has become a primary concern of the new European Union. The development of the Schengen agreement between the Benelux countries, France and Germany calls for the dismantling of all border checks, in return for a strengthening of internal procedures for vetting of the population. France and the Netherlands have already passed legislation allowing for identity checks on a much broader basis, and other countries are likely to follow.

The establishment of personal identity in the new borderless Europe is a contentious issue, but is one which appears (to many people) to be a broadly acceptable trade-off for the convenience of total freedom of movement within the union.

The use of a card for purposes of checking resident status depends on the police and other officials being given very broad powers to check identity. More important, from the perspective of civil rights, its success will depend on the exercise of one of two processes: either a vastly increased level of constant checking of the entire population, or a discriminatory checking procedure which will target minorities.

The two arguments most often put forward to justify the quest to catch illegal immigrants in any country are: (1) that these people are taking jobs that should belong to citizens and permanent residents, and (2) that these people are often illegally collecting unemployment and other government benefits.

The image of the illegal immigrant living off the welfare of the State is a powerful one, and it is used to maximum effect by proponents of ID cards. When, however, the evidence is weighed scientifically, it does not bear any resemblance to the claim. When the Joint Parliamentary Committee on the Australia Card considered the issue, it found that the real extent of illegal immigrants collecting government benefits was extremely low. The report described a mass data-matching episode to determine the exact number. Of more than 57,000 'overstayers' in New South Wales, only twenty-two were found in the match against Social Security files to be receiving government unemployment benefits. That is, twenty-two out of a state population of 5 million. The Department of Immigration and Ethnic Affairs (DIEA) had earlier claimed that the figure was thirty times this amount (12.4 per cent as opposed to 0.4 per cent of overstayers).

Once again, immigration authorities worldwide base their estimates on 'qualitative assessment' or guesswork. Again quoting from the Australia Card inquiry: 'It became clear that the estimates for illegal immigrants were based on guesswork, the percentage of illegal immigrants who worked was based on guesswork, the percentage of visitors who worked illegally came from a Departmental report that was based on guesswork . . . The Committee has little difficulty in rejecting DIEA evidence as being grossly exaggerated.'

4. They will facilitate discrimination
As I mentioned earlier in this section, the success of ID cards as a means of fighting crime or illegal immigration will depend on the exercise of one of two processes: either a vastly increased level of constant checking of the entire population, or a discriminatory checking procedure which will target minorities.

The irony of the ID card option is that it invites discrimination by definition. Discriminatory practices are an inherent part of the function of an ID card. Without this discrimination, police would be required to conduct random checks which, in turn, would be politically unacceptable.

All discrimination is based on one of two conditions: situational or sectoral. Situational discrimination targets people in 'unusual' circumstances, i.e. walking at night, visiting certain areas, attending certain functions or activities, or behaving in an abnormal fashion. Sectoral discrimination targets people having certain characteristics, i.e. blacks, youths, skinheads, motor-cycle riders or the homeless. ID cards containing religious or ethnic information make it possible to carry this discrimination a step further.

Several developed nations have been accused of conducting discriminatory practices using ID cards. The government of Japan recently came under fire from the United Nations Human Rights Committee for this practice. The Committee had expressed concern that Japan had passed a law requiring that foreign residents must carry identification cards at all times.

French police have been accused of over-zealous use of the ID card against blacks, and particularly against Algerians. The Greek authorities have been accused of using data on religious affiliation on their national card to discriminate against people who are not Greek Orthodox. ID checks by Belgian police sparked race riots in the early 1990s. During the campaign against the Australia Card, aboriginals and Jews expressed fear of discrimination, while in New Zealand, trade unions and civil liberties organizations warned of discrimination against minority groups and poor people.

5. They will create an unwarranted increase in police powers

The Privacy International survey of ID cards found claims of police abuse by way of the cards in virtually all countries. Most involved people being arbitrarily detained after failure to produce their card. Others involved beatings of juveniles or minorities. There were even instances of wholesale discrimination on the basis of data set out on the cards.

While it is true that cards containing non-sensitive data are less likely to be used against the individual, cards are often alleged to be the vehicle for discriminatory practices. Police who are given powers to demand ID invariably have consequent powers to detain people who do not have the card, or who cannot prove their identity. Even in such advanced countries as Germany, the power to hold such people for up to twenty-four hours is enshrined in law. The question of who is targeted for ID checks is left largely to the discretion of police.

The wartime ID card used in the UK outlived the war and found its way into general use until the early 1950s. Police became used to the idea of routinely demanding the card, until in 1953 the High Court ruled that the practice was unlawful. In a landmark ruling that led to the repealing of the National Registration Act and the abandonment of the ID card, the Lord Chief Justice remarked:

> . . . although the police may have powers, it does not follow that they should exercise them on all occasions . . . it is obvious that the police now, as a matter of routine, demand the production of national registration identity cards whenever they stop or interrogate a motorist for any cause . . . This Act was passed for security purposes and not for the purposes for which, apparently, it is now sought to be used . . . In this country we have always prided ourselves on the good feeling that exists between the police and the public, and such action tends to make the public resentful of the acts of police and inclines them to obstruct them rather than assist them.[15]

6. They will become an internal passport

Virtually all ID cards worldwide develop a broader usage over time than was originally envisioned for them. This development of new and unintended purposes has become known as Function Creep.

All compulsory ID cards – and even the majority of non-compulsory ones – develop into an internal passport of sorts. Without care, the card becomes an icon. Its use is enforced through mindless regulation or policy, disregarding other means of identification, and in the process causing significant problems for those who are without the card. The card becomes more important than the individual.

In most countries with a card, its use has become universal. All government benefits, dealings with financial institutions, securing employment or rental accommodation, renting cars or equipment and obtaining documents requires the card. It is also used in myriad small ways, such as entry to official buildings (where security will invariably confiscate and hold the card).

Ironically, many card subjects come to interpret this state of affairs in a contra view ('the card helps streamline my dealings with authority', rather than 'the card is my licence to deal with authorities'). The Australia Card campaign referred to the card as a 'licence to live'.

7. A 'voluntary' card will become compulsory

Any official ID system will ultimately extend into more and more functions. Any claim that an official card is 'voluntary' should not imply that a card will be any less of an internal passport than would a compulsory card. Indeed a voluntary card may suffer the shortcoming of limited protections in law. Comments by correspondents in many countries suggest that even where a card is voluntary it is so inconvenient not to have one that they are effectively compulsory.

8. The cost will be unacceptable

In the Philippines and Australia, the cost of implementing an ID system has been at the forefront of opposition. The Philippines proposal relied on government estimates that were drawn, as is often the case, from estimates calculated by computer industry consultants. These were found to under-estimate the true cost by 8 billion pesos over seven years.[16] The proposal lapsed because of this factor.

In Australia, the cost of the proposed ID card failed to take into account such factors as training costs, administrative supervision, staff turnover, holiday and sick leave, compliance costs, and overseas issue of cards. Other costs that are seldom factored into the final figure (as was the case in Australia) are the cost of fraud, an underestimate of the cost of issuing and maintaining cards, and the cost to the private sector. As a consequence, the official figure for the Australia Card almost doubled between 1986 and 1987.

Private sector costs for complying with an ID card are very high. The Australian Bankers Association estimated that the system would cost their members over $100 million over ten years. Total private sector compliance costs were estimated at around $1 billion annually.

The official figure for the Australia Card was $820 million over seven years. The revised estimate, including private sector and compliance costs, together with other factors, would amount to several times as much.

The UK government's CCTA (Information Technology Centre) advised that a national 'smart' ID card would cost between £5 and £8 per head, yet this figure does not include administration or compliance. The cost of a card system could ultimately be as high as £2 billion or £3 billion.

9. The loss of a card will cause great distress and inconvenience

Virtually all countries with ID cards report that their loss or damage causes immense problems for people. Up to 5 per cent of cards are lost, stolen or damaged each year, and the result can be denial of services and benefits, and – in the broadest sense – loss of identity.

There exists a paradox in the replacement of cards. The replacement of a high security, high integrity card entails significant administrative involvement. Documents must be presented in person to an official. Cards must be processed centrally. This process can take some weeks. A low value card can be replaced in a lesser time, but its loss poses security threats because of the risk of the potential for misuse.

People who lose a wallet full of cards quickly understand the misfortune and inconvenience that can result. A single ID card when lost or stolen can have precisely the same impact on a person's life.

10. A card will imperil the privacy of personal information

The existence of a person's life-story in 100 unrelated databases is one important condition that protects privacy. The bringing together of these separate information centres creates a major privacy vulnerability. Any multi-purpose national ID card has such an effect.

Privacy advocates argue against ID cards on the basis of evidence from various 'security threat models' in use throughout the private sector. In these models, it is generally assumed that at any one time, 1 per cent of staff will be willing to sell or trade confidential information for personal gain. In many European countries, up to 1 per cent of bank staff are dismissed each year, often because of their involvement in theft.

The evidence for this potential corruption is compelling. Recent inquiries in Australia, Canada and the United States[17] indicate that widespread abuse of computerized information is occurring. Corruption among information users inside and outside the government in New South Wales had become endemic and epidemic. Virtually all instances of privacy violation relate to computer records.

A UK National Audit Office (NAO) report (March 1995) revealed that computer hacking, theft and viruses are on the rise in Whitehall's developing IT network. Instances of hacking rose by 140 per cent in 1984, while viruses increased by 300 per cent. 655 cases of hacking were identified by the NAO. Most of these involved staff exceeding their authority by obtaining information on members of the public to disclose to non-authorized people.

II. The card will entrench criminality and institutionalize false identity

Remarkably, the main problem for all ID card systems is not the inevitable conflict with civil rights. It is the curious repercussion that a card actually entrenches crime. By providing a 'one stop' form of identity, criminals can easily use cards in several identities. Even the highest-integrity bank cards are available as blanks in such countries as Singapore for several pounds. Within two months of the new Commonwealth Bank high security hologram cards being issued in Australia, near perfect forgeries were already in circulation. The card manufacturing technologies are now all available for purchase or hire to criminal organizations.

This argument has been advanced in Australia, the UK and the Netherlands. It relies on the simple logic that the higher an ID card's value, the more it will be used. The more an ID card is used, the greater the value placed on it, and consequently, the higher is its value to criminal elements. Organizations come to rely on the card as an unquestioned proof of ID, and often abandon the checking systems that have evolved over many years.

12. They will compromise national identity and personal integrity

ID cards strike a nerve in the national psyche of some countries. ID cards are often viewed as inimical to the struggle for independence, freedom, autonomy and individuality that nations are proud of. The Australia Card campaign vividly illustrates this phenomenon.

Privacy protection involves resistance to the establishment or consolidation of monolithic information systems. Informational chaos among agencies has ensured that the individual has not become a servant of the State. Variety, choice, and chaos have also had the effect of ensuring the free movement, rights, and free choice of individuals.

The movements against ID cards in the US, Canada, Australia and New Zealand have highlighted a number of abstract fears, widely held throughout the population, such as that people will be de-humanized by being reduced to numbers; that the system is a hostile symbol of authority; and that society is becoming ruled by technology driven bureaucracy, rather than by elected government. While these fears may be dismissed by proponents of ID cards, they ultimately will be the fuel for public feelings.

CHAPTER EIGHT

SMART CARDS AND CLEVER ILLUSIONS

Swindon is an unlikely place to glimpse the future of the world's economy, but fate nevertheless has chosen it for the job. If the banking sector has its way, this featureless Wiltshire town will spearhead a global movement to eliminate cash. From mid-1995, 6,000 Swindoners joined a push to replace cash with electronic 'credits'.

Banks do not like cash. Nor do retailers. It is costly, cumbersome and messy. It is insecure and untraceable. UK banks estimate that they spend £2 billion a year on cash distribution, and the cost to retailers has been put at £800 million. Banks want to save money not only by taking cash out of the system, but also by charging customers and retailers for an alternative system that avoids the traditional drawbacks of cash.[1]

Governments are also anxious to eliminate cash. Without cash, the black and grey economies would suffocate. Forced to transfer their proceeds overseas for laundering, criminal organizations might be more easily identified. Furthermore, if 'legitimate' transactions were conducted by some means other than cash, then criminal uses of cash would be more easily traced and identified – or so the theory goes.

For all these reasons, every bank and every government in the world has looked closely at the alternatives to cash. The conventional solution, credit cards, has proved useless for small amounts, as well as being time-consuming and costly. In their place, technology has offered a remarkable solution: the smart card.

The smart card is a device which can store and process considerable amounts of information. Most smart cards contain a microchip, which can hold several A4 pages of data, but some embrace laser technology, and have a capacity of up to 2,000 A4 pages from 6 megabytes of memory. The microchip card can independently process this data, and present it in different forms according to requirements. Information on the chip can be 'locked' with a PIN number, and protected through a range of encryption methods. These cards have been developed in various countries for health, social welfare benefits, transport, and financial transactions.

The smart card is, in effect, a credit-card-sized personal computer. It is able to act as the 'interface' with large computer systems, giving and receiving data and instructions. It can store a comprehensive record of your personal details and transactions, and can even digitally store your fingerprints and handprints for verification by a scanner (see the section on the INSPASS biometric project in Chapter 3). Thus, depending on the system being used, the card can bring together in the one place a vast spectrum of your personal information. In a fashion similar to telephone cards, the smart card can also store money in the form of electronic units.

The Swindon experiment is at the cutting edge of smart card technology. It is being conducted by Mondex, an aggressive partnership of National Westminster and the Midland banks. They have also signed up Midland's sister company, HongkongBank, as the first overseas partner. HongkongBank has acquired the rights to franchise Mondex in Hong Kong, China, India, Indonesia, Macau, the Philippines, Singapore, Sri Lanka, Taiwan, Thailand and Malaysia. Trevor Blackler, NatWest's chief executive of group services, has said talks are being conducted with thirty banks in fifteen countries around the world. He described discussions with potential partners in Japan, Europe and the US as 'encouraging'.[2]

HongkongBank told *The Times* that it expected smart cards, as a replacement for cash, to be well received in the Far East, where consumers take to new technology quickly. HSBC, the parent of HongkongBank and the Midland, operates in sixty-seven countries worldwide, and it seems likely that other HSBC banks elsewhere in the world will also become partners.

The Mondex card can electronically store the value of cash authorized from a bank ATM machine or by way of specially adapted pay phones connected to the customer's bank. Instead of handing over cash to a store, you will hand over the card, which acts in place of cash. Because it is a debit card (that is, you have already paid for the value of cash contained in it), no signature or authorization is needed. The relevant amount is electronically deducted from the card. The big High Street retailers, including Boots, Asda, Safeway, J. Sainsbury, W.H. Smith, BP and McDonald's are participating in the scheme.

The difference between the Mondex card and other debit

cards is that the former is designed intentionally as a replacement for cash. It can be used for transacting very small amounts. It is universally accepted, is fast, and involves no expensive administrative overheads.

Although the card is a direct substitute for cash, it can be made more secure than cash. The owner can encode it with a PIN number which 'locks' the cash value, and thus makes the card useless for anyone else. The card can be topped up, or the security instructions changed, by using any ATM or modified pay-phone.

Other banks are not far behind Mondex. Barclays and Lloyds are in partnership with Visa International to pioneer a truly international system that may, in effect, create a single international cash unit of currency. The Visa International project is cooperating with bank-led groups in Belgium, France, Portugal, Spain, Taiwan and the US. Like Mondex, it plans to create an extensive network of shop-based card readers.

The concept of electronic cash is almost certain to take hold throughout Europe, particularly in the lead-up to a single unit of currency. In 1995, European Commission premises across Europe are to act as host to a trial of an electronic multi-currency payment system similar to the one being pioneered by Mondex. The technology is known more popularly in Europe as an 'electronic purse'. Under the EU's own research programme in Information Technology, a seven-country consortium of partners in industry and academia has developed the purse, which can be loaded with money from the owner's bank account, then used to meet expenses in ECU and national currencies by down-loading payments into compatible terminals in shops, pay-phones, toll roads, public transport and so on.

The trial is intended to check the feasibility of the scheme.[3]

At the same time, a specialized working group attached to the European Committee for Standardization (CEN) is on the point of developing a European standard that could open the door to cross-border use of electronic purses. An international standard has already been finalized for point-of-sale machinery for the purses. Thirteen European countries have been involved since 1991 in the effort. In 1994, the Council of the newly formed European Monetary Institute (EMI) – the precursor of the EU's projected European Central Bank – adopted a report on prepaid cards drawn up by the EU working party on payment systems. This calls on central banks to adopt an active but flexible regulatory role that will allow the market to develop. The report also asserts that the power to issue electronic purses should be restricted to banks and similar financial institutions. The report advises that the creation of the elecronic purse must be evaluated carefully, because it could change the role of banks in a major way.[4]

These electronic purses are particularly useful for small transactions such as payments at parking meters, public telephone boxes and automatic vending machines, though in theory they can store and transact an unlimited amount of money. National schemes such as Mondex which use prepaid cards as a general payment instrument are still at a relatively early stage of application, but other projects are forging ahead. The furthest advanced is a Danish initiative called Danmont which links commercial banks and telecommunications authorities. Trial projects involving service providers such as laundromats and automated newspaper vending machines are now being implemented in several

Danish cities. Other schemes now under way include the SEMP project in Spain which is being run by a consortium of banks, and the SIBS initiative in Portugal. In addition, Finland has now progressed considerably with the development of an electronic purse scheme. The Finnish project is unique in the sense that the work is being led by the country's central bank. More recently, Sweden has launched a scheme based on coordination between banks, with road toll payments a major focus.[5]

Other countries that have been involved in local purse projects range from Switzerland to South Africa. Internationally, both Visa and Mastercard are now showing interest in chip card applications including prepaid cards. Paradoxically, France – the country that has made most progress in applying chip card technology to standard credit and debit card payments – appears to be falling behind in developing prepaid card applications. Conflicting interests within the French financial community seem to be the main culprits. For example, France's commercial banks protested bitterly when the national post office – 'La Poste' – came forward with its own draft scheme.[6]

From the perspective of banks and governments, these schemes offer the promise of decimating the cash economy. From the perspective of privacy, they are likely to be bad news. Each cash card is linked to a bank account. Each transaction you make is linked to your card. Wherever you go – on public transport, in shops, or on the road – you will leave a 'transaction trail' that can be followed by anyone who has the know-how or motivation to track you. Despite the banks' claim of anonymity, electronic cash is anything but cash-like.

THE INDISPENSABLE FRIEND

In January 1995 the *Guardian* newspaper obtained a bundle of confidential Cabinet papers retrieved from an ex-government filing cabinet in a Camden junk shop. The papers revealed a plan to adopt smart card technology throughout the UK government. Included in the find was a seventeen-page report from the Government Centre for Information Systems (CCTA), a Whitehall agency under the control of the Cabinet Office, which describes a big research programme for introducing smart cards by the turn of the century.

The report reveals that Whitehall is involved in twenty-two separate inquiries into the introduction of smart cards. The Department of Transport is taking the lead, with seven pilot studies to investigate potential applications. These include road tolls – expected to be introduced after the next general election – and driving licences, which are already due to be replaced with a photo identity card. They could also monitor vehicles and taxation discs. The transport industry is also cooperating with the government to introduce smart cards to replace bus and train tickets, and to protect car radios and reduce car theft.[7]

The Department of Health has the second largest programme, examining applications to replace organ donor cards and store prescription information and medical records. The Home Office, along with the Passport Agency and Immigration Service, is looking at electronic photographic recognition for passports; replacing the British visitor's passport with a smart card; automatic passenger processing at ports and airports, and replacing residents' permits with a smart card.[8]

The Social Security ministry is considering electronic benefit payments and the use of smart cards to identify claimants at post offices with the intention of reducing fraud. The Departments of Employment and Education are looking at electronic benefit payments for training schemes; a card that could store a student's training credits, and security cards for the payment of grants.

The report for ministers says that fraudulent casual use of smart cards could be contained at a very low level. 'The addition of photographs to credit and debit cards has shown how a simple expedient using physical characteristics can markedly lower the level of casual fraud. The use of this, other biometrics, and passwords will make it virtually impossible for lost or casually stolen cards to be misused.' The report implies that the use of fingerprints would be ideal as a means of identifying individuals.

The report suggests that the driving licence would be ideal for the first cards, with people voluntarily adding information to cover everything from passports to pension payments. The report says: 'The cardholder would obtain the "primary use" card . . . and subsequently have it validated for its secondary use or uses by appropriate authorities. The cards would need to be re-issued every three to five years, to cope with wear and tear and to provide up-to-date photographs, which would have the dual advantage of allowing fraud to be forestalled by changing encryption mechanisms, and allowing greater capacity to be provided at each change.'

The report adds that the underlying technology is approximately doubling its capacity every two years, a process expected to continue for at least a decade.[9]

The public responded with indifference to these revelations. In New Zealand, however, news of a national smart card for health and welfare caused an uproar, and forced the Prime Minister to publicly disassociate his government from the technology. News of a proposed health smart card in Australia prompted a doctors' protest in 1992, causing the federal minister for health to publicly distance himself from the technology.

Public concern about smart cards was also reflected in the Clinton Administration's health reform Bill. Documentation released by the White House indicates that the administration is highly sensitive about the issue of smart cards: 'The Health Security Card will not be a "smart card" – which carries information in a computer chip – a national identification card, or a credit card. It does not hold sensitive information such as medical records. It's simply a way to streamline the billing process, reduce paperwork for doctors and patients, and assure people that they have a comprehensive set of benefits that can never be taken away.'[10]

Despite some clear benefits that smart cards may offer, many people do not trust the technology – or its designers. The card industry is trying to replace 'smart' with 'chip' to avoid a sense that people will be in some way subordinate to the technology. The damage may already have been done. People want intelligent toasters, but are nervous about technology that intelligently deals with their own personal data.

The newest generation of smart cards can transmit data and instructions without having to make physical contact with any other machine. Known as Radio Frequency ID (RFID) cards, they generate a signal which can be picked up and interpreted by computers. With these cards, you do not have to place the card into a reader. Instead, the reader scans your card from a distance. These devices are also being used for road tolling, personal identification, and for purchasing goods. RFID cards may provide a technical solution to the dilemma over a borderless Europe. A passport contained within an RFID card does not even have to be shown to an immigration control officer. Just walking past a scanner will determine whether you are in possession of a valid European passport. This technology is already being used on public transport, for access to buildings, and for travel on roads. Such an integration of technology and human activity could well lead to a situation where the card does become truly indispensable and mandatory.

SMART AND HEALTHY

It seems inevitable that as European union progresses so too will there be created a number of Union-wide smart card projects. These are likely, at some point, to become global, allowing patients to carry their medical records anywhere. The 'Good European Health Record Project' aims to establish a plan by 1996 for an integrated Europe-wide electronic health system. This will create an international technology system allowing the transfer of patient data across national borders, using smart card technology.[11]

One of the models being proposed will contain the essential health details of the owner, coded in such a way that it can be read in all European languages. The information is set out in several 'zones', according to the sensitivity and purpose of the data.

One of the key advantages proposed by the planners is that access to patient information on the smart card will be controlled to a greater degree by the patient. Not only will patients have the ability to gain access to their data, but they can also refuse access to whoever they choose. This, however, seems to be a theoretical construct which does not translate readily into reality. Few patients are aware of, or prepared to exercise, these rights. Confronted by a health professional, most people conform to the historical norm of divulging all that is necessary. All the same, the card's flexibility could be a boon for people who have sensitive medical conditions, a history of psychiatric care, or who use medication.

Some medical smart cards divide information into five zones:

- **Zone 1** Identification information. All care providers (and this may or may not include paramedical or complementary providers) will have access to this level. Only physicians, pharmacists and the issuing organization are permitted to make entries.
- **Zone 2** Emergency information. All care providers are authorized to read this zone. Only physicians are authorized to make entries.
- **Zone 3** Vaccination information. All care providers with the exception of ambulance personnel are authorized to read this zone, but only physicians and nurses may make entries.
- **Zone 4** Medication information. Only physicians and pharmacists are permitted to read or write in this zone.
- **Zone 5** Medical information. Only physicians are permitted to read or write in this zone.

Care providers (doctors, nurses, paramedics, etc.) are equipped with a reader, micro-computer and the necessary software. Each provider is given an accreditation card to gain access to the smart cards of patients. This card defines the zones to which access is allowed. A PIN number must also be entered before the smart card can be accessed.

The questions of access and security are central to the promotion of smart card technology. Several card organizations are currently working on a new generation of smart cards that will have multiple programmable levels of access. The only question is whether people will accept the complexity of the system. Ultimately, people can – and probably will – opt for a very simple, single-level access that allows anyone with a reader to view the card. If the card is used for many purposes, for example for vetting by employers, insurance companies and other organizations, security will be sacrificed for convenience.

SOME DANGERS

There can be no doubt that smart cards offer some fascinating possible solutions for age-old problems. There are, however, numerous drawbacks with the technology. Some are real, some are perceived. Either way, universal acceptance of the cards will happen only after the problems have been well and truly resolved.

Smart cards falter when they encroach on the rights and traditions of people and organizations. Australia is a harbinger of the problems UK authorities are likely to face in introducing the technology into general use. There, the medical profession learned that a card system similar to the

UK proposal was going to be introduced as part of a general strategy of health sector computerization. Despite the Health Department's insistence that the project was designed to create a system that was fairer and more efficient for all players, doctors saw it as a plot to undermine their profession.

The Australian Doctors Fund, a right-wing action group which led the charge, summed up the ill-feeling in a provocative brochure. 'To use the new system, all doctors will be required to speak the same language, use the same terminology, and communicate patient information in a uniform and universal manner.'

The brochure continued:

> Information will be communicated on demand from any area of the health sector, to any other area . . . What you say will be published throughout the health sector, and probably beyond it. You will have to comply with a costly and complicated system developed by bureaucrats and technologists. Every facet of your medical practice will, from 1995, have to conform to the standards set for you.
>
> Everything you do will be known by the authorities. No procedure, diagnosis or opinion will be confidential. It is one small step from this state of affairs, to one where you need approval from the system to make a clinical decision.

The Australian Doctors Fund felt that the technology was far from neutral. It was, in its view, a Trojan horse.

> The Smart Card plan has been adopted for two much more significant reasons. First, the Government intends using the smart card system to exercise total control over the medical

profession. All patient records will be centralized, allowing open access to such authorities as the Australian Federal Police, the Health Insurance Commission and the Bureau of Statistics. Of even greater importance is the reality that once all practitioners are locked into a universal computer system – once all transactions are dependent on the technology – control over the profession can be exercised by merely altering the programming of the system and demanding compliance with the changes.

'Second,' the brochure continued,

the proposal is being driven to a large extent by financial interests. A confidential consultancy planning document argues that a 'window of opportunity' exists to capitalize on the billions of dollars being invested in Australia's tele-communications infrastructure. Key people in the health sector stand to make huge amounts of money from its implementation, and are already lining up for a slice of the cake. Computer companies, systems designers and telecommunications companies smell a windfall. While the benefits to doctors and patients are very limited, the operators of the network stand to make tens of millions of dollars in profits.

Provocative stuff. And doctors' fears were further fuelled when they learned that a senior Health Department official had told a smart card planning meeting: 'We have to plot and plan – we must identify the enemies, and suborn them, buy them off and knock them aside to get this through . . .'[12]

Soon after the ADF published its views, branches of the Australian Medical Association (the Australian equivalent of the BMA) moved to oppose the government's proposal.

Within two months of the campaign, health minister Brian Howe issued a press release condemning the medical associations and pledging that the government would not proceed with a health smart card.

While elements of the response from Australian doctors were motivated by factors that were only tangential to the technology, there can be little doubt that the profession had identified some key concerns. Smart card technology is, after all, the end result of harmonizing other technologies, streamlining information administration and centralizing the passage of personal data. Such reforms can have many ends.

The data held on smart cards must be backed up in a series of 'data repositories'. These are distributed rather than centralized, but would be linked through the common numbering system. Any additional security of information held on the card itself would be well and truly outweighed by the added vulnerability of the personal information held elsewhere on the system.

In 1991, during the controversy in New Zealand over the suggestion that smart cards should be introduced for government benefits, one private company reminded a nervous television audience that the technology existed to encode a fingerprint into the card.[13] Australian and US banks are already issuing fingerprint encoded smart cards to staff who need to gain access to the inside of Automatic Teller Machines. The UK Cabinet documents describe a fingerprint system that will cost around one pound per smart card.

The uses of smart cards go well beyond the health care sector, transport or banking. Micro Card Technologies, a computer research company based in the United States, is proposing the use of smart cards which will include criminal histories, digital face image, fingerprints, medical histories, insurance information, driving licence, and driving history.[14] This is getting close to the official UK plan for a smart card that will include driving licence, health data, banking information, Social Security and passport. Right at the moment, this interlinking of functions is in its infancy and most attempts to 'educate' the consumer in the use of such complex card functions have failed. The development of more user friendly cards is likely to change this resistance.

The temptation to introduce these cards may be irresistible. Smart cards that house the biometric details of the holder may go a long way to eliminating fraud. A US company, Comparator Systems Corporation, has developed such a card, which was manufactured in Malaysia for worldwide distribution in 1993. The card, designed for multiple uses, will be produced by a new company 'Universal Heritage' and will potentially create a total linkage of all government and private sectors.[15]

The extension of use of the health smart card would be made far easier if it was generally carried at all times by the population. Overseas health authorities have tended to avoid the issue of whether the health smart card should be carried at all times, but the existence of emergency medical information indicates that there would be an expectation that it should be kept permanently in the wallet or purse. A briefing document for Quebec's 'Projet Carte Santé' subtly suggests that 'The credit card size of the Health Card is designed to enable the holder to carry it at all times.'

During the planning for the Australia Card, the Health Insurance Commission dreamed up the priceless expression 'pseudo voluntariness' to describe the ultimate status of their proposed card. Certainly if the card is of a high enough integrity (if it can be trusted to be highly accurate, perhaps with an encoded fingerprint or access codes), it would be a valuable document indeed for a range of other purposes.

Professor Yves Poullet, a Belgian expert in medical information systems, warns that one problem of having a smart card which is constantly carried around by the patient is that larger volumes of information can be inputted through increasing numbers of access points. 'Once this situation has been normalized, and people have become accustomed to the enhanced spectrum of information on the card, the information can be subjected to access by a multitude of people.'[16]

Just on the matter of the health smart card, the medical profession faces a number of difficult questions as it decides the merits or otherwise of any smart card project. A proposal to introduce smart card technology would be perhaps the single most important development ever envisioned for the British health care system. Assurances that its impact will be entirely positive simply cannot be believed. Legislation is unlikely to protect either doctors or patients from the worst effects of such a system. Legislation – if any exists – is likely to protect such facets as investigation of doctors. Law is likely to be a relatively ineffective method of controlling the misuse of a smart card system.

Likewise, assurances that the system is safe because it employs several computers rather than one major data base are deliberately misleading. A distributed data base is designed to act as if it were one single computer. Because it works with greater efficiency and across a broader spectrum of uses than does a single computer, it can be much more dangerous to privacy.

FURTHER DANGERS

The smart card can be used for a virtually limitless spectrum of purposes. Experiments are under way in a dozen fields and for 100 or more distinct applications. One newspaper warned, 'A troublesome teenager might be placed under curfew by programming his or her movements on public transport; a habitual drink driver could be prevented from buying alcohol.'[17]

Citing US privacy expert Professor James Rule, the article continued:

> A technology or database developed for a specific use may find itself serving purposes its architects never anticipated; this illustrates the need to anticipate, rather than react to, threats to privacy.
>
> In the future, government welfare agencies, determined that their handouts will be used for the social purpose intended, could make payments into the recipients' smart cards, which were programmed to force changes in spending habits. And the agencies would be able to police spending because many supermarkets already itemize their goods by scanning barcodes.

Speaking in Sydney in 1989, Rule warned that the creators and controllers of such systems had a great deal of trust placed in them. But regardless of the intended purpose of smart cards, the global experience seems to be that there is a huge gulf between the theoretical and the practical. Some smart card experiments have collapsed because consumers have failed to understand the complex programmes in the card. The several instructions and the various options are often ignored and are generally misunderstood. While it is true that procedures can be established to enhance security, few people use these mechanisms.

A common example of this reluctance to use more advanced features of technology is the deposit function of the automatic teller machine, which in the early years was almost never used by bank customers, and is still underused. Another example is the neon menu display screen of a modern VCR, which hardly anyone over the age of fifteen fully understands.

Smart card companies are now able to produce a multi-purpose card that can link, say, health, banking and Social Security information. Whether such a merging of functions would work in practice, given our experience with cash machines and VCRs, is anyone's guess. When Michell Venn from Quebec's *Le Devoir* newspaper travelled to France to interview Roland Moreno, the inventor of the smart card, he was told that the card was never intended for such complex use as health care, and was supposed to be used originally only for simple banking transactions. Moreno told Venn that purposes such as complex health data processing would create many unforeseen problems between the card holder and government agencies because of technical problems with the system.[18]

Was the response by Australian doctors hysterical? Not according to groups opposed to a similar scheme in Austria. Several organizations oppose the introduction there of a health smart card which would contain personal medical records. A press release issued by one group, Engagierte Computer Expterinnen, is headed 'Warning: Med-Card can damage your health'. It proclaims: 'Although dealing with the Austrian situation, the argumentation is general. Obviously only the industrial and government lobby is interested in such a card. Privacy rights and data security issues are endangered.'

The press release outlined the potential dangers: employers could request the Med-Card before deciding to employ a new worker and find out whether the applicant is going to provide a risk or not – evidence of diabetes, say, or alcoholism might count against the applicant; a landlord may investigate a new tenant. 'Even a card offered only on a completely voluntary basis can serve as an instrument of natural selection.'

The 'instrument of natural selection' is a powerful concept. It embodies the fear held by some people that the most intrusive technologies will be introduced as voluntary devices, outside the interest of law or the scope of regulation.

PRIVACY TECHNOLOGY

Smart cards are so named because they have the potential to perform many complex functions. One of those potential functions can be the protection of privacy. A smart card programmed with privacy in mind can disguise the identity of its owner. It can scramble personal information so that sensitive details do not get into the hands of large organizations. It can act as a buffer to stop information becoming centralized. A privacy smart card can help reduce the threat of technological intrusion by acting as an independent information processor, rather than being part of a vast centralized database. A privacy health card, for example, could store all your health data, without disclosing your identity to people or machines reading it. At the same time it could allow you to access all your data from throughout the health system. The flow of information would then be more balanced.

Will people demand smart cards that are privacy-oriented? Will they push for technology which reduces centralized control and minimizes the collection of potentially damaging personal data? According to several sources, the signs are not good. Customers using smart cards tend to prefer a full accounting of the goods and services they purchase. When the card is used to calculate road tolls or public transport, people are often anxious to ensure that they have not been ripped off by the technology.

It is not so much that the cost of privacy is any greater to the individual, but that the cost of not having it is yet to emerge as an issue. Until then, it seems smart cards will follow the trend of other technologies by eroding privacy and centralizing information and control. Technology that should have worked in our interests has been exploited and misused.

CHAPTER NINE

THE WATCHERS

If an award was to be given for the most haunting video footage of the decade, it might well go to the Liverpool surveillance camera that inadvertently recorded the last images of murdered toddler James Bulger.

For millions of people who viewed the fuzzy grey pictures of the young boy being led from the shopping centre, the experience only confirmed what most had already suspected: video surveillance is good for crime control, and we need more of it.

As a consequence of this grisly crime, Liverpool certainly did get more video surveillance. In 1994 the City Council, in conjunction with the police, set up an intricate web of cameras throughout more than three square miles of the central business district. Twenty state-of-the-art cameras located at major intersections can be made to zoom in from any angle on the comings and goings of everyone walking the streets, driving cars, or even eating their meals in restaurants.

The network is controlled from a secret location in a local shopping centre. From this room, security personnel and police can watch and record everything that happens in the city centre. Twenty monitors display crystal clear colour images of shop fronts, laneways, park benches and even Liverpool's red light district.

Inside the control room, half a dozen police and security personnel go about the business of monitoring the activities of the public. They are looking for 'the unusual – the different'. The cameras can be made to move in any direction. They can zoom up to reveal the minutest detail of a face, a licence plate, or even the contents of a paper bag. The clarity of the pictures from the cameras is startling. No more of the fuzzy grey images which have confounded the police time and time again in such cases as the Bishopsgate IRA bomb, which devastated the financial district of London. These cameras can read a cigarette packet in full colour at 100 metres. The system can even work in pitch blackness, bringing all images up to daylight level, and using computer enhanced shading to stop headlights and street-lights from 'whiting out' the image.

The £360,000 system is the central plank of a crime control strategy to clean up Liverpool's streets and bring people back into the centre. According to local police, the scheme is having the desired effect. Superintendent Howard Parry, responsible for Liverpool's Central Division, told the *Independent* newspaper: 'I'm not going to make any great claims, but all the indications are that the cameras are helping to bring crime down. We're making some very good arrests as a result of it.'[1]

Superintendent Parry is also delighted about some unexpected benefits of the CCTV (Closed Circuit Television) strategy. He explains that his resources can now be managed better. 'We can use the cameras to work out whether we should send one officer or four to an incident.'

Liverpool Council is hoping that the cameras will bring people back into the city. Eric Holden, manager of Liverpool Council's Traffic Control Systems division, says he hopes the CCTV initiative will make people feel safer when they walk the streets. The Liverpool authorities are so happy with the public response to the CCTV initiative that they plan to expand it to a sixty-five-camera system covering a large section of Liverpool. Since the shattering effect of the Bulger trial, the cameras have received almost universal approval by Liverpool residents.

THE ALL-SEEING EYE

On the other side of the country, the Norfolk town of King's Lynn has also been discovering the joys of CCTV surveillance. Since 1987, this end-of-the-line town of 30,000 has seen the construction of an impressive CCTV system involving sixty remote-controlled cameras linked to a central command. The system is being constantly expanded and it is likely by 1998 to comprise 120 state-of-the-art cameras located throughout King's Lynn and surrounding towns.

The expansion is being driven by the local council, a body which is immensely proud of its conservative heritage and its 'ear for the voice of the people'. Behind the initiative is a tiny group of middle-ranking bureaucrats who saw the promise of CCTV some years ago and went about promoting it widely. To give the technology added weight and appeal it was promoted as a 'partnership' deal. The partners include police, local businesses and the citizens of King's Lynn –

everyone, really, except criminals, hooligans, louts and the enemies of law and order.

From a cluttered control room on top of the council headquarters, police and private security personnel scrutinize the minutest activities of the residents, scanning the parks, streets and housing estates. Row upon row of monitors – two dozen of them – display images from the cameras. Banks of recording equipment routinely record everything thereon. Tapes are then stored for a month in the increasingly likely event that they are wanted for the purpose of evidence for investigation.

The project began in 1987 with seven cameras in the local burglary-plagued industrial park. It was a well-coordinated and well-financed partnership between business, police and council and it succeeded in dramatically reducing burglary and vandalism. Indeed, so successful was the scheme that other partners and other schemes soon emerged throughout the town. Five years later the system had expanded to thirty-two cameras to stop crime in car parks. Then it burgeoned further to include the housing estate. Then the sports complex. Then the city centre. At first, in an effort to protect privacy, only stationary cameras were installed near residential areas, but within three years these were replaced by cameras that could be remotely controlled. Now the city has plans for the hospital, the remaining housing estates, and the surrounding towns. It seems nothing can stop this surveillance juggernaut.

The King's Lynn system currently provides only black and white images, but this shortcoming is more than compensated for by the sophistication of the technology, which includes night vision, computer-assisted operation, and a motion detection facility which allows the operator to instruct the system to go on red alert when anything moves in view of the cameras. And, like the Liverpool system, the clarity of these pictures is brilliant. The cameras can even work in pitch blackness, bringing all images up to daylight level.

The justification for this remarkable piece of work is puzzling. King's Lynn never had a particularly serious law and order problem – particularly in comparison to else-where in Britain. With a negligible level of street muggings, rapes and murders, it was hardly the crime capital of Norfolk.

'What it comes down to is a perception of crime, rather than crime itself,' conceded council official Barry Loftus, the King's Lynn surveillance project director and founder. The surveillance system has grown because of the 'feel-good factor' it creates among the public, he said. Originally installed to deter burglary, assault and car theft, in practice the cameras have been used to combat what town officials call 'antisocial behaviour', including many such minor offences as littering, urinating in public, traffic violations, fighting, obstruction, drunkenness, and evading meters in town parking lots. They have also been widely used to intervene in other undesirable behaviour such as underage smoking and a variety of public order transgressions.

If anyone ever chose to criticize the omnipresence of the system, the local police would most likely be able to avoid the slur of authoritarianism. Even though they have absolute access and control, the system belongs to everyone. It is administered by the local council, paid for by the residents, and operated by a private security company.

THE FUTURE OF CRIME CONTROL

This, according to some experts, is the future of policing in Europe. Former Norfolk Police Chief Superintendent Ted Worby, now a CCTV consultant, believes the technology represents the 'greatest boost for policing since the introduction of radio'. John Major told the 1994 Tory Party conference that his government was committed to CCTV, and would provide funding to implement the technology. One initiative was to offer a funding pot to support local CCTV projects. The Home Secretary first announced the initiative on 18 October 1994. There were 480 bids from local authorities, community groups, schools and industrial estates. Nationally, more than one hundred schemes received a share of the £5 million funding, with a further £13.8 million levered in from other partnerships. National winners of the Home Office CCTV competition were announced in March. The Home Office also launched an 'instruction manual' which was sent to all councils, large businesses and police forces. The publication was, in effect, a device to promote CCTV.

Not that CCTV needs a helping hand. According to the Home Office, around 95 per cent of councils in Britain are already considering the establishment of CCTV systems. Eighty cities, including Blackpool, Swansea, Glasgow, Edinburgh, Hull, Torquay, Wolverhampton, Chester, Bath and Brighton, have installed sophisticated surveillance systems to watch main public areas, and more cities go on line every week. Bournemouth, for example, has installed 103 cameras since 1985, some of which are located on the cliff walks leading to the local beach. These cameras have infrared capacity, allowing accurate night-time surveillance.

The systems are expensive – typically more than £200,000 a year for equipment leasing and operation – but one by one, towns across Britain are installing them.

The motivation behind the establishment of these systems is crime – or, at least, the fear of crime. The type of crime varies by area, but in each case the prevalence of car theft, rape, vandalism or assault has galvanized virtually all sectors of the community in working towards the goal of total surveillance of public places.

The effort appears, at first sight, to have paid off. Glowing reports of the effectiveness of CCTV are announced regularly. Strathclyde police recently claimed a 75 per cent drop in crime following the installation of a £130,000 closed circuit TV system in Airdrie. Not only are people delighted because they are no longer afraid to go out shopping, say local police, but even criminals welcome the chance to prove their innocence by calling on evidence from the cameras. In King's Lynn, burglary and vandalism in the industrial estate has dropped to a tiny fraction of its original level. Car crime in car parks has dropped by 90 per cent. People say they feel safer. Indeed they should. Assaults and other violent crimes appear also to have been decimated in the centre of town.

The government believes this is because CCTV deters 'opportunistic' crime, where people take advantage of a situation on the spur of the moment. Phillip Edwards from the Home Office Crime Prevention Unit says the government is using CCTV as part of a long-term plan to reduce overall crime. 'Today's opportunist is tomorrow's professional criminal. If we decrease the number of opportunities for easy crime, we can reduce the number of people becoming professional criminals.'

The logic and the statistics are superficially impressive but some analysts are not convinced. In a report to the Scottish Office on the impact of CCTV, Jason Ditton, Director of the Scottish Centre for Criminology, argued that the claims of crime reduction are little more than fantasy. 'All [evaluations and statistics] we have seen so far are wholly unreliable.' The *British Journal of Criminology* went further by describing the statistics as '. . . post hoc shoestring efforts by the untrained and self interested practitioner'.

Ditton says the crime statistics are without credibility. They are collected over too short a time, in dubious circumstances, and without regard for the conventions that apply to conventional crime statistics. 'Different types of crime are often lumped together, concealing possible increases in some and decreases in others.' The King's Lynn detection statistics indeed reflect this: 'fighting and assault' . . . 'littering and graffiti' . . . 'theft and burglary'.

The cameras are also creating a vastly increased rate of conviction after crimes are detected. Virtually everyone caught committing an offence on camera in King's Lynn pleads guilty nowadays. Once people know they have been videotaped, they admit the offence immediately. Such is also the case in Newcastle, where the installation in 1992 of a sixteen-camera system has resulted in a 100 per cent incidence of guilty pleas.[2] Police are delighted at the time and money they are saving from long and expensive trials. Some legal experts are a little more wary of the implications of these results, arguing that – like DNA evidence – juries can be seduced and defendants intimidated in equal proportions by evidence that might not normally stand up to scrutiny. Indeed, some districts are now reporting that people are surrendering after the mere mention in newspaper reports that their activities had been captured on CCTV.[3]

ILLUSION OR REALITY?

Ditton and other criminologists say that the crime statistics cited in evidence for the benefits of CCTV rarely, if ever, address the hypothesis that CCTV merely displaces criminal activity to areas outside the range of the cameras. Discussing the justification for establishing a surveillance system of sixteen cameras in Manchester, Gordon Conquest, chairman of the city centre sub-committee of Manchester Council, candidly admitted, 'No crackdown on crime does more than displace it, and that's the best we can do at the moment.'[4]

The Crime Prevention Unit of the Home Office appears to agree. In 1993 it suppressed the findings of a survey of the crime impact of camera surveillance on the basis that the displacement effect had been all but ignored. In other words, crime may be merely pushed from high-value commercial areas into low-rent residential areas. One of the features of current surveillance practice is that the cameras are often installed in high-rent commercial areas. Councils often find that it is impossible to resist demands for such systems. The trend is fuelled in part by the insurance industry, which in some towns is offering a 30 per cent reduction in premiums to local retailers who pay a contribution to a CCTV levy system. A nationwide insurance discount scheme is currently being negotiated and should be in place by 1996. The systems are also increasingly being funded by a range of innovative partnership schemes in which levies are raised through parking fees, rents or rates.

Critics of CCTV fear that while some areas can become financially or politically organized to fund camera systems, others are left vulnerable to displaced crime. There is some evidence for this. In 1992, the year before the Airdrie CCTV system was switched on, 171 assaults were reported in the town centre. This dropped to seventy-nine the following year. Figures across the entire police district, however, show a different trend, with serious crime rising by 20 per cent.

CCTV continues, nevertheless, to gain momentum. Surveillance cameras now keep a watch over countless public places throughout Britain. Banks of them hang above the London Underground and throughout prestige areas of the city. They are concealed above doorways, inside vending machines, and behind two-way mirrors. They are being installed in bank cash machines, inside buses and on rooftops. Each week, more of these cameras are being installed at intersections, on top of police cars, alongside motorways, and in areas of high crime.

The video surveillance boom is likely to extend even inside the home. Andrew May, Assistant Chief Constable of South Wales, has urged victims of domestic violence to conceal video cameras in their homes to collect evidence. Michael Jack, then Minister of State at the Home Office, was reported as responding that the idea brought a 'freshness of approach' which highlighted the role of new technology.

While the incidence of surveillance cameras in the home may still be limited, their use on private property is becoming popular. Increasingly, police and local councils are placing camera systems into housing estates and red light districts. Residents' Associations are independently organizing their own surveillance initiatives. Residents in Belgravia and in the exclusive Hampstead Garden Suburb of London have installed privately operated CCTV systems. Local newspapers in London have begun to report on similar ventures, funded on a levy basis, that place residential streets under surveillance.

It seems that after decades of suffering vilification, Big Brother is finally being paraded as a loved member of the family. In the quest for a life that is quiet, a society which is safe, and an administration which is efficient, video surveillance is seen as a real answer. Wherever there is dysfunction, threat or disorder, one authority or another will seek the introduction of video surveillance.

BIG BROTHER: BIG MONEY

This activity has been a goldmine for security companies. According to the British Security Industry Association, the market for surveillance camera systems has quadrupled since 1989 and in 1994 accounted for an annual spending of around 170 million.[5] Other estimates put the total figure for capital and operation at more than £300 million. Already there are upwards of 200,000 cameras installed nationwide, and at least 300 towns and counties across the UK are planning to introduce these systems, many of which are controlled by local government but operated by private security companies.[6] American journalist Larry Tye, reporting from London for the *Boston Globe*, observed, 'You can't go anywhere in this city these days without feeling you're being watched.'[7]

The government is doing its best to encourage the trend. According to a glossy Home Office promotional booklet, CCTV can be a solution for such problems as vandalism, drug use, drunkenness, racial harassment, sexual harassment, loitering and disorderly behaviour.[8] Other innovative uses are constantly being discovered. Police in King's Lynn used CCTV evidence to challenge an insurance claim for theft of fishing tackle from a car. A woman who negotiated to buy a pay and display ticket from another motorist, after her own had expired, found herself immediately surrounded by police and council authorities. The cameras are particularly effective in detecting people using marijuana and other substances.

UNEXPECTED HOSPITALITY

Authorities in Britain are slowly pushing out the limits of camera surveillance. For the past ten years, hospitals have used Covert Video Surveillance (CVS) to monitor parents who visit their children. These videos are taken by concealed cameras and microphones located behind the walls of specially prepared surveillance rooms and are used in cases of unexplained injuries or illnesses. Where authorities believe there may be a case of abuse, the child is relocated into one of these rooms. Cases involving suspected suffocation of children are priorities.[9]

The Department of Health has been supporting these CVS schemes since 1987, even though no mention of the practice is made in the Department's own public documentation. The Department has recently endorsed a CVS protocol developed at the North Staffordshire Hospital.

Since 1986, thirty abusers have been caught through the CVS practice. Croydon Crown Court, for example, convicted a nineteen-year-old Bristol woman of cruelty to a child after the jury watched taped evidence from a hospital apparently showing the mother trying to suffocate the child.[10] Inspiring as such cases are to the cause of information gathering, there is still the unresolved question of the fate of unused videos, or indeed the sense of violation felt by parents who have been the subject of such surveillance. There are no statistics of the total number of CVS operations, though as an indicator, a recent survey by Anthony Butler, Chief Constable of Gloucestershire, revealed that of 15,000 video interviews of child witnesses, only 3,652 were submitted by police to the Crown Prosecution Service. Of those, forty-four were accepted by the court, and only twenty-five were actually used.[11] One issue of concern is the extent to which the unused tapes – aural or visual – will be used for the purposes of training hospital staff and social workers. The Health Department promotes the use of tapes for this purpose, though no mention is made of securing consent from the parents and children involved.

Gwyn Tenney is one mother who was victimised by CVS. Her *second* child had died from Cot Death in 1988, in circumstances that had not led to any suspicion of foul play. When Gwyn had a *third* child in 1991, she and the child were placed under surveillance by a hospital based monitoring programme. The baby had stopped breathing on several occasions, and hospital authorities were concerned that Gwyn may be responsible.

In 1992 Gwyn's child was taken in for observation to North Staffordshire hospital, Gwyn was asked to live at the hospital, in a room adjacent to where the baby was being kept. What she did not know was that for three weeks, four pin-hole surveillance cameras were watching her every movement. The cameras watched while Gwyn and her husband engaged in what she diplomatically describes as 'heavy petting'. What the cameras did not record was any instance of abuse of the baby. For sixteen days, the baby had been confined in isolation to the cot, with the mother under strict instructions not to take it out. As Gwyn later observed, perhaps the hospital should have been held responsible for abuse of a child.

For the moment, at least, unused CCTV footage from urban centres is recycled every few weeks. The constraint is one of cost. Keeping the tape permanently would impose a high financial cost. On the other hand, it would take only one or two instances where such footage would have been useful in the pursuit of a child abductor or rapist for the cost of permanent storage to be deemed bearable.

KICKING OFF THE CCTV REVOLUTION

The CCTV trend began in 1985, when – after a particularly bad year of football hooliganism – the Football Trust, a charitable body funded by the pools companies, gave grants to ninety-two clubs to establish CCTV systems in their grounds. This was closely followed by a similar gift to the police to establish mobile CCTV surveillance throughout Britain. In the absence of guidelines restricting their application, police found more uses for the systems. The word spread quickly that CCTV could be a boon to law enforcement both for evidence gathering and for social control. This extensive and unique promotional base of support for CCTV explains why Britain leads the world in visual surveillance. Although CCTV is being used in football grounds overseas, no other country has experienced such a broad base of support for CCTV.

Police were tremendously excited by the possibilities opened up by such systems. They could covertly monitor and record vast numbers of people without risk to officers and without fear of detection. One little-known feature of modern CCTV systems, for example, is their ability to track the movements of people. Like some bizarre computer game, the system can routinely track individuals as they walk through the city, switching cameras as the subject moves out of range. The fields of the cameras intersect, so that no one can escape their gaze. System operators and police often follow 'persons of interest' for miles, creating a comprehensive profile of all activities and contacts. All new CCTV systems, such as those in Liverpool and Glasgow, have this function as a built-in facility. The cameras are powerful enough to identify individuals from 300 metres.

To many people, the evidence of CCTV's success as a tool of crime control is powerful and persuasive, which explains why the technology has struck a chord at the highest levels of government. Nevertheless, despite the extraordinary success of CCTV, some councils have raised concerns over its use. In 1992, Exeter Council overturned a plan to construct a camera system, opting instead to use the money to pay for six extra police. In 1993, Birmingham City Council suspended an application for a city-wide network of cameras because of concerns about how the images would be stored and used. In the absence of privacy protection, the Council felt that the project should not go ahead. In response, six months later, Downing Street announced that laws would be passed prohibiting councils from blocking the installation of camera systems by making their installation exempt from the requirement to submit a planning application.

Most councils, however, do not concern themselves with the full impact of visual surveillance. Indeed, council officials cheerfully admit that they are motivated by the simple desire to make shoppers and residents feel safer.

In Bromley, once described by the *Independent* newspaper as 'London's most boring borough', the council has spent nearly one million pounds on a CCTV system to monitor a town centre almost devoid of crime.

The spread of CCTV can be explained as part fashion and part desperation. 'Those towns not covered are feeling very vulnerable,' says Ted Worby. Many small towns genuinely feel that the technology offers a real solution to a range of problems, and they feel nervous when surrounding towns are covered by the cameras. Another less flattering motivation might be that the architects of some CCTV systems have their own personal agenda. The competition between CCTV planners in different parts of the country is fierce, with each trying to outperform and outshine the others. King's Lynn's Barry Loftus, one of the first in the field, observed, 'They all want to get on to the national circuit and do seminars.' It's certainly true that politicians at a local level are seldom interested in whether CCTV will actually accomplish the appointed tasks. The technology makes everyone look and feel good.

THE FIRST PHASE OF *LAISSEZ-FAIRE* LAW ENFORCEMENT?

Anyone can set up a CCTV system. There is no licensing system. There is no government oversight agency. The technology falls outside the protection of law and, once the government makes it exempt from planning requirements, CCTV will be free of any constraint whatever.

The usual sequence of events leading to the construction of a system is that, first, one or two 'converts' in a council will seek the support of police and residents' groups before securing approval for the appointment of a specialist consultant. Once a preliminary feasibility study has been completed, potential 'partners' will be consulted in the lead-up to the development of a specific plan. As local media go about the business week by week of reporting on a variety of crimes, CCTV is publicized as a potential 'all-round' solution. The public consciousness – and, in turn, the political will – is whetted.

The problem in thrashing out the pros and cons of CCTV is that there has, to this point, been little or no public interest in a debate. So powerful and persuasive is the image of this technology that few people think beyond the promise of the moment. Support for CCTV is instinctive. This fact alone should set alarm bells ringing in the ears of anyone interested in the protection of civil liberties. It is true that everyone should have the right to walk freely and safely in a public place. It is equally true that everyone should be free from the dangers of unnecessary and unwarranted surveillance. Visual surveillance is a critical issue in that it has the potential to desensitize the population to other, less visible, forms of surveillance. The ready acceptance of video surveillance might be indicative of the creed 'nothing to hide, nothing to fear'. And a nation which happily accepts visual surveillance without debate may easily and happily accept a range of other forms of surveillance, from wire-tapping to identity cards. It is the absence of wide-ranging public debate which is the real problem.

Very occasionally, a dissenter will appear. *Sunday Telegraph* columnist Niall Ferguson complained, 'No sooner have the damned things been got rid of in the benighted East . . . than they start sprouting like giant hogweed throughout the West. My only consolation was the certain knowledge that free-born Britons would never tolerate such infernal devices, the tools of totalitarianism.' Another *Telegraph* columnist later that year wrote, 'Am I the only one who finds this trend disturbing?'

In September 1995 Privacy International published a damning statement which read in part: 'There is a grave risk that the CCTV industry is out of control. Fuelled by fear of crime, the systems take on a life of their own, defying quantification and quashing public debate. In a very short time, the systems have challenged some fundamental tenets of justice, and created the threat of a surveillance society. Other more traditional approaches to law enforcement and social justice are being undermined without due process.'

These isolated complaints excepted, the government most certainly believes that the public is happy about video surveillance. Home Officer minister David McLean bluntly told the *Guardian* newspaper: 'The public want more cameras and less crime.'[12]

The lack of concern among the public over these developments can be traced, partly, to the spate of 'real life' dramas such as the *Crimewatch* series. Video cameras are not merely prevalent, but their existence is promoted as a natural part of the public environment. This exception is not limited to an accident scene or a public place, it also extends to private spaces. Media organizations and consumer groups frequently use miniature cameras to record events inside private property. Cameras measuring 42 millimetres square and able to see in virtual darkness are freely available on the British market for less than £200.

In the very near future, the distinction between overt surveillance and covert surveillance will disappear. Cost and size will cease to be factors in visual surveillance. Bugging is already a national pastime, with something in the order of 200,000 covert surveillance bugs being sold each year. Before long, people will accept that visual surveillance is just one other function of ordinary products in their environment. The only space free of such surveillance will be the home – and even then there will be numerous exceptions.

Perhaps of greater significance are the hundreds of thousands of semi-professional and amateur cameras in the hands of the citizenry. Images from these cameras are eagerly sought by authorities anxious to collect evidence against wrongdoers. One Wolverhampton resident crouched along the roadside for hours with his camera, dutifully filming motorists who were making illicit use of a bus lane. The police treated the film as lawful evidence and prosecuted the offending motorists.[13]

The surveillance ethic, if it can be so called, appears to be that anything goes in public places and that surveillance in the pursuit of crime can be undertaken without limitation.

A 1992 Home Office report on video surveillance, entitled 'Closed Circuit Television in Public Places', highlighted a general lack of concern about surveillance. Between 80 and 90 per cent of people surveyed said they 'welcomed' the introduction of surveillance cameras. In late-twentieth-century Britain, people expect to be routinely videotaped during the course of their daily business. They accept that CCTV has become a key plank in crime control, traffic control and crowd control.

The use of such monitoring is not confined to the mere control of theft or vandalism. Since the 1960s it has become an integral part of a revolution in company management. Virtually every Western corporation has undergone a transformation in administration and organizational structure. Employees are often monitored to determine efficiency and productivity. Information is the lifeblood of the best management experts.

Not all uses of video surveillance are legitimate. Following some organizing activity by a local union, one US employer installed video cameras to monitor each individual workstation and worker. Although management claimed that the technology was being established solely for safety monitoring, two employees were suspended for leaving their workstations to visit the toilet without permission. The activity of union representatives on the floor was inhibited by a 'chilling effect' on workers who knew their conversations were being monitored.[14]

A spate of well-publicized cases of similar abuses of visual surveillance has prompted concern in the workplace. A 1991 survey of employees throughout the US revealed that 62 per cent disagreed with the use of video surveillance (including 38 per cent who 'strongly disagreed').[15]

There are virtually no legal constraints on video surveillance. Indeed, unlike the laws of Austria, Germany, Norway and Sweden, under which employers are obliged to seek agreement with workers on such matters, the UK law generally obliges employees to accept the technology.[16] The International Labour Office has advised that there is 'no specific statutory provision' covering any form of workplace surveillance.[17]

THE ALTERNATIVE VIEW

Given that at least some crime is lessened because of the cameras, can there be an argument against them? The short answer is 'yes'. Among the supportive responses to the 1992 Home Office survey was a thread of caution. Thirty-six per cent of those surveyed did not agree with the proposition 'the more of these cameras we have the better'. This minority raised a number of concerns about where the line should be drawn at surveillance. They also expressed concern about possible abuse of surveillance systems, the risk of erosion of civil liberties and the uncomfortable feeling of being watched.

Then there are legitimate concerns about the sort of technology that is in use. Infrared systems, for example, have become very popular in recent years. Sanyo promotes its high-resolution IR Spy cameras by promising: 'Because of the unique design, people remain unaware that they are being monitored.'[18] Infrared is useful for detecting such crimes as urinating in a public place, indecent exposure and drinking in public, where the naked eye might not detect the incident. While it is true that this enhanced technology is likely to deter some major crimes, it is in less spectacular circumstances such as these where the cameras could be used in an unforeseen and unfair manner.

All technology constantly expands and converges. In the absence of a healthy public awareness, this process is incremental and invisible. The creation of a nationwide network of CCTV cameras does more than establish a visual surveillance canopy. The technology cannot operate effectively without a comprehensive voice and radio system. All CCTV control rooms have direct links to police operation rooms, but some have gone further by providing direct radio links to retailers and other organizations. King's Lynn has organized a radio system involving forty local retailers. Any suspect activity or person is immediately reported to the control room, which activates the appropriate camera. The merging of two technologies creates a powerful and ubiquitous surveillance synergy.

Police are now moving to the second phase of visual surveillance: CCTV registration. The Met in London have approached security industry groups with the intention of gathering support for a camera registration scheme. This scheme would identify each camera system in Britain, its coverage, capacity and the person or organization controlling it. The registry would allow police to determine whether any reported crime was likely to be captured on tape, and to know where to find such evidence. It would also give police the ability to communicate directly with all CCTV operators, perhaps with the result that operators could be notified about information that might be useful to police. Contemporaneously, the Association of Chief Police Officers (ACPO) has been floating the idea of supporting a scheme to create a video liaison officer in each district, responsible for promoting CCTV and ensuring that police are active partners in all schemes. Within a decade, an estimated half million camera systems could be in operation, each dutifully registered with authorities, and each able to instantly exchange and compare images.

THE NEXT GENERATION OF CAMERAS

But the merging of surveillance technologies does not stop there. The modern surveillance camera has become truly awesome. Connect it to a moderately priced computer, and it can achieve what the Stasi could only dream about. As every motorist knows, roadside cameras can now detect whether you are travelling over the speed limit. Having accomplished that, they will cheerfully scan your number plate, identify your vehicle, communicate with the Driver and Vehicle Licensing Agency (DVLA) and police computers, and send you a nasty surprise in the mail. All within seconds. The latest version operating on the M1 even displays your car's details – and your offence – on a giant neon sign for all the world to see. Known as the Speed Violation Detection Deterrent, the device not only publicly displays the driver's offence, but it also sends a comprehensive visual record to the local police headquarters.[19]

Across the Atlantic, computer research companies have succeeded in creating surveillance systems that can work the same magic with human faces. Known as Computerized Facial Recognition (CFR), these systems can convert any face into a sequence of numbers. The NeuroMetric System can match the images from surveillance cameras, with facial images held in computer databases. The Florida-based company has developed a system that uses a range of powerful computing technologies which can scan a crowd at the rate of twenty faces a second, digitize the faces (converting them into code that can be electronically stored) and match the images with varying degrees of accuracy against identities in a database.

The machine cannot easily be fooled by a change of facial

hair, expression, or hairstyle. Three-dimensional imaging technology and neural networks which mimic the functions of the human brain have made this technology magnificently powerful.

By 1997, according to the manufacturers, this type of machine will have the capacity to scan a database of 50 million faces in something less than a minute. Images from any closed circuit camera can be linked into the system, as long as those images are processed and transmitted in digital form.

Several police and commercial organizations in Britain are developing this technology, and it is likely that within a decade it will be in wide use across Britain. In 1995 the first CFR system opened for business at Manchester City Football Club's Maine Road ground. The system is intended to detect football hooligans automatically, but in a decade the application is likely to be far more universal. By then, the DVLA and the police will probably have constructed a database containing the digitized face prints of virtually the entire population. How? The new photo drivers' licences, to be issued from 1996, will almost certainly be digital.

The revolution in CFR will inevitably produce a national face recognition system that can be accessed by a range of authorities. This process recently commenced in a limited fashion with a service by the UK company Secure Imaging, which has introduced a network system called Crime Link. Images of criminals are digitized by the company, and these are then cross-referenced in a minute way so that reported details from a crime can be matched against the existing file of CCTV digitized images.

Such projections are not the province of paranoia. The

government of Massachusetts is in the final stage of developing a state-wide database containing the digitized photographs of 4.2 million drivers. Within about one second, the state will be able to match any face against the database images. The system is similar to NeuroMetric in that it can look past hairstyles and spectacles into the essential light and shade created by the facial structure. The facial templates created by the system are called eigenfaces. The system has been motivated by a crackdown on fraud through false ID. It does not require a suspicious mind to imagine what would happen if Massachusetts had the CCTV web that Britain has developed. The possibilities for state surveillance would be virtually limitless.

If current trends continue, cameras on motorways will not merely scan number plates, but will routinely peer straight into the vehicles and scan the occupants. Tens of thousands of cameras in public places, phone booths[20] and automatic teller machines will do the same. Barclays has pioneered the use of pinhole cameras in its cash machines, and this lead is likely to be followed by other banks.

If these applications worry you, consider what will happen if the cameras are able in the future inexpensively to incorporate high resolution from the non-visible light spectrum. Such technology is now used in the form of the (somewhat inaccurately named) Forward Looking Infrared Radar, a hand-held device designed to look through the walls of buildings with an accuracy and clarity similar to an early video camera. The FBI has introduced these devices for a range of purposes, including detecting drug manufacture, kidnapping and trespass.

A similar, though less sophisticated, device will shortly be available to police and customs authorities. Called Millivision, the hand-held device is being marketed for the purpose of covert frisking and can be concealed behind a door or thin wall to conduct an infrared scan of passengers or suspects. Clothes are virtually invisible to the system, which can detect objects being carried in the stomach, bowel or mouth, as well as weapons or other objects concealed in clothing.

SEEDS OF UNREST

Alvin Toffler once predicted, 'We will be living in the pupil of a thousand different eyes at any given moment.' Most of the British public currently see this as a positive trend, but adoration of visual surveillance is by no means a universal response. On the other side of the globe, Western Australia's police and road traffic authorities announced a plan in 1992 to install surveillance cameras at intersections in the capital city, Perth. There was an immediate outcry. Demonstrators marched in the city while the media carried stories calling for open debate on the issue.[21]

For many Western Australian citizens, the proposal to install cameras entailed important questions of state power and civil liberties. Such devices, it was claimed, should not readily be placed into the hands of law enforcement agencies. This threat was well recognized by the students involved in China's pro-democracy demonstrations, who had disabled the city's surveillance cameras before taking to the streets. Closer to home, French, German and Dutch citizens may be passive about some facets of police power grabbing, but they have had a long-standing suspicion of visual surveillance.

It can, of course, be argued that Britain has already made its choice, and it has chosen to have safer streets. This may be so, but we need then to ask whether the decision is based on reality or illusion. Return for one moment to the criminological work of Jason Ditton and others who tell us that the very basis of our reasoning may be thoroughly flawed. We may be safer underneath the cameras, but what about elsewhere? The cameras may appear to be a boon for crime prevention, but are they in fact causing detrimental changes to law enforcement? Some towns, for example, no longer have a routine police presence at pub closing time. Police now prefer to react only to what they see on their monitors.

The popular argument put forward by police and local authorities is that the cameras are doing no more nor less than a vigilant police officer. Little is said of the risk that the images will be misused. Bolton Council's John Watson told a Manchester newspaper, 'It's a matter of trust at the end of the day.'[22] Trust is all we have. British law offers virtually no protection over the use of CCTV.

The police in every city have a video repertoire of 'greatest hits' showing crimes captured on camera. These are played at every opportunity to promote the technology. While some of the scenes show genuinely distressing crimes like assault, most are incidents of minor vandalism or graffiti. One, recorded at 2 am, shows a middle-aged husband and wife trying to get into their Jaguar. He is too drunk to get the key into the door. She sets about the task while the husband playfully fondles her behind. As soon as she manages to open the door he swings into the driver's seat, oblivious to the patrol car which has just pulled up. The intimate communication between CCTV headquarters and the police operations controller has struck another blow for safer roads.

Some councils have gone so far as to place these 'greatest hits' videos on the open market. The King's Lynn Council put together on a promotional video a sequence of incidents including assault, drug use, graffiti, and theft, and has so far sold more than 400 of them. Most of the people caught on camera can be identified.

Police and other officials are unrepentant about the activity. After all, many are on a crusade to sell CCTV for almost every social ill in the book. Not everyone, however, is prepared to meekly accept the technology. The King's Lynn Council admits that there have been several occasions where people have tried to destroy or disable the units using a range of weapons from air rifles to spray cans. One man on a local housing estate attacked a camera that was placed too close to his home. In each case of vandalism the culprits have been recorded, either by the camera being attacked, or by a nearby camera. Most integrated CCTV systems are designed so that the cameras can watch each other. Some, such as the Liverpool system, go a step further by programming the cameras to pan automatically across to a fellow-camera under attack. Most centres place their cameras in a very open position, ostensibly to ensure that villains know they are being watched, but also to minimize the risk of attack. Increasingly, cameras are being sheltered behind unbreakable plastic domes which incorporate several dummy lenses, designed so people have no idea whether they are being watched.

In what was possibly the first public call for civil disobedience, the London based cyber-culture magazine *Wired* advised, 'Try disabling the cameras by throwing blankets over them.' People in other countries are not so passive. In California, where the prevalence of guns is a real threat to CCTV, highway cameras have had to be placed in bullet-proof casings.

THE URGENCY OF DEBATE

Any serious debate over CCTV will require a vast amount more honesty and openness than has been offered to date. Icons should be replaced by facts; trust should be replaced by rules and safeguards. It is not just that CCTV systems are operating entirely without guidelines. Most systems have an unofficial code of practice which limits the activities of the operator and the use of the data. The key problem is that no limits have been placed on the purpose for which cameras are used. The secondary problem is that no limit has been placed on the sort of technology that can be used within these systems.

Once a national debate does begin, councils must then have the authority to decide if a CCTV scheme is appropriate for the local area. If it is, they should have a legal right to exercise control over its establishment and use. Of equal importance is the need for a national law to limit and regulate the use of cameras. The nature of the information collected, the uses to which it is put, and the type of technology used should all be subject to a thoughtful and forward-looking law.

The former Deputy Commissioner of the Metropolitan Police, Sir John Smith, warned a London computer seminar in 1995 that fear of crime had become 'almost pathological'.

'Such unwarranted concerns could result in the creation

of crime-free enclaves protected by the best that money could buy, yet surrounded by a sea of criminality and disorder.' Those who could afford to protect themselves would do so at the expense of poorer neighbours, who would suffer an even larger burden of crime.

This is not a question of sacrificing safety for democracy. It should be the duty of all players to demand both.

SATELLITE SURVEILLANCE

As Privacy International observed in its 1995 surveillance statement, 'CCTV is emerging as one of this century's most profoundly important developments'. It has been known for some years now that the Superpowers have placed spy satellites in orbit which are capable of recognizing objects on the surface of the earth of twenty to thirty centimetres. Pictures leaked in the mid-1980s to *Jane's Defence Weekly* show just how remarkable is the clarity of these images.[23] Depending on the day, these satellites are able to produce images clear enough to indicate which newspaper you are reading. Objects of only a few centimetres' diameter can be clearly made out. Beyond that, little is known about these satellites. Governments rarely even acknowledge their existence.

The spy satellites, however, are only a small part of the massive stratospheric surveillance web currently being constructed. The end of the Cold War, coupled with the release of military satellite technology, means that space-based surveillance of surface activities will soon be within the reach of many government and commercial organizations. President Bill Clinton's decision in 1994 to allow the commercial sale of high-resolution remote-sensing imagery was the official starting gun for a rush by US aerospace firms to capitalize on a rare opportunity – an emerging market with billions of dollars in potential revenues.[24] France, Germany, China and Israel are all believed to be considering marketing military reconnaissance-quality satellite capabilities. Their aim: to use satellites to extract the maximum amount of information from the surface of the earth.

Satellites are being used for a variety of purposes: urban mapping, rural monitoring, vehicle tracking, monitoring by media organizations, geological exploration, drug control, communications interception and pollution monitoring. They are, increasingly, being linked to surface databases to check on such activities as building extensions, farm subsidies, swimming pools and water usage. Potential applications of higher-resolution satellite imagery include mapping, pictures for broadcast and print news and even industrial espionage.[25]

Many modern satellite systems are capable of recognizing small objects such as a car or a garden shed. Others are able to detect objects by way of the non-visible spectrum. It is, therefore, possible to monitor the insulation used in houses, or the presence of life-forms, even under cover. The LANDSAT satellites are the most comprehensive spies. They cover seven wavelength bands ranging from the blue, green and red of the visible spectrum, down through three relatively near infrared bands which permit the identification of vegetation, and some chemicals and minerals, as well as a thermal infrared spectrum to monitor and picture heat transmission.[26]

The earliest SPOT satellites had an ability to discern objects of five to ten metres' diameter. The most recent commercial satellites have greatly improved on this resolution. To date, one-metre systems planned by Lockheed and a GDE Systems/ Orbital Sciences/Litton team have been licensed by the Commerce Department, while Ball Aerospace says it expects a licence for its proposed one-metre system to be granted in September. In addition, WorldView Corporation has been licensed since early 1993 for a three-metre system.[27]

High resolution is not necessary to undertake mass surveillance of the earth. Two French SPOT satellites and two American LANDSAT satellites with a ten-to-thirty-metre resolution capacity are currently being used to scan all farms in Europe to monitor crops and livestock. This information is then matched against the European Community's farm subsidy database.[28] The French satellites have manoeuvrable 'eyes' that can look sideways, forwards and backwards to take pictures through cloud cover.

Satellites are now used for international communications. They have the ability not only to accurately receive and transmit telephone messages, but also to pinpoint the precise location of some mobile-phone users. Motorola's Project Iridium, involving a web of seventy-seven satellites, will create an international tracking system for phone users.

There are relatively few legal constraints on the development or use of satellites. National security and espionage laws do have an effect, provided the information is actually physically present in a country. There may also be some limited constitutional protection, such as the Fourth Amendment to the US Constitution. In a case involving aerial photography of a chemical plant used to prosecute a pollution violation, the US Supreme Court barred agencies from using classified satellite imagery without first getting a search warrant.[29]

Many countries are nervous about the implications of satellite surveillance. In the 1980s, several international conferences were established to hear grievances about the technology. African, Latin American and Middle East nations were particularly sensitive about the issue.

A number of governments, with Brazil at the forefront, identified large-scale export of economic strategic industry and national resource information encroaching their national interests, through the use of satellite technology. The conferences highlighted the practice of photographing and analysing crops and mineral resources to influence foreign commodity market prices.[30]

In Quebec, a Geographic Information Strategy aims to merge satellite and demographic data to create a province-wide inventory of unprecedented accuracy. The system will involve a comprehensive database of a vast spectrum of human activity, physical objects, vegetation and economic activity in each square metre. The great problem, from the perspective of privacy, is that in time the sheer mass of information from these satellites will be brought together in a form that is cheap and readily available. The watchers will be even more difficult to evade.

CHAPTER TEN

THE END OF
TELEPHONE PRIVACY

21 November 1994 was a momentous day in the life of Britain's telephone users, for it was on that day that they fell victim to one of the greatest hoaxes ever perpetrated by a telecommunications company.

Accompanied by slick ads and high-sounding statements of public interest, British Telecom introduced two new services: Call Return, and Caller Display. Both claim that they will let you identify the number of the calling party, even before you pick up the phone.

With Call Return, which was automatically connected to three-quarters of BT customers, you can find out the number of the last person who called you. No more the frustration of leaping up the stairs two at a time to face the anguish of wondering who was trying to ring you. With this new service, all you have to do is pick up your receiver, dial 1471, and a mechanical voice will tell you the number of the person you just missed.

The second service BT introduced on that momentous day was an intriguing device called Caller Display. This is a small grey box that can be fitted on to your telephone cable.

Whenever the phone rings, say the advertisements, a screen on the device displays the number of the person trying to call you. The device does not concern itself about whether you answer the phone, or whether the calling party refuses to leave a message on your answering machine. Its sole job is dutifully to record the number of every person who dials your telephone, even if that person has an unlisted number. The unit stores details of the last fifty callers.

Apart from the obvious advantage of being able to get back to people who weren't able to reach you, the device allows you to screen calls and to decide whether or not to answer them. Callers will have the right to 'block' their number from appearing on your screen by using the code '141' before dialling, but you will see a message 'Number withheld' informing you that they have done this. The mere fact that you have refused to disclose your number may invite some suspicion.

BT's Service Development Manager, Carol Rue, told the *Daily Telegraph* that the introduction of these services represents the most important change to the telephone system since the introduction of STD. 'What we have here is a wholesale change to the telephone service that affects every user.'[1]

Ms Rue's assessment is accurate. The Caller Display service is indeed going to create a wholesale change to the telephone service. What is at stake is nothing less than an obliteration of privacy on the telephone. BT's technology poses fundamental questions about the control and disclosure of personal information in the telephone network. The central issue is whether the telephone user or the telephone customer should have the right to control the disclosure of personal telephone numbers. This question is one of the most important privacy issues of modern times and will have a bearing on the privacy of future generations.

When the technology made its début eight years ago in North America, the immediate reaction of customers was largely positive. People quite naturally felt they had a right to know who was calling them. Telephone companies argued that the Caller Display device (or Caller ID, as it is known over there) was just like having a peephole on your front door. You have a right to see who is contacting you, so say the overseas telephone companies, so you can make a decision whether or not to pick up the phone.

BT is running the same argument. Announcing the service, BT's group Managing Director, Michael Hepher, gushed, 'These two services will give our customers a level of control and choice that they have never before experienced.'

The overseas experience tells a different story. Caller Display and Call Return have caused widespread controversy in the US and Canada. Some states and provinces have been so worried about the hidden implications for privacy and intrusion that they have either banned the service or made its introduction impossible.

It turns out that far from being a simple and popular 'peephole' technology, Caller Display has generated hostility and vulnerability on an unprecedented scale. Indeed, rather than being a peephole, it is a means of allowing businesses to photograph and profile visitors passing their front door. Among the many problems that the service has caused in North America are:

- Some people who have installed Caller Display on their phone have inadvertently put their children in danger. After instructing them to answer calls from only two or three particular numbers, they discover that they are unable to speak to them in an emergency, say, if they have been involved in a car accident and need to call from a public telephone.

- Telephone users who use the special prefix to block the sending of their number sometimes find they are denied access to certain numbers. Some of the people they call become suspicious when they see that the number has been blocked. Friends won't pick up the phone. Some businesses treat them like a second-class customer. The local pizza shop insists on ringing them back for verification. The school, bank, radio talk-back programmes and even government departments do the same.
- People making what they believe to be anonymous calls to government departments find themselves the subject of an official visit some weeks later.
- Anonymous enquiries to find out the price of merchandise often result in a flood of unwanted calls from direct market companies and sales people.
- People ringing around to get quotes for engine parts or for household repairs have their evenings ruined by businesses who return aborted calls to their answering machines or switchboards.
- Some telephone users who accidentally dial a wrong number find that the other party rings them back with the accusation that they are making nuisance calls.

Such concerns led Judge Lemke of the Californian Public Utilities Commission to rule against Caller Display. In his summing up, the Judge remarked, 'The Caller ID service would not be in the public interest, because the significant detriments associated with the feature would offset the scant benefits it offers to only a very small minority of customers.'[2]

The Scottish Advisory Committee on Telecommunications (SACOT), the official telecommunications watchdog for Scotland, was opposed to Caller Display from the outset. It believed that the humble answering machine could do the job just as effectively, and without the inherent risk to the privacy of the caller.[3] SACOT also warned about the impact that Caller Display may have on very simple everyday situations:

- You've seen a job advertisement about which you want to obtain information. You don't want to be identified, but you also wouldn't want it to be known that you were blocking information.
- Children not home at the appointed times, supposedly at a friend's house. Do you want a phone call from the children to let you know they will be home late, or, instead, no phone call because they are not at the friend's house, and don't want you to know this?
- You have an ex-directory number, and do not wish your number to be displayed, but if the person being called sees that you are blocking your number they may decide not to answer.

SACOT's chairman, William Begg, said he was 'anxious that users are encouraged to think about the use and implications of the introduction of new technology'.[4]

Is SACOT defending deceit? Probably, but it's in good company. American sociologist Gary Marx explains that the automatic tracking of calls is likely to imbalance delicate social relationships. 'Our sense of autonomy and self are enmeshed in a complex web of privacy, secrecy, diplomacy and fabrication. Anything that curtails social manoeuvrability and alters these delicate relationships, whatever its other benefits, is likely to be morally ambiguous.'[5]

Before introducing the services, BT conducted trials in Scotland. While claiming that there was widespread support for both Call Return and Caller Display, BT failed to publicize the fact that businesses in Scotland had exploited the service in ways that were at best ethically dubious, and at worst, grossly invasive of individual privacy.

While it was certainly true that people who had the Caller Display device enjoyed the ability to see who was ringing them, life was made worse for the majority who didn't have the device. Anonymity disappeared. No longer could you shop around unfettered among a range of business and service providers. Once businesses had your number, they made use of it. In Scotland, as in North America, the era of anonymous shopping came to an end.

For business, the service has been a boon. One of the people who participated in BT's trial, a Perth driving instructor, told me that his business has benefited enormously from Caller Display. He said people are reluctant to leave messages on his answering machine, resulting in a string of annoying bleeps. 'I've recorded 200 phone calls where people didn't leave a message on my answering machine. Many of them became customers when I rang them back.'

An Edinburgh clairvoyant who also participated in the trials said, 'I would call people back even when they hadn't left a message. People were astounded, which was good for my image. Caller Display has made me a lot of money.'

Indeed BT thinks this procedure is just perfect. It believes such behaviour is a natural part of an open and friendly telephone network. Such practices are promoted in an in-house article entitled 'Your numbers up – new services to keep track of every caller'.[6] Businesses, naturally enough, also agreed with this position. Ninety per cent of those polled were in favour of Caller Display.[7]

But what of the ordinary telephone users? Whad did they think of all this? Surprisingly, neither BT nor Oftel, the national Telecommunications Authority, bothered to canvass the views of the ordinary telephone customer involved in the trials. The evidence both here and overseas, however, is that many people end up having bad experiences as a result of Caller Display. Ringing the number on a Caller Display box has the same effect as broadcasting the caller's private business. You are, after all, ringing a premises rather than a person.

The clairvoyant, for example, admitted he rings people back only to find sometimes that people at the other end are reluctant to talk to him. 'Sometimes I have to stop because I think if I push this I'll just cause someone trouble.' As for the driving instructor, he says he occasionally ends up creating hostilities when he tracks people through the service. 'You sometimes get an argument. They say, "Now listen Mister I'm telling you that wasn't me." When I tell them I have their number, it turns out it was their son or daughter. It's just one of the complications, but I've done well out of it. I've no complaints.'

And what happens if you use the 141 blocking option to stop your number being sent through the telephone system? The Caller Display unit at the other end then shows the message 'Number Withheld'. In Canada, this message was viewed as discriminatory, and telephone companies were forced to change the message to 'Number Unavailable'. In this way, subscribers to the Caller Display service would not know whether a number had been withheld, or whether the telephone system itself was unable to provide the information because of technical reasons.

One father in Edinburgh mentioned to me that while Caller Display had been a well-used novelty in his home, the new service had created a degree of suspicion that they had not known before. 'We used to innocently answer the phone. Now we gather around while it's still ringing, scratching our heads and wondering whether to answer it. We can also track where the kids are.'

SACOT, which had been largely excluded from the trial planning and evaluation, issued a press release containing a thinly veiled attack on BT: 'The trials, in restricted areas, were not in themselves fully representative of normal use of such a system . . .'[8]

Meanwhile, OFTEL was sleeping throughout the lead up to the introduction of the service. Compared to the actions of other regulatory authorities overseas, it did almost nothing to question the implications of Caller Display. This lack of interest is rather strange considering that British telephone consumers are more privacy-conscious than those of just about any place on earth. Around a third are ex-directory. Some of these customers were surprised and angry to discover that their numbers were being routinely transmitted without their knowledge. BT's advertising campaign had intentionally understated the issue of privacy. The campaign failed to get the message across that ex-directory numbers were going to be dealt with in this fashion, or, indeed, that there was a means of permanently blocking the transmission of a number.

Consumer groups in North America have also raised a number of questions about the actual benefits of Caller Display, including whether the service is in fact more useful than a telephone answering machine or voice mail. Both of these services allow callers to provide actual identity and the reason for the call. They may also be less costly than Caller Display. Despite the existence of these less dangerous options, OFTEL and the carriers are creating an environment in which Caller Display becomes universal. OFTEL says it wants to 'encourage' BT and other providers to offer equipment that will automatically reject any number that is blocked.[9] As a consumer, you will not be able to win either way.

THE WIDER PICTURE

The British telephone system is currently going through a major upgrading. Instead of the old copper cables routed through physical switching systems, the multi-billion-dollar network is changing to optical fibre and digital exchanges. Some people have called this the emergence of the Intelligent Telephone Network. The new technology will also mean that the telephone carriers are able to transmit several 'layers' of information simultaneously down the same wire.

The Intelligent Telephone Network is going to mean that we will use the telephone not just as an instrument to speak through, but also as a device through which we transmit and receive a vast spectrum of information. The new system is interactive. That is, information and instructions are passed backwards and forwards down the line. By pressing numbers on your telephone at the appropriate time, you can send instructions down the line to a receiving computer. Pressing 1, for example, might mean 'yes' to the offer of a product, or pressing 2 could mean 'charge this to my credit card'. Using a series of numbers, coupled perhaps with a PIN code, could give complex instructions to the building department of a local government, to an embassy for a visa application, or to a health computer for advice.

This means we can organize our banking over the phone, do our shopping, or book theatre or airline tickets electronically. With digital technology, a computer terminal can be linked to the phone line to produce rapid and reliable two-way communications. The options for education (long-distance, correspondence and Open University education) are magnified magnificently.

Overseas, the provision of this technology has made possible a range of valuable new services. With Call Trace, for example, you can take action against harassing or obscene calls. A facility in the network will allow you to transmit the details of the telephone number to the telephone carrier, where it will be stored for later action (unless you receive the call from a public phone). With another service, Call Screening, you can instruct the network to block a certain number of incoming numbers. If, for instance, you did not want to receive calls from a creditor, your mother-in-law, your landlord or employer, instructions could be provided via your phone, and any calls originating from those numbers would be blocked. A recorded message would advise the caller that you did not wish to receive calls 'at this time'.[10] Call Forwarding is a means of instructing the telephone network to re-route your calls.

These are all beneficial services that most people would

gladly welcome. However, not all the services made possible by the new technology are so agreeable. Caller Display, for example, is being portrayed by the telephone companies as a customer-friendly, privacy-friendly service. The person receiving a call, they claim, has a right to protect privacy, because the person making the call is the privacy invader. Telephone companies argue that the person receiving a call has a right to control whether or not a call should be answered.

Privacy advocates also argue that Caller Display represents a control issue, but their position is that the issue is not control over the answering of a call, but control over the disclosure of the telephone number. This has been the status quo since automated exchanges were introduced more than eighty years ago. To reverse the onus of disclosure would create a diminution of privacy for all telephone subscribers.

The purveyors of the Caller Display service also argue that their facility will all but completely eliminate harassing, hoax and obscene calls. If malicious callers know their number will be displayed at the other end – and police can then trace the address from that number – who would take the risk? Sounds logical.

The problem is that the arguments advanced by BT and the overseas telephone companies are deceptive and inaccurate. Obscene and threatening callers only need to either use their blocking facilities, or use a public telephone. Police departments in the US are cautious about giving unfettered praise to Caller Display. Indeed, many people are angry at the police because instead of dealing with the problem of obscene callers, they often merely advise that the victim subscribe to Caller Display.

Some consumer groups in the United States have argued

that the use of Caller Display as a mechanism for dealing with objectionable and threatening calls constitutes telephone companies offering less service to their customers, not more. Mark Cooper, Research Director of the Consumer Federation of America, observed: 'Before the advent of new technology, call trace was considered by the phone companies to be part of the basic service for which there was no extra charge. It was unwieldy. It took a long time to get it installed. You had to keep a log of all your calls. But the service was unbilled, part of the phone company's obligation to monitor the network. Now that they have a new and very potent technology, the phone companies are trying to take it out of basic service and profit from it.'[11]

Addressing a telecommunications privacy conference in Melbourne, Rohan Samarajiva, a telecommunications expert from Ohio State University, also threw cold water on the technology.

> [Caller Display] is not very useful in providing a lawful and effective response to the real problem of obscene and harassing calls. The called party cannot identify the obscene or harassing caller's name and address without accessing a reverse directory or calling back the deviant caller and asking for the information. The information that an obscene or harassing call was made at a particular time can be recorded on the Caller Display display device, but that information is likely to be of minimal evidentiary value since the machine was under the control of the aggrieved party and in any case does not indicate what the call was about.[12]

While offering at least the illusion of security, Caller Display has also created grave danger for some subscribers.

In 1995 the New York Public Utilities Commission revealed that one in fifteen telephone subscribers in New York who had chosen to have their lines made private against Caller Display ended up having their numbers inadvertently sent through the system. The new computer exchanges failed to maintain the Caller Display block that these subscribers had paid for.[13] Among the aggrieved customers was a psychiatrist who realized that his home details were now in the hands of violent patients.[14] As a result, the Rhode Island Public Utilities Commission immediately forced Nynex to stop offering the Caller Display line blocking facility.

Such technical problems also beset the British telephone system. The presenter of the BBC's consumer programme *Watchdog*, Anne Robinson, found that despite the line block on her private phone, her number was still being transmitted by the telephone system to the people she was calling.[15] Although BT told the programme that it knew of only three such instances, *Watchdog* was able to produce a sheaf of other complaints. Within two months of the grand launch of the service, BT was quietly compensating angry customers with £50 and a new number.

Caller Display is fraught with other problems. The greatest use of the facility will be by commercial organizations, law enforcement agencies, government departments and direct marketing companies. Many people who genuinely want or need to protect their anonymity will find their number published at the other end of the telephone line.

The provision of these services overseas has caused public protests. In North America, Caller Display has become the single biggest privacy issue in memory. In its report on the introduction of Caller Display, the Australian Telecommunications Regulator AUSTEL observed: 'The overseas experience with CLI based services suggest that Australia should adopt a cautious approach to the introduction of such services in Australia. Although there are instances in which the service has been introduced in a trouble-free way and with consumer and business benefits, the overseas trends are in the direction of giving greater weight to the consumer-based privacy concerns and towards telephone companies and regulators being in conflict.'[16]

According to Professor Marc Rotenberg of the Electronic Privacy Information Center in Washington DC, Caller Display is no more than a dangerous gimmick that allows telephone companies to take control of personal telephone numbers.

The telephone companies insist Caller Display is in everyone's interest. Surely no one would mind transmitting their telephone number to the person they are calling. Surely everyone has the right to know who is calling? Telephone companies throughout the world have argued that the Caller Display debate has opened up a privacy 'conflict'. Regulators, while being more sympathetic to the privacy view, agree that there is a potential problem. On the one hand, they claim, the caller has a right to privacy. On the other, the called party has a right to be free of intrusion. Privacy advocates are not so unclear about this dilemma. Indeed, there is unanimity in the privacy community that the status quo should be maintained.

There is a very cogent reason for this solidarity. When we talk about the Caller Display facility, we have to keep in mind all the information attached to it. As more of our affairs are conducted over the telephone, we leave an ever broadening trail of transactions – intimate details of our purchases, wants, needs, and even our interests and fantasies.

Many people and organizations have an interest in securing this information. The Electronic Privacy Information Center (EPIC) recently discovered that the toll records (details of activity on a telephone) of more than a million people had been subpoenaed by law enforcement agencies. The FBI has run 'dragnets' over the telephone records of entire groups of people. In 1992, for example, it secured the toll records of 600 environmental activists. Police in the UK call this practice 'metering'.

In 1993, multinational giant Procter & Gamble convinced a Cincinnati judge to order the seizure of the toll records of virtually the entire Cincinnati population to detect who had been leaking company information to a *Wall Street Journal* reporter. The company secured the toll records in electronic form and then had the entire mass scanned to reveal the origin of calls to the reporter. Thirty-five million records from 850,000 homes and offices were searched.[17] The culprit was never found.

Twenty years ago, the release of a telephone number meant just that: a number. Now there is a vast spectrum of personal data that can be revealed through the release of the number. Reverse directories will soon be available in the UK. These are computer-based services that give a number and address from a telephone number. That means at the touch of a button a person or organization receiving your call knows not just the incoming telephone number, but also the address of that number and the name of the subscriber. The possibilities go beyond this. A whole range of information is legally available which can instantly provide a profile on the basis of a telephone number. You are, in fact, doing much more than communicating your telephone number to the person you call.

In an effort to demonstrate this Pandora's box, the Canadian consumer programme *Marketplace* commissioned a private investigator, Harry Lake, to discover all he could from a telephone number displayed on a Caller Display facility. Within three hours, Lake had traced not just the subscriber's address, but also his full name and birth date, his wife's name and birth date, the date of purchase of his home and the price he paid, details of the mortgage and to whom it is paid, his employer and his wife's occupation, his credit card numbers, credit rating, vehicle details and licence plate number.[18] If Lake had had better technology, these and other details would have been available far sooner than three hours.

Practices such as these, involving information mercenaries, are part of the reason why telephone companies in North America have dropped from being the most trusted public organizations to the fifth most trusted in a period of nine years.[19]

There can be no doubt that there is big money to be made. Bell Canada made $89 million in one year from Caller Display in Quebec and Ontario alone, not including rental of the equipment. The more people use the Caller Display system, the more attractive it is to businesses. All telephone companies are aiming for a 'critical mass' of users.

Privacy advocates have argued passionately that the public interest fell against the technology. EPIC's Marc Rotenberg, one of the technology's most eloquent critics, told the United States Telephone Association:

What is technically possible is not the same as what is good public policy. Our system of government, through the regulatory framework, is designed to ensure that citizens have some say over the technical forces that affect their lives. The protection of the environment and public safety depend on the efforts of law makers to draw boundaries around technologies that could make our world less safe, and our lives less secure. And this includes personal privacy. It is a mistake to assume that because something can be done, it should be done.[20]

THE NEED FOR ANONYMITY

A surprisingly large number of people have reason to fear the introduction of Caller Display. It is not a service that will bring joy to anyone who desires privacy or anonymity. Apart from the millions of people who have unlisted numbers, there are many instances where people would want to preserve their privacy and anonymity in the course of any day:

• Women and children who need protection from violent estranged husbands do not want their whereabouts known if they need, for any reason, to speak with either the husband or his acquaintances.
• People who work from home make many phone calls in the course of their work, but do not necessarily want their number identified and treated by others as a 'free for all' commercial number.
• Doctors and other professionals who make calls to patients from home value their privacy and the time they spend with their families and might not want clients and patients ringing back on the home number.

• Police and other law enforcement agencies conducting investigations risk the secrecy of their operations if a suspect notes that the incoming number is suspicious. (Law enforcement authorities in the United States have complained that drug traffickers are using Caller Display to monitor incoming calls and thus minimize the risk of a wire-tapped conversation.)[21] In addition, it allows criminals under investigation to identify informants and investigators, placing the lives of police in danger.

PRIVACY PROTECTION FOR THE TELEPHONE

Telecommunications companies in other countries have successfully highlighted an apparent contradiction in the privacy argument: that of the right of privacy of the called party. The distinction is not challenged by privacy advocates. Only the manner of identification of the caller is challenged. If a subscriber felt a need to answer only those calls from a fixed number of people, this can best be achieved by using code names rather than numbers. There is a real consumer issue here because identification of a caller by a number limits the mobility and options of the calling party. If you are known only by your number, you are restricted to using that number. After a century of striving to remove geographical limits, the telephone companies are now imposing them. The technology already exists to achieve coding of names, but telephone companies have been slow to introduce it.

Telephone companies grudgingly admit that the overwhelming use of Caller Display will be for purposes which have nothing to do with the protection of the called person's privacy. While it is true that in a very small number of cases the interests of the called party will be genuinely served, the advocacy argument is clearly that the balance of public benefit is not served by Caller Display, and that the benefits of the service lie elsewhere (i.e. with commercial uses).

Advocates argue that on the basis of the overall diminution of privacy, Caller Display should not be offered unless under very strict guidelines. It should, for example, be an 'opt-in' service. In other words, the default is the withholding of the number instead of its release, and callers will have to enter a code to transmit their number.

Perhaps the most persuasive, though most complex, privacy factor is the issue of overall diminution of privacy for society. The intelligent telephone network will generate a vastly increased amount of personal information throughout the telecommunications network, and this increases the risk of privacy violation for all people. The existence of large quantities of personal information is dangerous where adequate protections are not in place. In Britain, there is limited protection against the amassing of personal data. As long as the database is registered with the Data Protection Registrar, the information is legitimate.

It is not surprising to see the telecommunications carriers and telemarketers arguing in unison the case for unrestricted use of Caller Display. Their view generally is that all telephone numbers should routinely be sent down the line at the time of each call unless the caller takes the trouble to enter a code. Experience in Scotland and elsewhere indicates that many callers simply don't bother to go to the trouble of doing this. During the BT trials in Scotland, the blocking option was used less than once per 2,000 calls, yet 30 per cent of people polled said they saw reasons to use the blocking option. As a result, the vast majority of calls on the network are picked up by Caller Display.

The United States and Canada have no single ruling on the blocking option. Each state or province is responsible for drawing up its own guidelines. Most of North America has an 'opt out' system. Much of the central and western US has yet to make a decision on the matter, leaving the option to each individual carrier. Naturally, they choose default line transmission, sometimes even without the facility of call blocking. On the other hand, it is clear that as the dangers of Caller Display become better known, regulators take tougher and tougher stances.

CONVERTING A TELEPHONE CALL INTO A PERSONAL PROFILE

Until now, the only direct marketing issue of interest to Britons has been junk mail and the generation of mailing lists. With the introduction of Caller Display, a new and far more invasive form of direct marketing will be spawned.

Each time you call a company or government department which has Caller Display facilities, your number may be registered and stored on their database. This can be linked to a reverse directory disk which gives addresses from a given telephone number. Thus, by making one anonymous telephone call, the company or department knows who you are and – in many instances – where you live. In some instances, there may be a data protection issue in doing this, but no one is prepared to gamble on the outcome of a court hearing on the matter.

The organization you called can then link this to data from the Census Office to indicate your probable financial status, family type, age and occupation. Other local government and government databases can also be instantly accessed through tapes and disks. Presto. One call and a profile has been compiled.

This information can be used for any number of different purposes. It can be sold to direct marketing companies who can either send mail to you, or – more likely – make telephone calls to your home.

As if the standard telemarketing calls are not intrusive enough, tomorrow's direct marketers will have access to a new generation of technology. Automatic Calling Equipment will dial numbers from a list and play a pre-recorded message down the line. The lists used by these machines overseas have often been generated through Caller Display registration. Some classes of this equipment (predictive diallers) will call until you answer, and then hand the call over to a human operator.

Rohan Samarajiva calls the new telecommunications environment 'electronic space' and advises: 'Right now, this is where the ground rules of electronic space are being defined, and the Caller Display debate, whether we like it or not, is one place where these rules are being debated in public.'[22] Samarajiva warns that if we do not take advantage of the opportunity for debate, the rules will be made for us. 'That's the way these things go.'[23]

The debate over Caller Display is much more than a discussion about the release of telephone numbers. Privacy International says it is for the telecommunications companies 'a means to the end of having the public become accustomed to data being transmitted as part of telephone usage'.[24] For some architects involved in the construction of the global surveillance web, it is a strand of inestimable value.

CHAPTER ELEVEN

FORECASTING THE FUTURE

The long-term implications of the ultimate fusion of flesh and machine are anyone's guess. Humans have always been hopeless at predicting the future. Indeed, if the past teaches us just one lesson, it is never to trust fortune tellers. Long-range forecasts are overwhelmingly wrong. The few that endure do so invariably through good luck or the simple law of averages. Or, as Arthur C. Clarke put it, 'The future is not what it used to be.'

In 1948, the founder of IBM demonstrated his visionary prowess by predicting that as many as twelve companies may some day have their own computers. And, according to the May 1967 edition of *Popular Science*, 75 per cent of all US college graduates would go, within a decade, into jobs in the computer industry. Little wonder then that we no longer fear the future: the prophets have let us down so often that we are cynical – and largely optimistic.

Nevertheless, many scientists and researchers are happy to dip their toes in the waters of the future, even if the stench from a millennium of dead prophecies has made everyone nervous. Most people now generally agree that the margin of viability in prophecy appears to be ten years.

John Naisbitt, for example, wrote a magnificent bestseller in 1982 called *Megatrends*, in which he used complex research methods to identify forces which would shape our destiny. The book was widely viewed as a masterly study on the future and for some years it seemed to be right on target. Twelve years later, mysteriously, his predictions started to go off the rails.

Naisbitt went for the Big Picture. He argued, for example, that short-term thinking would become long-term thinking, yet a world recession created business and political practices which reversed this. He predicted that centralization would yield to decentralization – yet throughout the world, predatory corporate practices have helped to kill this hope. As soon as a trend emerges, it instantly throws open a range of new forces that mutate it. The irony in long-term, forecasting of humans is that they deliberately go against the grain.

Closer to home, a consortium of high-profile British organizations joined forces in 1994 to calculate what life would be like in the future.[1] Recognizing the fallibility of long-range forecasting, they decided to opt for the safe bet of a five-year prediction. Their project – *Wiring Whitehall* – is a hard-nosed probe into the sort of technology that is likely to be in use by 1999, and the sort of society it is likely to create. The report makes scintillating reading. Some of its predictions are optimistic: crime will be lessened, government will be more efficient, and people will have access to a vast range of services and information.

LOOKING TO A TECHNOLOGICAL NIRVANA

For the technologically literate generation, the next ten years are going to be good ones. A top-of-the-range personal computer will, for example, most likely have the power of a basic present-day military research system. It is likely that you will be operating your computer through voice recognition. Keyboards will be largely redundant. People will find more satisfying uses for their hands. A new generation of software will transcribe the human voice at the rate of 100 words a minute. The 'tuning' process will be fine enough to produce an accuracy just slightly worse than the average professional typist. Instant language translation using artificial intelligence will be in general use. The barrier of language will be removed.

The speed and capacity of personal computers will be such that 100 gigabyte hard drives the size of a paperback novel and capable of storing the equivalent of a small library will cost less than £500.

Powerful Virtual Reality (VR) systems will be common-place, though they will then be cheap enough to suit the pocket of most households, and spectacular enough to actually deserve the name 'virtual reality'. Sensual and erotic VR will be extremely popular. Used in combination with designer drugs, it will provide a unprecedented form of recreation that makes computer games and television insipid and obsolete.

The consensus among experts is that computer technology will have reached the point of total compatibility. Virtually all machines will be able to talk with each other. Around 200 million people worldwide will be connected to the worldwide 'web' of computers, the Internet, which by the year 2005 will be so complex that one- and two-year university courses will be offered to help people find their way around the system (see Chapter 2). Schools will finally have caught up with the information revolution through the Internet, mainly because it will offer a range of low-cost, high-impact education packages. As a result, face-to-face teaching will be directed more to low achievers, disadvantaged students, and to lessons in languages and crafts.

Computerized 'remote' health systems will regularly check a growing number of the ageing population, with a diagnostic accuracy much the same as the average GP (and at a half of the cost to the NHS). Patients will still have the right to see a GP, but the waiting time for an appointment will be much longer. Shopping channels using 'interactive' cable television will allow people to shop in their living-room – a boon to housebound parents, the disabled, the lazy and the isolated.

In the year 2005, you will possess at least two 'smart cards', each containing an embedded microchip. These cards will store a massive volume of information. One card will be your driver's licence, and will store administrative details, your history of traffic violations, a digitized photo and signature and basic health data. This card will probably also contain your medical records, programmed in a 'univeral' code that will allow them to be read in any major language. The second card will be issued by your bank. It will also act as an 'electronic purse', containing cash credits that can be used throughout the world. This card may also contain credits for public transport, as well as your entitlement to certain government benefits.

A network of satellites will make it possible for you to be contacted wherever you are on the globe. By 2005, many people will have been issued with cradle to grave 'universal personal numbers', which will follow them wherever they are, and allow them to be contacted in any circumstance. Mobile telephones will be as cheap as ordinary fixed wire phones.

THE FUTURE OF FUSION

The physical bond between human and machine is destined to be strong. Most researchers in the field of neural prosthetics appear to be confident that their science can, in the medium term, create a basic interface between the brain and the major organs of the body. Patients will be able to 'feel' artificial limbs. Blind and deaf people will be able to see and hear. Paralysed patients will increasingly have their sexual function restored.

In the field of neural communication, which is concerned about the flow of nerve impulses and thought within and outside the body, most experts are confident that complex 'telepathy' between human and machine will become viable within a decade. Computer companies are competing fiercely to achieve workable Virtual Reality technology. Neural links could well provide the key.

Some of these procedures have genuine medical applications, but many do not. These are most likely to fall into three streams:

1. Some ID chips will be voluntarily implanted for the purpose of identification, tracking or automatic provision of medical data. Children in 'at risk' situations and Alzheimer's patients are among the groups who may be

viewed as requiring this technology. Some patients who have undergone major surgery may also be routinely implanted.

2. Some criminals will be implanted as a condition of their sentence.
3. Advanced microprobe technology will have the ability to interface with memory and mind function.

Mark Ferguson, a professor of cell biology in the University of Manchester, has suggested that within two decades, personal health maps or what he calls 'passports' showing a person's genetic likelihood of developing particular diseases could be held in a microchip implanted in the body. Ferguson says the ethical and religious implications of wholesale genetic profiling and identification are immense.[2]

Colin Humphreys, a professor of materials science at Cambridge University, told a recent London medical conference that it was realistic to envisage a day when surgeons would be able to attach tiny artificial memory circuits etched on microscopic silicon chips to the living circuits of the brain to augment memory and intellectual prowess.

'If we can understand the interface, the boundary, between silicon chips and brain cells, then there is a prospect of implanting silicon chips into the human brain,' he said. 'This could be a possible partial treatment for Alzheimer's disease, the degenerative brain disorder in the old. Or it may be a way in the future for man to extend his intelligence.' He said the ultimate goal was to create a silicon implant 'for the brain to think it's just got another piece of brain there'.[3]

In the long term, implants may be situated in 'pleasure

centres' of the brain, or in areas that could open up the possibility of external control or even new methods of interrogation. It is feasible that microprobes and microchips could at some point in the future make it possible to retrieve information from the mind that the subject did not want discovered.

The use of microchip identification is limited only by the reaction of the general public to the technology. Given that biometric identification was unthinkable and repulsive twenty years ago, it is possible that a multi-purpose implant would be acceptable within a few years. A chip which provided secure identity, and which replaced all cards and documents, would be an attractive proposition for some. Young people, in particular, who feel no threat from technology and feel no particular vulnerability to large organizations, may adopt the technology for expedience, fun or image.

Such an application would depend on harmonization of several external information systems (government benefits systems, banking systems, immigration, etc.). This process is under way, but will not be complete for some years. It is likely that when major credit and information systems are compatible, mass-market commercial applications will be found for identification microchip implants.

The use of brain activity to control, or interface, with external technology may also find a mass-market application. It requires no great stretch of the imagination to envision a commercial 'games' package that allows computer users to train their thought processes in order to provide rudimentary instructions to their machines. Such packages could be available within five years, at an extremely low cost. Once this sort of device is available as a mass-market item, the concept of direct human-to-machine telepathy will be entrenched. The next phase might be an extension of Virtual Reality in the reverse direction, where the brain received direct input from a computer.

Such projections are not spectacular, and they are likely to remain on target. Just consider the remarkable advances in computer technology since the 1950s. A modern £20 multi-function digital wristwatch can perform the functions of the million-pound computers of the 1960s. The same advances in the automobile industry would mean that we should now be able to snap up a 2,000-mile-a-gallon Ferrari for less than £2.

THE DARK SIDE

This breathtaking progress involves one inevitable result. It means that in the course of our day-to-day contact with organizations, we will generate mountains of personal information, which will become known to more and more computer systems. These computers will become so much a part of our life and fortunes that we will scarcely notice their existence.

When governments began establishing massive computer systems in the 1970s, it was common to hear people complain resignedly, 'They know everything about us anyway.' This surrender was premature. 'They' had only just begun. By the 1990s, 'they' really were starting to know a great deal about us. More than a million people in the UK are employed full time in the business of collecting our personal information. The average British adult is identified on 200 files.[4] But what 'they' know now will be a drop in the bucket compared to their future knowledge.

First, 'they' will know our movements. By 2005, most public areas in major population centres will be under the gaze of high-tech surveillance cameras. The images from these cameras will be routinely matched with digitized facial images stored in police computers (see Chapter 9).

Most motorways and A-roads will also be monitored by sophisticated surveillance systems that automatically identify vehicles and scan occupants. Traffic violations of all kinds will be detected and acted upon by this computer. Private security firms also will operate these systems in residential areas, many of which will have seen an unexpected increase in crime as a result of the displacement of crime from surveilled commercial areas.

The smart cards you use several times a day will act as a real-time tracking mechanism, following your movements and monitoring your transactions with banks, retailers, petrol stations and toll gates.

'They' will bring together all information about you. All government computer systems will have been linked through a national data-matching scheme that commenced in 1992. The nightmare for ordinary people is that an offence committed against one government agency (say, Social Security) will cause a domino effect which disturbs – or even suspends – your relationship with other government agencies. Outstanding tax means that other government benefits may not be paid. Failure to pay a television licence, traffic fines or child support may produce a similar outcome. This 'cross-debt' policy was pioneered by the Australian government in the late 1980s, and is becoming popular in other countries. Its effect will be to vastly increase the power of the State.

THE MYTH OF NEUTRALITY

However sophisticated we make our conversation about the impact of computers, we invariably have to keep coming back to one simple theme: it is the computer which makes these threats possible. It is the computer which is the tool of surveillance and control. Smart people are so enamoured of computers that this often becomes a blind spot in their otherwise thoughtful outlook.

The Information Technology (IT) industry throughout the world has enjoyed a dream run since the 1970s. So important was the industry to the growth and prosperity of nations, and so fundamental were its products to administrative reform, that despite public misgivings about the downside of some new technologies, governments have uniformly avoided the temptation to interfere with or pass laws to regulate the industry. The computer industry stood for all that was positive about free enterprise, and so the honeymoon period has continued.

There are rare exceptions. In some countries, new technologies are portrayed as a tool of enslavement. In others, IT is condemned as a vehicle that might bring about invasions of privacy and individual freedoms. Technology itself is considered 'bad' because its use and even its mere existence entails certain risks to society. The Constitutions of Germany, Portugal, Austria and Hungary, for example, have outlawed the establishment of a national personal numbering system. The French technology watchdog body, the National Commission on Data Processing and Freedoms (CNIL), has regularly outlawed the uses of some photographic and identification technologies. Britain, India and other countries have started to regulate against some genetic developments.

Computer professionals have long argued that their products are neutral. They insist that it is only the use and application of the technology that deserves scrutiny. Perhaps, in a perfect world, this may have been so. In the real world, however, the IT business will be seen increasingly as possessing features in common with the arms trade. Both industries, after all, have fooled themselves into believing that their technology is neutral (as if to imply that it is inherently harmless). Both industries believe that ethics are the province of use rather than creation. Both industries have steadfastly avoided the application of law in their business. And, perhaps most irritating of all, both industries treat themselves as if they were cases worthy of special consideration. Few other industries – and certainly none with the influence of the computer industry – have ever managed indefinitely to make these arguments stick.

British computer manufacturers have feasted off the profits of the surveillance trade for many decades. Cameras supplied to the Chinese government were used to track down the Tiananmen Square demonstrators. Police computers were used to support the South African apartheid regime. Miniature bugs manufactured in the UK are sold to the secret police of repressive regimes. The Guatemalan government's death lists were drawn up on Western computers. These are not neutral technologies.

It is important to differentiate between *neutral* and *passive* technologies. IT may well be neutral while it remains in the lab, but it is never passive. Tobacco may be neutral in the field, but it loses its neutrality the moment it is processed and packaged. Computer matching as a technology is only neutral so long as it remains an unfulfilled concept. After that point it becomes an act of mass surveillance. Even the printing press, widely viewed as a sacred cow technology, had its downside. Some commentators believe that the invention of printing and the development of newspapers has retarded democracy by eroding public life and creating monopolies of information.[5]

FRAGILE FREEDOM

We are living in an aberration. Democracy occupies the tiniest corner in time and space of the history of the world. It has been in existence only a short time, and few countries maintain it. Democracy is a delicate petal and can be destroyed as much by innocent surrender as it can by the imposition of despotism. Allowing the creation of a web of surveillance is as potentially harmful to a free nation as would be the handing over of past powers to the State.

Lord Browne Wilkinson observed in 1990, when contemplating police powers to collect records, 'If the information obtained by the police, the Inland Revenue, the Social Security services and other agencies were to be gathered together in one file, the freedom of the individual would be gravely at risk. The dossier of private information is the badge of the totalitarian state.'[6]

This is a polemical issue. It has no choice but to be so. True, we cannot deny that technology has brought many magnificent benefits. People who are handicapped use it to participate more ably in the community. People who are lonely or isolated can communicate with the outside world. We can in many ways function faster and more efficiently. But Information Technology should not be treated like a gift from some benign god. Its development and use demand deep and careful thought. Our contract with the technology cannot be unconditional. The 'good' uses of such machines cannot be used as credits to counterbalance the threatening uses of technology.

If we are indeed constructing a society which worships efficiency and conformity, we should keep in mind that – in theory at least – nothing will stand in the way of a massive erosion of democracy and rights. This will not happen as a result of the jackboot of authority; it will come about incrementally, and by voluntary consent. Robert Maynarde Hutchins expressed this dilemma as: 'The death of democracy is not likely to be assassination from ambush. It will be a slow extinction from apathy, indifference and undernourishment.' There exist few barriers to such a trend. Geoffrey Robertson QC sums up the current situation in the words, 'Liberty in Britain is a state of mind rather than a set of legal rules.'[7]

This, then, is the gravest problem of the information age. In a society which honours conformity and efficiency and which is suspicious of difference, few people have an inclination to stand in the way of technological change. As soon as an inefficiency is identified in government, there is an unquestioning agreement that it must be rectified. Technology is usually the solution. Notable failures aside, we are moving steadily to a government administration and a corporate sector which is compatible and ruthlessly efficient. The big accounting companies move in to 'reorganize' companies, destroying in the process corporate culture, corporate identity and any humanness that might have once existed.

In their 1986 book *On the Record*, Duncan Campbell and Steve Connor argue, 'Society has been best protected from autocratic excess not by the altruism or honesty of administrators, but by their incompetence.'[8] In time, computers will remove much of this incompetent behaviour. Privacy advocates, too, are in general agreement that the greatest force for the protection of our freedoms is administrative chaos. It may be more financially costly, but it prevents an environment in which people lose their liberties.

Civil rights advocates have been aware since the 1950s of the risk that computers might facilitate the formation of a Big Brother state. They always presumed that two conditions would prevent this from happening. The first is that computers, ultimately, would fail to actually work as an integrated unit. The second condition is human nature: people would refuse to accept mass computerization, and would rebel. To their surprise and horror, both conditions have been met. All the circumstances are now ripe for the emergence of a surveillance society.

CHAPTER TWELVE

COUNTDOWN TO CATASTROPHE

The date is a Tuesday some time in the very near future, and in the Dutch city of Utrecht, a respectable-looking young man walks into the computer laboratory of a research institute affiliated with his university. Using a fellow student's pass code to operate the system, he accesses the huge Datanet 1 public computer network. On the pretext of sending a series of chemical formulae to another computer lab in Amsterdam, he loads into his terminal a disk on which he has placed a computer virus.

Viruses are custom-made computer programmes (programmes are sets of instructions that operate computers) and are designed – usually – to disrupt or even destroy a computer system. Such programmes are not uncommon, but this one is special. Known as a 'Stealth Worm', this virus boasts artificial intelligence and has a structure similar to DNA. It is possibly the most dangerous virus ever devised, and has been the subject of extensive investigation by military and national security agencies for more than a decade.

This intense man watches as two years of programming

effort come to life in the terminal, and travel out over the public network, eventually bringing hundreds of computers throughout the Netherlands to a sudden crash.

The worm is transmitted from the Rotterdam computer installation to other international transmission and exchange centres, and it infects other major public data networks. Via the X25 and X75 gateways, where computer transmission signals are processed, the Stealth Worm spreads rapidly through the Tymmet, Telenet, Infonet and Compuserve networks. As the business day begins in the Eastern United States, the worm reaches the teleport serving New York City, and within fifteen minutes causes a crash of the Clearinghouse for Interbank Payments Systems (CHIPS), the Federal Reserve Network, the New York Stock Exchange and American Stock Exchange automatic trading systems, and New York's Automatic Teller Machine (ATM) network. The Federal Reserve Bank responds with panic, and suspends the national payments system while the problem is investigated. The US macro-economy is dealt a severe blow. The worm spreads so rapidly that within another twenty minutes every Automatic Teller Machine, bank computer and Stock Exchange system throughout the USA is halted. The Canadian stock trading system is also infected and sections of the Canadian economy are then similarly paralysed.

Meanwhile, in Europe, the worm penetrates the key regional networks in Brussels and creates a major crisis. Many computer systems in Belgium are infected with the worm. One small security flaw allows the worm to penetrate the huge Society for Worldwide Interbank Financial Tele-communications (SWIFT) mainframe. The worm quickly spreads to infect every banking computer in the world. A

243

chain reaction causes the suspension of international banking activity. From Brussels and Datanet 1, the worm invades the European Community's network, and spreads itself, paralysing networked computers throughout Europe. The worm accesses the West German and Austrian Data-P network and halts the processing of oil prices in Vienna. The oil market collapses. Gold pricing in Johannesburg is also paralysed. The world's monetary infrastructure faces collapse. By the start of the Japanese business day, all financial transactions have had to be suspended, a state of affairs that is replicated throughout Asia and the Far East.

Some interconnections of networks permit the worm to access sensitive government computer networks around the world. Within hours, the command, control, intelligence and communications capabilities of the world's major powers are severely diminished. Economies start to collapse. There is talk of war.

Less than sixteen hours have passed since the worm's introduction from a Dutch terminal. None of the standard defences stood a chance of working against the worm. No one part of the financial system would dare disconnect from the networks, because to do so would cause massive damage to the industry (the currency or stock index would plunge) and there would never be any hope of voluntarily shutting down the entire international finance system to stop the spread of the worm. Ultimately, the virus would infect most of the world's networked computers, with little hope of the virus ever being exorcized.

THE PROBLEMS OF A WORLDWIDE COMPUTER NETWORK

The above scenario, originally suggested by US security expert Wayne Madsen,[1] might sound like fantasy, but most computer security professionals agree that there is nothing in principle to prevent such a crisis occurring. All that is required would be the right programme.

The right programme will depend on the existence of three factors: knowledge of the security procedures in the major computer networks, money and resources to develop and unleash the right Stealth Worm, and the malicious motivation to disrupt the world's computer systems.

The motivation already exists. Countless terrorist organizations, anarchist groups, revolutionaries, hackers and crackers all have reasons to inflict damage. It follows that money and resources are probably there in one form or another.

There is a view – and it's a view that is gaining widespread acceptance – that computers and computer terrorism will replace conventional terrorism. The prediction that computer-based fraud would eclipse standard crimes such as bank robbery have already become reality. The difference between mere computer fraud and network virus terrorism is that the latter threatens the stability of entire nations, and ultimately the relationship between nations. The US National Security Agency (NSA) calls this 'information warfare' and has recently placed it as a key international threat.

On a financial and political level, virus terrorism is no less a threat than the spectre of nuclear warfare.

The world's financial system now depends on the intricate interlinking of trillions of microchips. Transactions are calculated to hundredths of a second and fortunes can be lost in less than the time it takes to push a button. Major multinational corporations depend as much as the corner small business on the proper functioning of information technology. The lives and fortunes of hundreds of millions of people are tied inexorably to their computer terminals.

The emerging threat to the world's computers comes in many forms – trapdoors, logic bombs, worms, viruses and Trojan horses. All variations are malicious computer programmes, deliberately designed to infect and sometimes completely destroy computer systems.

The programmer who creates the worm constructs a complex series of instructions similar in some ways to the instructions encoded in DNA or a biological virus. Most worms start by hiding in a computer's existing software, waiting for a particular date or an event, and then coming to life, corrupting the hard disk of the machines, or instructing the host computer to do the same. More than 1,000 key viruses have so far been detected, and more than fifty new strains are being found each month throughout the world.

Many of the people behind these viruses are new frontier criminals; usually male, between the age of sixteen and twenty-five, and right on the cutting edge of computer software development. Some produce the viruses as no more than an intellectual challenge. Others do so through a particular motivation or goal. An 'AIDS' virus uncovered in 1989 was designed to blackmail the recipients of complementary computer programmes to pay money to a Panama postal address. The complementary programmes had been sent on disk to 20,000 computer operators. Much to the horror of the recipients, the AIDS programme, rather than being an educational programme, was a lethal Trojan horse virus – a time bomb that would ultimately destroy all data on the computer system.[2]

The new hackers and crackers have developed an extraordinary intelligence network. They use nationwide and transnational electronic bulletin boards to swap information on security systems, and ways to break them. Networks of virus writers are forming around the world. Vital, and often confidential, program information is posted and distributed through these networks.

Hackers in the US even have a glossy magazine called *2600 – the Hacker Quarterly*, containing articles with such titles as 'Secret Frequencies', 'Hacker News', 'Build a tone tracer' and 'Magnetic stripes (how to copy them)'. Considerable amounts of sensitive information about computer security systems are freely circulated around the hacker community, many of whom believe that corporations and governments are the real criminals who deserve to be brought to justice. Information networks are commonly interpreted as either the new heart of international socialism, or the engine room of capitalism. A great many viruses are unleashed on to systems because of the writer's hatred of what the network stands for.

It is difficult for many members of the older generations to comprehend what has been spawned by the computer revolution of the past decade. We often think in titillating terms of how much faster, or bigger, or smarter information technology has become. It is harder to think in terms of the quantum shift in human attitudes and values. Millions of youngsters around the world live in a different life matrix – a sort of network reality – a virtual reality where tangibility is confirmed through prompts, flags, and programme instructions. An entire generation of young people see reality and change in terms of networks and network communications. The older people might complain about how video is keeping their kids indoors. Well, the networks are achieving the effect of confining young people to a terminal, but liberating their movements in time and space. These youngsters have inherited a new dimension known as 'cyberspace'. In the US they call it 'living on the net'. This new lifestyle is an electronic frontier no less impressive than the old pioneer frontiers of the eighteenth century.

Richard Hollinger of the Department of Sociology of the University of Florida told the Computers, Freedom and Privacy Conference in San Francisco, 'To them [the young computer hackers] pirating software, sharing passwords, illegally accessing remote computers, browsing through electronic files, is not deviate behaviour. Instead, the real "criminals" in the world of computers are the private corporations, institutions and government agencies who wish to deny them access to this wealth of information.'

The hackers know that the technology of the present and future will not bring a new and glorious prosperity for everyone. One of Australia's leading computer experts, Roger Clarke of the Australian National University, believes that the end result of rampant technology will be anarchy. He says this will happen because the new richness and availability of information will prompt attacks upon social institutions. As the institutions respond with ever more repressive measures to defend themselves, the community takes possibly violent measures to remove them.

Little wonder, with such knowledge and passion behind them, that the new generation of viruses and worms are so effective.

The Stealth Worm is the most dangerous virus yet

devised. Once introduced into a computer system or network, the Stealth Worm issues instructions to the computer to hide its presence. This means that even though a computer operator constantly scans the computer to see whether there is any disk space unaccounted for (which may indicate a hidden virus), the Stealth Worm will instruct the computer to lie. The virus then reproduces itself, travelling through and between networks, leaving a ghost of itself at each new point. At the appropriate moment, the worm will destroy the system it has infected.

HOW IS THE WORM USED?

There are numerous examples of malicious worm and virus attacks on computer networks. In November 1988, a Cornell University student devised and released a particularly vicious and fast worm which ended up shutting down or crashing thousands of computer systems throughout the United States. Defence networks, as well as the National Science Foundation's network, were also infected.[3] Another virus introduced via electronic mail in 1987 gridlocked and infected hundreds of IBM mainframe computers around the world.[4] On a smaller scale, a US financial company suffered an infection in July 1994, and 2,200 computers were down for a week. In Sydney, a major bank recently shut down its entire dealing network on the mere suspicion that a virus had entered its system.[5]

The threat of the dreaded Michelangelo virus has caused widespread concern among corporations and persuaded some companies either to doctor their programmes or to shut down completely on the day of the great artist's birthday.

Telecommunications systems are particularly vulnerable to virus attack. On 15 January 1990, American Telephone and Telegraph (AT&T) suffered a major virus attack that virtually shut down its national network.

The crisis first came to notice in AT&T's long-distance control room fifty miles west of New York City. The huge video maps of the United States cover an entire wall, and are illuminated by countless green lights, indicating that the network is functioning satisfactorily. At 2.30 pm, the lights started changing to red, indicating that the network was breaking down. Tens of thousands of callers were failing to get their calls through.

The crisis had begun when 'switching computer' number 50 in New York found a small but unidentified error in its software, and automatically took itself off the network to 'reboot' (switch on again). The computer first notified the other switching facilities that it intended to go off-line, and the calls were thus diverted elsewhere in the network. Once the New York computer had re-established itself (a process that took less than two seconds) it sent out an OK message to other facilities, which then reset their routing tables accordingly. So far so good.

A domino effect was then sparked when the virus in the New York computer caused the OK messages to be re-sent. This threw all other computers in the network into a spin, triggering their shut-down. As they came back on-line, the same bug caused them to issue multiple OK messages, compounding the network's collapse.

Within ten minutes, all 114 switching stations were affected, and 50 per cent of calls on the world's largest and most sophisticated communications system were unable to connect.

Although the technical problems were largely resolved by the following night, the damage to AT&T was incalculable. The tangible loss for the day was $75 million, but the overall effect on business for the company was far greater. The public relations damage caused by the failure was quickly exploited by rival companies.[6]

The chance of such a major catastrophe occurring on an international basis in the key computer systems is still considered remote, but Jim Bates, a leading British virus expert, recently warned, 'My experience is that speculation from twelve months ago is beginning to become reality.'[7]

One very clear example of vulnerability can be seen in the world's satellite control systems. Although the main satellite control systems are invariably mainframe computers, and thus less likely to be infiltrated by viruses, the satellite tracking stations are not. They are connected to PCs. A worm or other virus can infiltrate these tracking systems, and just slowing the mechanism minutely can change the path of a satellite. As the world's telecommunications organizations move to universal personal numbering systems, in which people can be tracked anywhere in the world, satellite integrity will be even more vital.[8]

WHY THE GLOBAL THREAT WILL AFFECT PRIVACY

This gloomy sequence of events has important ramifications for privacy. There can be little doubt that the computer virus will soon be regarded as the single greatest threat to the stability of the international economy. As the world moves towards one compatible, integrated computer canopy, the vulnerability of the system will increase.[9] As the vulnerability increases, opportunities for terrorism will also become more apparent.

As the world and everyone in it becomes more dependent on sensitive and vulnerable computer systems, the need to protect them may well override the rights of users and, eventually, the rights of everyone. The government in the United States is attempting to pass legislation to allow routine and mass surveillance of computer communication, partly in an attempt to monitor information that may threaten computer networks.[10]

To minimize the possibility of terrorist attacks or sabotage, government may well demand more and more access to our personal computers and our communications. It is feasible, as has been suggested in the US, that a national biometric identity card would be used to access computer systems. In this scenario, everyone who wanted to access any computer network would have to use a card which verified (through fingerprints or voice recognition) that they were who they said they were. This would make it easier for the police to track down any malicious action. As more and more people need to access these networks either because of their work or their day-to-day business, a compulsory national or international biometric smart card is quite feasible.

In the United States, privacy advocates fear that law enforcement agencies will impose invasive initiatives to track down virus writers and control the flow of information within systems and networks. There is a widespread fear that if the stakes are high enough, governments will invoke anti-terrorism powers that will override civil rights.[11] The US government has already sought through Congress to require that communication service providers make available the 'plain text' version of encrypted (coded) computer communications. This effort was successfully opposed by privacy advocates, and computer and communications companies, but the FBI and other agencies continue to work to those ends.[12] If we are not allowed to communicate privately, and to speak in a way that protects our privacy, one important plank of individual rights is destroyed. Cryptography will remain one of the battlegrounds for communications privacy for the foreseeable future.[13]

Law enforcement has always been one of the greatest threats to privacy and rights. National security and terrorism give law enforcement extraordinary scope for intrusion. Computer terrorism is likely to provide this opportunity. Extremist political groups which have traditionally depended on brutality to exercise their intention may take the option of going down the technological road. If, for example, some practical aspects of regional collaboration are made possible through computer linkage, it's only natural that enemies of collaboration will direct their energies to destroying the computer facilities. And since the facilities are frequently well protected, the damage must be achieved through the system itself.

In the eyes of law enforcement agencies, every computer user is a potential hacker and therefore a potential threat. The executive editor of the US based *PC Magazine*, Gus Venditto, believes that no special genius is required to develop and launch a computer virus. 'Any programmer could make a virus. There are maybe 300,000 programmers in the world who could do it if they wanted to do it, pretty simply.'

The development of the global computer canopy has the

potential to make aspects of our lifestyle more fruitful and productive. It clearly also has the potential to create an international police state in which access to the network is essential for survival, but dependent on the surrender of privacy and rights.

FACING THE PROBLEM

Knowledge of these potential crises leaves most people feeling dazed and powerless. Such a reaction is well and truly justified. The harsh reality is that nothing of substance exists to protect us from the web. Our media have difficulty coming to grips with the issues. Our politicians seek simple solutions to extract more revenue. Government regulatory agencies have failed to put a stop to the construction of the web. Law often gives the intruders a licence to proceed with their plans by permitting surveillance schemes instead of restricting them. Advocacy groups and civil liberties organizations are so impoverished that many can hardly afford to pay their phone bill, let alone hire staff to raise awareness and run campaigns. Meanwhile, the bureaucrats increasingly act within the scope of administrative regulations rather than under the authority of direct law. They succeed, therefore, in escaping the restraint of public scrutiny.

Just who is accountable for these invasions should be a matter of serious and ongoing debate. Given the depressing wall of evidence about the growing surveillance web, we have every justification for feeling dazed and powerless. The surveillance question has become so complex that few people understand even a small part of the issue.

I do not know how we are going to come to grips with the emotive argument advanced by the government about the desirability of catching cheats and criminals. Maybe it would be nice if we could safely and easily weed out every crook. The answer to social problems, however, is not necessarily tighter and more authoritarian government. The more tightly controlled a population becomes, the greater will be the incidence of victimization. The authoritarian system itself will ultimately become the justification for ever more rigid controls.

The government's cost benefit justifications are, as I have discussed throughout this book, based in many instances on flimsy figures and creative calculations. Still, even if the various surveillance systems could bring the promised returns, the money would hardly justify the sad outcome for liberty.

WHAT SHOULD WE EXPECT FROM GOVERNMENT?

For this questioning to begin, we have to clarify precisely what mechanisms should be scrutinized. We need to identify the surveillance web as being at the same time both a separate and an integral part of government administration. Surveillance machinery is not necessary for good government. It can be a useful parasite, but not all parasitical relationships are beneficial to the host.

To keep abreast of the government's strategies and to become empowered to do something about them, we ultimately will have to stop viewing government administration as one unchangeable integrated mechanism, and

255

instead take the view that each of its parts can be examined and judged in isolation. We do this regularly with revenue and benefits issues, so there is no reason why we should not scrutinize the government's internal mechanisms.

The mind of the bureaucrat highlights the essential privacy problem so often identified in the preceding chapters. Modern technology, bringing power and prestige to those who use it, can be a dangerous weapon in the hands of the shortsighted and arrogant. The technology is no more neutral than an atom bomb. The people who have been entrusted to manipulate the technology have a responsibility to ensure that it is used for the benefit of humankind. It is so often the case that a greedy, stupid madness takes hold of technologists and bureaucrats, enticing them to set aside reasoned and intelligent consideration of the impact of their innovations.

The private sector, banks, insurance companies and the like, should not be exempted from this criticism. They have been responsible for some of the most heinous intrusions into the rights of the individual. Free marketeers base their reckoning of social justice on the equation that if it's good for competition, then it's good for the stockholders and therefore good for society. That reasoning has changed little in several centuries.

It is tempting to excuse the private sector as a fairly harmless player compared to the government. This might have been true (at least to an extent) a decade ago, but not so these days. The capacity of the insurance sector to intrude into the lives of people and control the interactions in society has become so massive that it cannot be overstated. The finance sector has become a virtual arm of government, and nearly all our information held in banks and other institutions will soon be passed routinely on to government. This working relationship between public and private sector will grow in importance over the next two decades to the point where all personal information may ultimately be subjected to government scrutiny and control.

The last nail in the surveillance coffin is the fusion of the biological and the technological. When our masters decide that biological identification will be mandatory to operate their wonderful technology, the surveillance web will be complete. Human and machine will be as one. Every individual that interacts with the information infrastructure will be personally known to that machinery. That technology exists right at this minute. Only the circumstance and the will stand in the way of its implementation.

WHERE DO WE GO FROM HERE?

First, we have to call a spade a spade. What is happening is nothing short of an orchestrated effort to bring the public to heel. There is no doubt that the government and the bureaucracy have acted with breathtaking arrogance in setting up the surveillance web.

In order to take action to change any entrenched policy of public administration, we need two commodities: facts and fury. Every concerned Briton should demand that elected representatives closely scrutinize what is happening, and report back to the electorate. If enough elected members – especially backbenchers – raise the issue in the party room, the environment of support and compliance will soon vanish.

IS THERE ANY HOPE?

People keep telling me that my warnings are too little, too late. I am told by well-meaning colleagues that the surveillance mechanisms are now in place and cannot be removed. Organizations, I am assured, have made massive investments in information holdings, and they will not dismantle these.

I agree with these views only to a point. The awareness of privacy invasion is at the same level now that the environmental movement was at twenty years ago. Back then, the greenies were assured that their quest was fruitless. Industry serves a legitimate function. There has to be a cost. In any case, nothing can be done. The polluters are not going to budge. Like the modern privacy advocate, the environmental activist in the 1960s and 1970s was viewed widely as a ratbag who worked against the interests of society.

There are still a few wild cards in the privacy pack, and those wild cards hold the key to slowing the surveillance juggernaut. At the moment, privacy has been all but engineered into extinction, so the odds are stacked in favour of the Superhighway supremos. It is not politically correct to assert one's right to privacy. Surely only those with something to hide would have something to fear.

Thankfully the justification of efficiency and law enforcement will hold only as long as people feel they are on the winning side of the equation. That will not last. In the end, the irresistible force will confront the immovable object: people with a commitment to sovereign rights will rebel against an order which enforces universality. As the global Superhighway moves towards its goal of omnipotence, it will marginalize and antagonize a growing number of groups.

Will Quebec, poised on the brink of secession, accept a Superhighway dominated by the United States? Will Scotland, in the wash of historical reflection, meekly accept a London-centred information society? States and territories whose culture or economy is threatened by a neighbouring power are acutely tuned to sovereignty and privacy. The UK itself is unlikely happily to surrender its data to an information-hungry Europe. Given that pub conversation is dominated by tirades disparaging our European partners, it will be a long time, if ever, before people will cheerfully accept the idea of a global information system. Claims that culturally vulnerable groups can more easily assert and protect themselves on the Superhighway are unsupportable. The television medium is dominated by the most powerful cultures.

Resistance against the global information society will be fierce. Christian and survivalist groups in the US and elsewhere are unlikely to become happy travellers along the superhighway. Once its surveillance nature becomes known, these groups will either disconnect, or they will engage in programmes of sabotage.

The 'modern-day Luddite', a term of abuse in this age, may become a source of hope in the future. Luddism, the organized rebellion against new technology, is actually a legitimate political response to a major social and economic change. Although it is a metaphor for backward thinking in the 1990s, in the future it may well be the last remaining mechanism to disrupt the construction of a global surveillance web. Organized civil disobedience, implemented by disaffected groups and individuals, will introduce elements of uncertainty into the structure. As people become aware that secrecy, anonymity and even seclusion have been

259

eradicated, a gut-level reaction could ensue. As new technology devastates more and more employment in the West, and as the wealth gap increases between the haves and the have-nots, civil resistance may become a common and well organized activity. The Superhighway will be used as a tool for its own destruction.

The new technologies feed on a diet of mass passification. Compliance and dependence give the Superhighway its strength. In an age of obedience, the information age will thrive. In a different time, it will become a target for losers. The race is on to develop an information infrastructure that becomes invisible and inviolable, before the trouble begins.

I started out this book by warning that Britain is witnessing its last years as a free society. Nevertheless, gloomy as I am, I believe that we can fight successfully to regain lost liberties, and to put in place powerful and meaningful safeguards so that future generations will never have to experience the threat of the surveillance web. All we need is a belief that we are at least as powerful as the technology we managed to create.

NOTES

INTRODUCTION

1. Derek Wheatley, 'Big Brother has his eyes on your bank account', *Independent*, 14 April 1993.

CHAPTER ONE: FUSING FLESH AND MACHINE

1. Neils Birbaumer, 'Think to move – and move! Self regulation of movement related brain potentials', Institute of Medical Psychology and Behavioural Neuroscience, Tübingen.
2. Author's interviews with staff of the Defence Research Agency.
3. Adrian Levy, 'The internet: it's all in the mind', *Sunday Times*, 16 April 1995, p. 15.
4. Kathleen Wiegner, 'Giving Surgical Implants Ids', *Los Angeles Times*, 17 August 1994, Part D, p. 5.
5. S. Davies, 'Bionic Man comes of age', *The Times*, 17 October 1994.

6. For an overview of the science of nanotechnology, see K. Eric Drexler, *Engines of Creation*, Anchor Press, New York, 1986.

7. Richard Muller, Director, Sensor and Actuator Center, University of California at Berkeley, quoted in Curt Suple, 'Bioengineers Construct Microchip Health Care', *International Herald Tribune*, 17 September 1991.

8. Jon Turney, 'Building the new world, one atom at a time', *The Times*, 27 February 1995, p. 16.

9. Ed Regis, *Nano – Remaking the World Atom by Atom*, Bantam Press, New York 1995.

10. 'Nowhere to Hide', *Time*, 11 November 1991.

11. Nick Rufford, 'China moves to ban babies with defects', *Sunday Times*, 5 February 1995, p. 17.

12. *Daily Telegraph*, 4 April 1995.

13. Office of Technology Assessment (OTA) Protecting privacy in computerized medical information. US Government Printing Office. Washington DC. 1993.

14. D. Campbell and S. Connor, *On the Record*, Michael Joseph, London, 1986, p. 20.

15. Alan F. Westin, *Privacy and Freedom*, Atheneum, New York, 1967, p. x.

16. Californian Supreme Court, White *v.* Davis (13 Cal. 3d, 757, 1975).

17. Westin, *Privacy and Freedom*, p. 7.

18. Arnold Simmel, 'Privacy', *International Encyclopaedia of the Social Sciences*, 12 (1968), pp. 480, 482, 485.

19. John M. Carroll, *Confidential Information Sources, Public and Private* (2nd edition), Butterworth-Heinemann, MA, 1991.

20. 'Technology and the New World Order', *BYTE Magazine*, December 1992, p. 324.

CHAPTER TWO: **MAKING A KILLING ON THE INFORMATION SUPERHIGHWAY**

I. Andrew Grosso, 'The National Information Infrastructure: implications for commerce, security and law enforcement', *Federal Bar News and Journal*, August 1994, Vol. 41, No. 7, p. 481, Washington DC.

2. ibid.

3. *Information Super Highways*, CCTA, London, 1994.

4. Mitchell Kapor and Jerry Berman, *Building the Open Road*, Electronic Frontier Foundation (EFF), Washington DC, 1993.

5. ibid.

6. Peter B. White, 'Australia's Information Future: Superhighway or Toll Road?' (paper presented at the Stanley Foster Foundation symposium 'What stories are we telling our children? The effects of the electronic media on Australian quality of life and the environment', Regent Hotel, Melbourne, 20–21 August 1994).

7. For further discussion of the impact of technology on organizations and national security, see Paula Swatman and Roger Clarke, 'Organizational, sectoral and international implications of Electronic Data Interchange' (paper presented at the Conference on Information Technology Assessment, the 4th IFIP TC9 World Conference on Human Choice and Computers, 1990, Dublin).

8. Interview with former National Security Agency staff member, Sydney, June 1992.

9. James Bamford, *The Puzzle Palace*, Penguin, New York, 1983.

10. ibid., p. 391.

II. ibid., p. 271.

12. Author's interview with Ralph Nader, January 1995.
13. Wolfgang Munchau, 'Fears of economic rifts temper the rush to cyberspace', *The Times*, 27 February 1995, p. 13.

CHAPTER THREE: **IN SEARCH OF PERFECT IDENTITY**

1. Bill Hart, 'Big Brother's watching . . . the family pet', *Phoenix Gazette*, 24 July 1994.
2. ibid.
3. Heather Mills, 'Private sector to supervise tagging of criminals', *Independent*, London, 22 September 1994.
4. Jon Van, 'Fingerprint scans pose uses, abuses', *Chicago Tribune*, 6 June 1994.
5. S. Davies, 'Touching Big Brother: How biometric technology will fuse flesh and machine', *Information Technology and People*, MCB University Press, Bradford, UK, Vol. 7, No. 4, 1994, p. 43.
6. ibid.
7. ibid.
8. *Biometric Technology Today*, November 1993, Vol. 1, No. 7.
9. ibid., p. 7.
10. S. Davies, 'Touching Big Brother'.
11. 'NTT Develops Rapid, Highly Accurate Fingerprint Recognition Technique', Telecommunications Association *New Era*, 15 August 1993.
12. Interview with project manager, 19 January 1994.
13. Sherman, Robin L.,'Biometrics futures' in *Journal of Electronic Defense*, January 1933; EW Design Engineers' Handbook & Manufacturers Directory.
14. ibid.

15. US Department of Health and Human Services, Workgroup on Computerization of Patient Records, 'Toward a national health information infrastructure', report to the Secretary, April 1993 (HHS, 1993).
16. Office of Technology Assessment (OTA), 'Protecting Privacy in Computerized Medical Information', US Government Printing Office, Washington DC, 1993.

CHAPTER FOUR: **NUMBERED LIKE CATTLE**

1. *Data Protection News*, No. 18, Summer 1994, p. 2.
2. L. B. Weiss, 'Government steps up use of computer matching to find fraud in programs', *Congressional Quarterly*, Weekly Report, 26 February 1983. Office of Technology Assessment, 'Federal Government Information Technology. Electronic record systems and individual privacy', OTA-Cit 296, US Government Printing Office, Washington DC, June 1986.
3. Parliament of the Commonwealth of Australia, report, 'Matching and Catching'. Report on the Law Enforcement Access Network, House of Representatives Standing Committee on Banking, Finance, and Public Administration, Chapter 8; see also audit reports on the United States General Accounting Office, and the 1993 report of the Australian National Audit Office.
4. Law Enforcement Access Network Dead Privacy Law and Policy Reporter, Vol 1 no 2 April 1994, Sydney.
5. Roger Clarke, 'Computer Matching', unpublished paper, 31 March 1991.
6. *Data Protection News*, No. 18, Summer 1994, p. 5.
7. Interview with the project manager of Metro Community

Services, Toronto, Ontario, 20 January 1994. This figure is viewed within the agency as an underestimate. The internal figure is ten times the official government estimate.

8. Submission of the Australian Department of Social Security to the Joint Select Committee on an Australia Card, and interview with Peter Roberts, head of fraud prevention, Commonwealth Attorney-General's Department.

9. New Zealand estimates in 1991 were 30–100 million NZ dollars out of a total budget of 10.4 billion NZ dollars, higher than some Canadian estimates, but lower than Britain's.

10. Commonwealth of Australia, Attorney-General's Department, submission to the Parliamentary inquiry into fraud on the Commonwealth, 30 May 1992, p. 5.

II. Perhaps the most obvious of these is the element of deterrence, which is rarely considered in a full audit, but which often counts as a major factor in informal estimates.

12. Roger Clarke, 'Profiling: A Hidden Challenge to the Regulation of Dataveillance', *Journal of Law and Information Science*, 4,2 (December 1993), pp. 403–19.

13. ibid.

14. Office of Technology Assessment (OTA), 'Federal Government Information Technology: Electronic Record Systems and Individual Privacy', OTA-CIT-296, US Government Printing Office, Washington DC, June 1986.

15. Maria Scott and Neasa MacErlean, 'Wired up to fight fraud', *Observer*, 11 June 1995, p. 16.

CHAPTER FIVE: **THE FAILURE OF LAW**

1. Tenth report of the Data Protection Registrar, June 1994, p. 26.
2. Alan Shipman, 'Scanned and Deliver: mailshot marketing', *International Management*, Vol. 49, No. 2, March 1994.
3. ibid.
4. David Flaherty, 'The emergence of surveillance societies in the western world: Toward the year 2000', *Government Information Quarterly*, Vol. 5, No. 4, pp. 377–87.
5. Cited in David Flaherty, *Protecting Privacy in Surveillance Societies*, University of North Carolina Press, Chapel Hill, 1989, p. 385.
6. Jan Holvast, 'Vulnerability of Information Society', in *Managing Information Technology's Organizational Impact*, ed. R. Clarke and J. Cameron, North Holland, Amsterdam, 1991.
7. Hansard, Standing Committee on Legal and Constitutional Affairs (Senate), 19 October 1990.

CHAPTER SIX: **THE IDENTITY CARD: BLUEPRINT FOR AN INTERNAL PASSPORT**

1. 'The Population Identification Number Project', brochure published by the Department of Local Administration, Bangkok, 1989.
2. ibid.
3. 'The Fear of Big Brother', *Bangkok Post*, 17 February 1991.
4. Christopher Lockwood and Helen Cranford, 'What They

Do on the Continent of Europe', *Daily Telegraph*, 16 January 1995.

5. David Hencke, 'Howard's ID smart card plans found in junk shop', *Guardian*, 16 January 1995, p. 1.

6. ibid.

7. Flaherty, 'Emergence of Surveillance Societies', p. 226.

8. ibid., p. 227.

CHAPTER SEVEN: **THE DARK SIDE OF IDENTITY**

1. Graham Greenleaf, *Law Society Journal*, Sydney, October 1987.

2. Report of the Joint Select Committee on an Australia Card, AGPS, Canberra, 1986.

3. These comments were published in an Australian Privacy Foundation booklet entitled 'Why the ID Card must be stopped NOW'.

4. *West Australian*, 12 September 1987.

5. *Australian Financial Review*, 28 August 1987.

6. Health Insurance Commission, Planning Report of the Health Insurance Commission, 26 February 1986.

7. *Daily Telegraph*, Sydney, 8 September 1987.

8. *Sun Herald*, Sydney, 13 September 1987.

9. *Daily Telegraph*, Sydney, 19 September 1987.

10. *Sydney Morning Herald*, 14 September 1991.

11. *New Zealand Herald*, 14 September 1991.

12. The meeting was held in Auckland on Friday, 13 September 1991.

13. Agence France Presse, 'New Zealand Government denies watchdog computer, ID card plans' by Michael Field, 13 September 1991.

14. Commonwealth of Australia, Attorney-General's Department, submission to the Parliamentary inquiry into fraud on the Commonwealth, 30 May 1992, p. 5.

15. Wilcock *v.* Muckle (1952) 1 KB 367, at p. 369.

16. Privacy International submission to the Senate of the Philippines, Manila, 8 May 1991.

17. In 1980, the Krever Commission in Canada investigated the abuse of patient health record confidentiality by private investigators, and concluded that the practice was 'widespread'. For an explanation of the methods adopted by the Commission to uncover these practices, see the Federal Privacy of Medical Information Act, S Rept 96–832 Part 1, 96th Congress, 19 March 1980, pp. 24–6. Investigations by the US Office of the Inspector General of corruption involving computerized files held by the Social Security Administration are cited in United States Congress, Office of Technology Assessment, 'Protecting Privacy in Computerized Medical Information', US Government Printing Office, Washington DC, 1993. More recently, the Independent Commission Against Corruption in New South Wales concluded an extensive investigation in 1993 and found that abuse of personal information among government information users was 'endemic and epidemic' (ICAC, Report on unauthorized release of government information, Vol. 1–3, 1992, Sydney).

CHAPTER EIGHT: SMART CARDS AND CLEVER ILLUSIONS

1. Patricia Tehan, 'Banks dream of "electronic wallets" for every shopper', *The Times*, 22 October 1994.

2. ibid.

3. 'EU invites involvement in pilot scheme for electronic wallet', European Information Service, European Report, 7 September 1994.

4. Michael Rowe, 'Europe's Central Bankers tighten electronic purse strings', *Financial Technology Insight*, 7 September 1994, Information Access Co., Elsevier Advanced Technology Publications.

5. ibid.

6. ibid.

7. David Hencke, 'Howard's ID smart card plans found in junk shop', *Guardian*, 16 January 1995.

8. ibid.

9. ibid.

10. Health Security Bill 1993, explanatory notes.

11. One of the goals of European union has been the establishment of legal and technological conditions that will allow the free and unrestricted passage of data across national borders. The European Data Protection Directive has been issued in draft form to provide minimum Europe-wide data protection standards. This situation will have a profound impact on the use of medical data in Britain.

12. Australian Health and Aged Care systems seminar, Sydney, December 1991, remarks made in the summing-up remarks of the conference.

13. TV1, 13 September 1991.

14. Presented at the Third National Court Technology Conference, Dallas, Texas, 1991.

15. *Australian*, 23 June 1992.

16. Yves Poullet, 'The medical Data Card – data protection issues', in *Computer Law and Security Report*, September/

October, November/December 1990, January/February 1991.

17. *Australian Financial Review*, 15 May 1989.

18. Venn's interview with author, Montreal, February 1992.

CHAPTER NINE: **THE WATCHERS**

1. S. Davies, 'They've got an eye on you', *Independent*, 2 November 1995.

2. 'CCTV – Looking out for you', brochure published by the Home Office in 1994, p. 11.

3. Tim Dawson, 'Framing the villains', *New Statesman*, 28 January 1994.

4. 'Who's Watching Who', *City Life*, 27 July 1994.

5. 'Use of police cameras sparks rights debate in Britain', *Washington Post*, 8 August 1994.

6. ibid.

7. 'Britons find some comfort under cameras' gaze', *Boston Globe*, 9 July 1993.

8. 'CCTV – Looking out for you', p. 12.

9. L. Gerard, 'Video traps catch abuse of children by parents', *Observer*, 26 September 1993.

10. 'Hospital filmed mother trying to stop baby breathing', *Independent*, 30 October 1991.

11. 'In the frame', *Community Care*, 28 October 1993.

12. Cited in 'Who's watching who', *City Life*, 27 July 1994.

13. 'Amateur's video spies on drivers', *The Times*, 17 July 1993, p. 5.

14. United States Congress, Office of Technology Assessment (OTA), *The Electronic Supervisor: New Technology, New Tensions*, US Government Printing Office, Washington

DC, 1987, p. 104. Cited in *Workers' Privacy, Conditions of Work Digest*, special report, International Labour Office, Vol. 12, No. 1, p. 20.

15. Society for Human Resources Management, 1991 SHRM, Privacy in the Workplace survey report, Alexandria, Virginia, 1992.

16. Creswell *v.* Inland Revenue (1984) IRLR 190, cited in Brian Napier, 'Computerization and Employment Rights' in *Industrial Law Journal*, Vol. 21, No. 1, 1992, p. 3.

17. *Workers' Privacy, Conditions of Work Digest*, p. 267.

18. *Security Industry Journal*, October 1993.

19. 'Speeding drivers shamed by hi-tech trap on the M1', *The Times*, 1 June 1994, p. 1.

20. *Daily Telegraph*, 16 October 1993.

21. Simon Davies, *Big Brother*, Simon & Schuster, Sydney, 1992.

22. 'Who's watching who', *City Life*, 27 July 1994.

23. Cited in Peter Zimmerman, 'Civil Remote Sensing: New Technologies and National Security Policy', in *New Directions in Telecommunications Policy*, Vol. 2, ed. Paula R. Newberg.

24. Joseph C. Anselmo, 'High-resolution Satellite Competition Heats Up', *Aviation Week and Space Technology*, 11 July 1994; *Aerospace Daily*, Vol. 141, No. 2, p. 56.

25. James Asker, 'Pressure Builds to Free Satellite Imaging Sales', *Aviation Week and Space Technology*, 15 November 1993, Vol. 139, No. 20, p. 26.

26. Zimmerman, 'Civil Remote Sensing', p. 107.

27. Anselmo, 'High-resolution Satellite Competition Heats Up'.

28. 'Spy satellites keep watch for fraudsters on the farm', *The Times*, 26 May 1993, p. 8.

29. Asker, 'Pressure Builds to Free Satellite Imaging Sales'.
30. G. Russell Pipe, 'Protecting Data – Has Anything Really Changed?' *Transnational Data and Communications Report*, TDR Services, Amsterdam, 1994.

CHAPTER TEN: **THE END OF TELEPHONE PRIVACY**

I. S. Davies, 'OK Anon your number's up', *Daily Telegraph*, 6 November 1994.
2. Public Utilities Commission of California, proposed decision of A. L. J. Lemke, mailed 21 January 1992.
3. 'The introduction of Calling Line identification', OFTEL policy paper, London, July 1994, p. 3.
4. SACOT press release, 9 August 1994.
5. Gary Marx, 'When anonymity of callers is lost, we're that much closer to a surveillance society', *Los Angeles Times*, 3 May 1989, Part II, p. 7.
6. *Business News*, Winter 1995.
7. 'The introduction of Calling Line identification', p. 3.
8. SACOT press release, 9 August 1994.
9. 'The introduction of Calling Line identification', p. 6.
10. This is the message used by Bell Canada for its call screening service. Other carriers use different, sometimes less subtle, messages.
II. CFA News, March 1991.
12. CIRCIT Conference on the Intelligent Network, Melbourne, December 1991.
13. *New York Times*, 2 February 1995.
14. Information obtained in interview with David Banisar, Electronic Privacy Information Center, Washington DC.

15. *Watchdog*, BBC 1, 20 February 1995.

16. AUSTEL 'Telecommunications Privacy' final report, Melbourne, December 1992, p. 71.

17. Alicia Swasy, *Soap Opera: the Inside Story of Procter & Gamble*, Random House, New York, 1994, p. 295.

18. *Marketplace*, 17 December 1991.

19. Survey cited by Rohan Samarajiva in seminar on the intelligent telephone network organized by the Centre for International Research on Communications and Information Technology (CIRCIT), Melbourne, 1991.

20. Speech to the United States Telephone Association, 13 September 1989, Washington DC.

21. 'Caller ID is a hit with Maryland's drug dealers', *Capital*, 7 May 1990, p. A4.

22. *Marketplace*, 17 December 1991.

23. ibid.

24. Privacy International General Meeting, 17 March 1992, Washington DC.

CHAPTER ELEVEN: **FORECASTING THE FUTURE**

1. *Wiring Whitehall* is a report organized by the London-based industry research group 'Kable', and involves experts from British Telecom, Ernst and Young, and Hoskyns.

2. Author's interview with Professor Ferguson.

3. Author's interview with Professor Humphreys.

4. Geoffrey Robertson, *Freedom, the Individual and the Law*, p. 116.

5. See David Lyon, *The Electronic Eye*, p. 44, and Harold Innis, *The Bias of Communication*, University of Toronto Press, 1951.

6. *Financial Times*, 1 December 1990.
7. Geoffrey Robertson, *Freedom, the Individual and the Law*, p. xiii.
8. Campbell and Connor, *On the Record*, p. 19.

CHAPTER TWELVE: **COUNTDOWN TO CATASTROPHE**

I. This scenario was originally published in *Information Age*, Vol. 11, No. 3, 3 July 1989, pp. 131–7.
2. Peter Huck, 'Tracking down the computer terrorists', *Sydney Morning Herald*, 26 October 1991, p. 42.
3. *Information Age*.
4. ibid.
5. Huck, 'Tracking down the computer terrorists', p. 42.
6. David Davies, 'Anatomy of a disaster', in *Computer Law and Security Report*, July–August 1991.
7. Huck, 'Tracking down the computer terrorists', p. 42.
8. Motorola's Iridium project will place seventy-seven satellites in orbit for this purpose.
9. The development of Open Systems planning means that computers in many different environments will have the capacity to communicate fully.
10. Bill s.266 of 1991 specified that people encrypting (encoding) their communications through the computer networks had to tell the government how to unscramble the code.
II. See the proceedings of the first Computers, Freedom and Privacy Conference, San Francisco, 1991.
12. The FBI has already placed another Bill before Senate which will require telecommunications companies to ensure that all technology can be intercepted by law enforcement

agencies. This is currently being opposed by the civil liberties lobby, but the Communications Assistance and Law Enforcement Access (CALEA) Act was passed by Congress in October 1994.

13. See *Proceedings of 1991 Cryptography and Privacy Conference*, Washington DC, June 1991, National Academy Press, 1991.

GLOSSARY

Active badge   Also known as an 'electronic tag', this is a smart card which emits a frequency that can be read and identified by receivers located in various parts of a building or along a road. (See also **radio frequency ID card**.)

Australia Card   A national identity card scheme proposed by the Australian government in 1986. The card sparked one of the biggest civil protests in Australian history, and was scrapped in 1987.

Automatic Teller Machine (ATM)   Technology which dispenses cash and accepts instructions relating to bank or other financial accounts.

Biometric technology   Any technology which captures, processes, or stores identifiable details of the physical characteristics of an individual (retina scans, thumb scans, fingerprints, hand geometry, digitized photographs, DNA readings and lip prints).

Caller Display   Also known as Caller ID. A telephone service which transmits the originating telephone number at the time the call is placed.

CD-ROM (Compact Disc Read Only Memory)   A disc

which can store vast quantities of information. The latest CD-ROMS are able to store video clips and even full movies.

Closed circuit television (CCTV)   Camera technology connected in real time to a monitor or video recorder.

Data matching   Computer matching (also known as parallel matching, bulk matching, record linkage, cross matching or joint running) is the process of automatically comparing and analysing records of a person from two or more sources.

Data profiling   A process of automatically processing computerized information to identify targets on the basis of their characteristics.

Data protection   This is the legalistic interpretation of privacy. That is, a circumstance which involves a control, or limit, on the collection, use and disclosure of personal information. Data protection is a quantifiable set of conditions for the use of personal information. Popular movements against technology tend not to be based on problems with data protection, but, rather, on problems of power, authority and accountability.

Digital cash   Cash in the form of electronic credits, dispensed when a smart card instructs a 'till' to withdraw the currency from its memory.

E-mail   Short for electronic mail. Messages sent in electronic form from one computer to another using a modem attached to a phone line.

Electronic tolling   A means of automatically charging vehicles for use of roads. This tolling uses smart card systems which have units deducted as the card passes through gateways at points along the road.

Encryption   The process of converting information into a form of 'code' that, in principle, cannot be read by anyone other than authorized people in possession of a 'key'.

Identity card   A document which contains identifying and other information relating to an individual, and which has the primary purpose of interfacing between the individual and an organization. Any document which is of a high enough integrity to be required as a condition of provision of benefits or services would be an identification document. If this document is issued for the primary purpose of ease of identification, it would be considered an ID card.

Information Superhighway   Metaphor for a system of electronic pathways connecting homes and businesses, along which can travel large quantities of information at high speeds.

Information technology (IT)   Any technology that automatically processes electronically stored information.

Interactive technology   Any information technology which responds and changes according to instructions by the user. Television is not interactive, but new cable-based services will be.

Integrated Services Digital Network (ISDN)   The technological infrastructure for the emerging intelligent telephone network.

Internet   Short for 'Inter network'. A network of networks joining together 10,000 smaller networks in 100 countries, and used for the transfer of messages, files and software.

Kiwi Card   A national social security card issued to welfare beneficiaries in New Zealand.

Neural prosthesis   The branch of medical science concerned with fusing technology with flesh. Some operations now implant microchips into the circuitry of the brain and major organs.

Photograph digitization A way of processing and storing photographic images in electronic form.

Privacy The relationship between people and the world around them. This concept of privacy follows the definition used by Privacy International, and involves relationships of power and situations of intrusion. Unlike data protection, privacy is an often intangible concept that takes into account the possibility of future threat. Privacy has also to be separated from the science of security, which is concerned with the parameters of access to data.

Radio frequency ID (RFID) card A smart card which emits a frequency that can be remotely read without the need for the card to make contact physically with any other machine.

Remote sensing Term used to encompass the information gathered by satellites relating to activities on the surface of the earth.

Smart card A plastic card which can store considerable amounts of information. Most smart cards contain a microchip, which can store several A4 pages of data but some, which embrace laser technology, have a capacity of up to 1,000 A4 pages from 2.7 megabytes of memory. The microchip card can actually independently process this data, and present it in different forms according to requirements. The smart card is, in effect, a credit-card-sized personal computer.

Stealth Worm A complex computer virus with artificial intelligence and the ability to mutate and replicate itself. The worm can penetrate well-defended computer systems.

Virtual reality A computer programme which responds to outside stimuli to give the appearance that it is an extension of the real world.

LIST OF ACRONYMS
AND ABBREVIATIONS

ACPO	Association of Chief Police Officers
ADF	Australian Doctors Fund
AUSTEL	Australian Office of Telecommunications
BMA	British Medical Association
BSIA	British Security Industry Association
BT	British Telecom
CCTV	Closed circuit television
CD-ROM	Compact Disc Read Only Memory
CEN	European Committee for Standardization
CFR	Computerized Facial Recognition
CLI	Calling Line Identification
CNIL	Commission on Data Processing and Freedoms (France)
CSIS	Centre for Strategic and International Studies
DPA	Data Protection Act
DPR	Data Protection Registrar
DSS	Department of Social Security
DVLA	Driver and Vehicle Licensing Agency
EFTPOS	Electronic Funds Transfer at Point of Sale

EPIC	Electronic Privacy Information Center (Washington DC)
GAO	US General Accounting Office
INSPASS	Immigration and Naturalization Service Passenger Accelerated Service System
ISDN	Integrated Services Digital Network
IT	Information technology
LASSY	Licensing Administrative Support System computer
NHS	National Health Service (UK)
NSA	National Security Agency (US)
OFTEL	UK Office of Telecommunications
OTA	US Office of Technology Assessment
PC	Personal computer
PI	Privacy International
PIN	Personal Identification number or Population Identification Number
RFID	Radio frequency ID cards
SACOT	The Scottish Advisory Committee on Telecommunications
SOFI	Social Security and Fiscal number (Netherlands)
SSN	US Social Security Number
VR	Virtual reality

INDEX